# NEVER A DRAGON

# NEVER A DRAGON

## DRAGON'S DAUGHTER™ BOOK 1

KEVIN MCLAUGHLIN

MICHAEL ANDERLE

DISRUPTIVE IMAGINATION®

Copyright © 2020 LMBPN Publishing
Cover Art by Jake @ J Caleb Design
http://jcalebdesign.com / jcalebdesign@gmail.com
Cover copyright © LMBPN Publishing
A Michael Anderle Production

LMBPN Publishing
PMB 196, 2540 South Maryland Pkwy
Las Vegas, NV 89109

First US Edition, November 2020
Version 1.01, December 2020
eBook ISBN: 978-1-64971-293-6
Print ISBN: 978-1-64971-294-3

THE NEVER A DRAGON TEAM

**Thanks to our Beta Readers**
Rachel Beckford, Mary Morris, Nicole Emens, Larry Omans

**Thanks to the JIT Readers**
Misty Roa
Dave Hicks
Deb Mader
Dorothy Lloyd
Diane L. Smith
Peter Manis
Paul Westman

*If we've missed anyone, please let us know!*

**Editor**
The Skyhunter Editing Team

# CHAPTER ONE

*Somewhere north of Kugaaruk, Nunavut. Canada.*

It was no mystery why the dragons had ceded the land below Hester Diamantine to the dwarves. This was a barren, icy place, especially in January. What few trees grew there were all windswept, scraggly pines that looked like they'd rather be incinerated by dragon flame than grow another year in the cold.

Every single body of water—and there were many of them on this peninsula that looked like it would prefer to be dragged into the frigid ocean—was frozen solid with ice. They had left the town of Kugaaruk behind them an hour before. The dwarves there hadn't wanted to tell Cesar Tormentus where they were hiding the rogue mages, but they had told him all the same.

"I have something," Rubonus said. He was the youngest of the three dragons on this mission to capture a group of renegade mages, although he was still far older than the last member of their group, a mage by the name of Lara Cooper who was bonded to Hester. He made up for his lack of experience with enthusiasm and had not hesitated to show the dwarves that even though their skin was impervious to dragon flame, their homes and businesses were not.

"If it's another fucking fish shack, I don't want to hear about it," Tormentus said.

They had already leveled three fishing shacks, only to find—what else?—people fishing inside.

"I appreciate that, sir," Lara said to Tormentus.

"It's not your job to approve, Mage Cooper." He said the word "mage" like it was a slur. To him, it was. "It's your job to obey the dragon you are bonded too."

"What do you see, Rubonus?" Hester asked. She knew Lara could use her magic to keep herself warm while she rode on her back, but there were limits to her powers, especially since she wore a dampening cuff on her wrist that rendered them more impotent than they might have been. The dragon didn't want to flatten any more fishing shacks, but she didn't want to be out there until Lara froze to death either. She liked the little mage.

"I hate to bust your horns, Tormentus, but it is another fishing shack."

"I'm waiting for the part where you tell me why I should care," their leader snarled.

"This one doesn't have any lights on," he replied. In his eagerness, he made Hester think of a fox hunting a vole. Honestly, that was an apt comparison. The idea of a modern mage killing a dragon was about as preposterous as the idea of a vole killing a fox. To be sure, both happened.

A fox might choke on a vole or get rabies from one, and groups of mages had been known to get lucky and hurt dragons —but not with even odds and not during a retrieval. Tormentus called this a hunt, but that was not what it was. This was a mage retrieval, plain and simple. Hester was his lieutenant, and part of that meant reminding him of such discrepancies.

"Then how do we know there are people there at all?" Their leader did not sound amused.

"I can sense magic signatures," Lara whispered to Hester. She relayed the information to Tormentus. It usually went better that way.

"How many?" he asked Cooper. He knew full well that it took a mage to sniff out a mage, exactly like it took a dragon to sniff out a dragon.

"Uh…they're trying to suppress their powers so I can't sense them but—"

"Tell me how fucking many of these traitorous mages there are," he growled.

"I sensed five, sir, but it's now only four," Lara responded and tried to keep her voice strong over the wind.

"That has to be them, sir." Rubonus flapped his wings and flew a little lower to point his nose at a fishing shack in the middle of the lake.

"Rubonus, grab a tree trunk and try to drop it on the building. You need to practice your accuracy and even if you miss, it'll shatter the ice and drown the cowards."

"Sir, if I may," Hester interjected before Rubonus swooped to retrieve his missile. She didn't wait for Tormentus to respond because she didn't want to wait until spring. "We haven't made contact with these mages since they left the United States and entered dwarf land. Protocol states that we need to give them a chance to explain themselves and take a cuff."

"They made their choice when they ran," he said.

"If they weren't running from the duties of their American citizenship, they wouldn't be suppressing their powers," Rubonus pointed out as casually as if he commented that it was cold out rather than trying to deny a group of citizens their right to cooperation.

"Still, sir, if Cooper and I can get them to wear the cuffs, that would be four more mages for our department. Reports show that two of them are at least third-level mages. As a commander, you get a commission based on their placement—correct, sir?"

"It's hardly commission but yes, you've made your point, Diamantine. You have five minutes to see if you and the mage can get them to put the cuffs on. After that, we burn that shack and melt the ice beneath their feet."

She nodded, ignored the fact that he insisted on using her formal dragon name, and flew out over the lake. Experience was a powerful reminder that Tormentus was already counting time. She spread her wings to slow her flight to a gentle glide as she approached the structure. It was tiny and made of rickety boards and a corrugated tin roof. A few fishing poles leaned up against the outside of it. But Lara was right. There were people inside.

Hester could smell smoke from a hastily extinguished fire. She pumped her wings twice and blew snow drifts away from the fishing shack and out across the frozen lake. Beneath the snow was the crystalline blue sheen of the ice. It reflected the moon above them as if both the sky and the lake watched what would transpire there that day.

Seconds before she landed, Lara leapt from her back with a magic-augmented gust of wind to slow her fall. Before the dragon touched down on the ice, she shifted into her human form. Her momentum was such that when her feet landed, cracks spread from her impact. Still, the ice seemed solid enough. She took a few steps forward and the surface didn't crack further.

"We know you're in there," Hester called into the night. In response, the clouds, heavy and gray, moved in to block the moon.

"We don't mean you any harm. We merely need you to come home to your country and serve your fellow people. You all have gifts. We want to help you use them."

She received no response except from the clouds, which began to drop big fat flakes of snow on the scene. Hester stood in silence for a moment. The falling snow swallowed all sound. She could hear nothing from inside the shed and nothing from outside except the sound of wind moving over the wings of the two dragons who circled overhead.

"One of them stopped suppressing their magic," Lara whispered through the snow.

"That was a stupid thing to do," she muttered, knowing the mages inside couldn't hear her. She stepped forward and knocked on the brittle, wooden door. Even if she didn't have a well of dragon strength to call on, she had a feeling she could have knocked the door off its hinges if she wished to do so.

She was about to do exactly that when a light blazed inside the dilapidated building. Orange light glowed around the poorly framed door and the wood exploded outward in the wake of a massive fireball. Hester, no stranger to fighting fire, raised her arms to block her face, but the heat and pressure of the blast were too much. She was hurled from her feet, thrown back, and cracked the ice with her shoulder, but thankfully didn't fall through.

One of her hands screamed in pain when she tried to push to her feet. The fireball had done far more damage than she had expected. Her dragon healing powers seemed to have trouble mending the wound.

"And you! You're a fucking traitor to your people!" the mage who had thrown the fireball yelled at Lara. Hester knew it was the same mage because his hands were wreathed in flame. This was most likely the leader of the little squad they were tracking. The reports had been wrong. He was more advanced than third-level. The flames on his hands danced and made his sweat-streaked brow glisten and his eyes look even crazier than they would have in the hidden moonlight of the growing snowstorm.

"Mages who don't work with the dragons are killed!" Lara shouted and used a spinning disk of air to deflect a blast of fire, then another. "Help me change the system from the inside."

"Says the slave. You're worse than a slave. You're a slave who hunts men brave enough to be free." The other mage launched a blast of fire and she flinched and allowed the attack through her disc of air to knock her off her feet.

"You don't deserve her pity," Hester said, done with playing nice and ready to take this mage by force for what he had done to Lara.

She readied herself for a retaliatory attack but never had the chance.

Tormentus and Rubonus swooped in from opposite sides and completed a damn near perfect ring of fire maneuver. Each dragon exhaled narrow blasts of flame at the ice surrounding the fisherman's shack. The ice—as thick as it was—was no match for dragon fire, and by the time the two dragons completed their loop, the surface beneath Hester's feet was no longer solid but an ice float.

"I'd rather die free than live as a slave!" the mage shouted at the two dragons and hurled balls of fire into the night that they dodged easily.

"And what about your allies? Do they wish to die on their feet or live for decades?" Hester shouted at the man and tried to draw his attention.

"She's trying to use her aura powers on you, Jason. Don't fall for it!" A female mage emerged from the shack and rocked on the now tilting and shifting piece of ice. The snow whipped behind her and revealed her magical ability to control the wind.

"Lara," Hester said.

"On it." The mage grunted. She pushed to her feet in time to throw a blast of wind at the newcomer. She was far more practiced and funneled her gust into a tight cylinder that drilled toward her opponent's chest, but the raw power of the unbound mage exceeded what power she had available to her while she wore the magical dampening bracelet. The rookie mage and the magic master's powers collided, created a swirling dervish of snow and sleet that zig-zagged between the two dueling women, and threw sleet and frigid lake water everywhere else.

The dragon had no doubt that if Lara were unbound, she would have been able to defeat the mage easily but of course, no mage could go about unbound. That was why these had tried to escape.

"You have no right to your power!" the fire mage yelled at Hester. "You're not a predator but a parasite." Another blast of fire followed and she dodged it. He could heat his attacks hot enough to burn a dragon, which was no easy task. Her right hand still hadn't healed and it didn't feel like it would.

But he was only human and she was a dragon who had trained for centuries in combat. She moved forward and stepped around his assaults with practiced ease. It took the mage a great deal of effort to throw the superheated fireballs, so every one of them was easy to anticipate—or easy for someone with dragon reflexes anyway.

She settled into a rhythm—step, step, dodge, step, step, step, crouch. Step. Step back. In moments, she had covered the distance between them. She thrust her left hand into his chest and the mage catapulted away. Her intention had been for him to collide with the shack, but she had misjudged. Instead, he tumbled across the snow-covered surface of the lake.

Hester glanced briefly at the shed. Why hadn't the other two mages come out? It was surely obvious by now that the two who currently fought wouldn't win. What were they waiting for?"

A scream jerked her head away from the shed, her opponent, and back to Lara. She turned in time to see a great wave of water rise from the lake and pound into her to sweep her feet out from under her.

It seemed the mage she had been fighting could control more than a single element. This was unusual in a rogue mage but not unheard of. While the woman's control of water might be rudimentary, it was still a threat, especially with the cold.

But it was fire that proved to be the decisive element in this battle. The mage Jason blasted Lara with flame. At first, the dragon thought he had missed but the ice melted and cracked beneath her and in seconds, her mage fell into the icy water.

"Lara!" Hester screamed and scrambled after her. She had to get her out. The mages could wait. Humans were squishy little things. If Lara got too cold, she would die. Her rescue took priority for now. She reached her and extended a hand but was too late. The water had already iced over.

The dragon straightened and turned toward the mage with the wind powers. Had she frozen the surface of the water to kill Lara? But no...she now ran back toward the fisherman's shack and pointed at the sky—or more specifically, the dark shapes of two approaching dragons—and screamed.

Then, Hester understood. In the doorway of the shed stood a third mage, an old man. He had refrozen the lake and killed Lara.

"Murderer!" she shouted and ran toward him as the two dragons swooped overhead.

They flew in a tight formation so when they exhaled flames, it was as if a single inferno engulfed the rickety structure.

Surprisingly, it didn't burn.

In the flames, Hester saw the fourth mage silhouetted, a young man who wrapped the entire hovel in some kind of shielding energy. His power was stronger than anything she had ever seen in a mage. To stop Tormentus was a feat in itself, but to stop him and Rubonus was beyond comprehension.

It was almost a pity that he didn't fully understand the power of the dragons he now faced. The flames didn't burn the shed but they did melt the ice all around it. In one moment, three mages stood in their shed and tried to defend it. In a split-second, they were on a tiny island of ice made top-heavy by the shed on it. It tipped into the frozen lake and spilled the three defenders into the water.

The old man had the wherewithal to attempt to freeze the water so he could climb out, but Tormentus's third strike came much sooner than his second had. He incinerated the old man and the shed in one blast.

The only mage left was Jason, the fire mage who had turned a simple retrieval into a goddamn slaughter.

His attention wasn't on Hester, though. It was on the pine tree falling from the sky directly toward him.

She knew that many mages could use their powers to move objects but Jason didn't seem to be one of them. Rather than redirect the falling tree, he blasted it with fire. All he achieved was to transform it into a burning trunk that impaled him and thrust him into the frigid lake to end the fight.

Hester wasted no time. She doubled back to where Lara had fallen under the ice. "Lara! Lara, dammit, you're better than this!" she screamed at the icy surface. This far from the dragon's twin inferno, the lake was still frozen from the old man's magic as if it had never been broken at all. "Lara!" she shouted.

"That mage complained about the cold of the wind. She's as good as dead," Tormentus boomed from the sky.

"She could have made a pocket of air to breathe. She might still be alive."

"It's doubtful," the leader grunted. "We're heading south. Mission accomplished."

"Mission accomplished!" Rubonus echoed.

"I can't leave her down there," she shouted at the two dragons. She had lost control of her aura and knew they could both taste her grief for the dead mage—no, dying. She could still be saved. The young woman had to be saved.

In return, Tormentus let Hester feel his aura plainly. Disdain was what he felt, disdain for her and achievement for the mission. He counted it a success even though Lara was dead.

"The plane in Kugaaruk will leave at dawn. If you miss it, you'll have to fly to Boston," The leader didn't even bother to slow as he banked in a wide circle to return from whence they came. "While you're at it, make sure there are no other survivors."

"I'm sorry about your mage!" Rubonus said. "She was a cute one. If they give me a good one, you can have first choice if you want it, yeah?"

With that almost insulting response to her grief, they were gone.

Hester turned to the lake and tried not to let despair over Lara's death overwhelm her. It was incredibly hard to not blast a hole in the ice and try to dive for the mage's body, but she was no swimmer. Some dragons were but she wasn't one of them. If she broke the ice, she wouldn't be able to peer through it. Instead, she searched for her friend's body—that was what Lara was, a friend. She didn't think of the woman as her mage but she did think of her as her friend.

And she had let her die.

After a long, fruitless search, she finally dropped to her knees and let herself grieve for her friend's death. She was gone. And for what? A few more dead mages? Why did they have to die? They had run from their duty, yes, but they hadn't hurt anyone. It was such a shame that the dumbest one had answered the door with violence. It was his fault they were dead and yet, if she truly believed that, why did she feel guilty about it? Why did she feel that if she had handled herself with more caution, not only Lara but all the people there might still be alive?

There was nothing to be done about it now. Hester pushed to her feet and proceeded to follow her commander's orders. She found no survivors. The old man had managed to freeze himself into the ice when the dragons had blasted him. His charred and blackened head and right arm were starkly different than the pale-blue frozen flesh of the rest of his body trapped beneath the ice.

The wind mage had fared no better. She had been seared with enough fire to kill her but not char her. Her blood marked the ice float she was on with red.

She saw no point in looking for Jason. A tree trunk had taken him in the chest and sent him to the bottom of the lake.

That only left the mage with the curious shielding power. Hester poked around the hole in the ice where the shed had stood. Debris from it was all over. A fishing pole lay on the ice and an insulated cooler—used to keep warm things warm in the cold climate—floated in the water. But where was the mage?

The dragon moved as close to the edge of the broken ice as she dared.

It was so quiet in the north of the world. The snow continued to fall, oblivious to the deaths that had taken place under its white flakes. She wondered if anyone would even know what had happened there in the morning. If the lake froze and the snow fell indefinitely, it seemed likely that no one would so much as suspect that anything had happened at this lake until the spring—if people even came then. There was so little of the shed left and no big pieces at all.

Well, there was something out near the middle of the hole in the ice.

It was big and long—maybe a canoe? But how could a canoe have survived Tormentus?"

As Hester considered this and poked around for the last mage's body, she heard something. It was extremely faint but it was there. It sounded like something was crying and came from whatever floated in the middle of the hole in the ice.

She vaulted skyward but transformed after she left the ice so as to not crack it any further and flew out over the hole. The object was indeed a canoe, and she picked it up in her talons and carried it to the shore.

There, under the dark pine trees, she changed into a human and looked at her catch.

She had found the dead mage. He was in the canoe, along with a pile of blankets and an explanation for why they had all fought so hard.

A tiny baby lay in a hand-carved bassinet in the craft and cried loudly for help.

Hester took a step forward, feeling chills despite the cold. Had that been the fifth source of power Lara had felt? Why had the mages come out there with an infant? Why risk its life if they cared so much about it? It seemed obvious—given the pristine condition of the canoe—that the mage had expended the last of his power to protect it and its passenger. Why?

The baby answered none of these questions, of course, but only continued to cry even louder. It of course didn't realize that with every shriek it expended what limited energy it had.

The dragon could bear it no longer, scooped the baby up in its parcel of blankets, and cradled it in her arms.

"There, there, little baby. There, there. The crazy people who dragged you out here are all gone."

Somehow, this calmed the little crying bundle. The infant's mouth closed and quirked into a kind of slobbery smile. It stared at Hester with big eyes that—in the light of the moon—appeared to be the same color as Lara's had been.

It spoke some unintelligible baby babble, freed one of its arms from its swaddling, and reached up to her face.

She leaned in and let it touch her nose, but when it did, something remarkable happened.

Scales rippled from the finger that touched her and covered the baby's hand and arm while the bones seemed to extend. Its head changed shape and its body grew awkward and knobby in the crook of her arm. In moments, she wasn't holding a baby at all but a dragonling instead.

"But that's impossible!" she exclaimed.

"Goo!" the little dragon burbled in reply.

But it wasn't a dragon, stolen or otherwise. If it was, she would have felt—would still feel—its aura. And Lara had felt a fifth power—a fifth mage power. But how could this little bundle be a mage? No mage could change shape— well, not in the last thousand years anyway. Hester's mind raced with legends of some long-ago stories about evil mages who could take the shape of a dragon, but those were merely stories intended to scare dragonlings and explain how the world worked and why mages should not be trusted.

Yet the little dragon in her arms had no aura. And, despite now looking like a dragon, it still had Lara's eyes.

Hester Diamantine decided she didn't care how this was possible. This baby was special. She couldn't let anything bad happen to it and the intensely protective urge that flooded through her seemed a natural reflex. Whatever else she did, she had to protect the baby. She had to. Quickly, she tucked its little arm inside the blankets, found a bag in the canoe that looked like it had been made expressly for carrying the infant, and tucked it inside. A silver and turquoise pendant on a silver chain lay inside. The baby began to play with it like it was a familiar toy. Hester couldn't help but smile.

She transformed into her dragon body, picked up her precious parcel, and headed south.

As she flew, she considered the certainty that she had to protect this infant. She had never felt anything as strongly as she felt that. But it meant keeping it secret from Tormentus. He could be vicious while he hunted but he wasn't stupid. Far from it. If he saw her return from the wreckage of the site with this baby and noticed it didn't have an aura, he would remember what Lara had said about a fifth mage.

And it wasn't unheard of for a runty dragonling to be culled either. Tormentus would make sure this one—as stunted as it was, he would claim, since it had no aura—was snuffed out before it had a chance to become the somebody she knew it would be.

Without a doubt, she couldn't allow that, even if it meant her flight home had suddenly become considerably longer.

# CHAPTER TWO

_**Sixteen years later: Somewhere outside Little Water, New Mexico, USA.**_

The wind felt amazing under Kylara Diamantine's wings and so much better than the stuffy air of their home—more like cave—half-buried in a mountain. The red rocks and sands of the New Mexican landscape below her had baked in the sun all day. They belched heat into the air that she caught with her wings as she spiraled higher into the sky.

She wasn't strictly supposed to be out flying—not without her mom—but what Hester Diamantine didn't know wouldn't hurt her. The young dragon was almost seventeen now, but her mom still treated her like she was nothing more than a dragonling.

There was no reason why she couldn't fly by herself. She was certainly good enough at it. She flapped her wings and forced herself into a dive that took her from the cool air that lingered high above the mountains to the heat-baked landscape below. As the air grew hotter around her, she whooped with delight. This was living!

Instinctively, she spread her wings and caught another

thermal of hot air to drift higher again as effortlessly as a bird. She circled continuously and increased speed as she added her strength to the power of the heated air to drive herself so high that the air became cold enough that when she breathed it in, it almost hurt.

When she reached that elevation, she leveled off and studied the landscape below her. Kylara had never known any landscape but New Mexico. She longed to see a lush forest, a meadow, a jungle, or even a city, but she could admit that she lived in a beautiful place. Below her, different shades of stone battled for dominance of the high desert landscape. Red rocks, yellow rocks, and pink boulders flecked with crystals that glimmered in the sun all poked from the sand and scrubby soil. Some people might see a wasteland, but not her. She saw a hundred kinds of cactus, dormant grasses, and scrubby trees ready to force out a year's worth of growth whenever the sky decided to let it rain again. It was beautiful there, yet she wanted to see what it looked like somewhere else—anywhere else.

She had been to nearby Farmington any number of times and even to Santa Fe a precious few, but she wondered what else was out there beyond the beautiful reds, oranges, and yellows of her home. Sometimes, she envied the cars that gleamed in the sunlight as they moved freely through the landscape. They only needed gas to escape their environment, not their mother's permission.

Kylara sighed and her gaze followed an old beat-up truck until it rounded a mountain road and vanished. Another glint caught her eye, this one higher up. A plane? No, it was too low for that and there wasn't an airport in that direction, anyway.

She almost gasped when she realized that it wasn't a plane but a dragon. It was a long way off but she had seen it bank and saw its dark silhouette against the reddish earth below. Its wings and tail were unmistakable. This was a dragon—the first she had ever seen besides her mother and herself.

Curiosity surged through her. She seldom had an issue with her aura as her mother constantly reminded her. While it was what Hester described as closed off, even the lizards hiding in the scrub below, she was certain, could feel her desire to find out more about her kind.

The curiosity was as quickly followed by caution. Her mom had forbidden her from meeting other dragons. It was the number one rule she had to follow and Hester had drilled it into her head since before she could fly. For whatever reason, she had never told her why.

At times—especially over the last few years—the rule had been frustrating, but it hadn't exactly been difficult to follow. Kylara had never even seen another dragon. To attempt to break the rule would have involved either stealing her mom's car or flying hundreds of miles through the desert. Neither was an option that she particularly wanted to take.

But now, one flew in view of her land.

Kylara thought about her mother's rule and how serious she had always been about it. She was not to meet another dragon... but could she look at one? After all, it wasn't like she had been raised in a vacuum. Her mom had taught her about dragons, their history, and even their current events—an especially exciting topic for the young dragon, as the exploits of the Steel Dragon and the new organization she had created a year before were more exciting than any book. She had told her daughter not to meet a dragon. It seemed logical that there was probably a reason for that. But to peek at one? How could that possibly hurt?

Her mind made up, she tucked her wings and dropped to glide over the arid landscape. She wanted to see this dragon but that didn't mean she wanted to be seen. Fortunately, her dragon form was perfectly suited for her environment.

In this light, her scales varied from copper to red. In reality, they were like her mother's—the color of a diamond—with the same hard, crystalline edges that made her mom's dragon form so tough. But the underlying shade was different, exactly like her skin was only a few shades darker than Hester's.

In the light of the late afternoon sun, she looked like a mirage floating over the desert, an apparition of heat hardly any different than the colors of the desert itself. She looked nothing like her mom, not in her dragon form or in her human body, but Hester had always explained that the magic in dragon blood made hereditary traits more interesting than they were in humans.

Kylara flew low and slow over the landscape, keeping her gaze fixed on the dragon as she drew closer to it. She could not sense its aura yet. If she did, she did not know what she would do. Even that might be enough to satiate her curiosity. But she couldn't sense it yet so she flew closer.

It was hard to tell in the light, but it looked like the dragon was coming closer. Did that mean it had seen her too? She had been up quite high—higher than her mom liked her to fly when they were anywhere but the very center of their land—but had the stranger seen her before she had seen it?

She knew these questions would not be answered. Certainly, she'd be lucky to even see the true color of the dragon's scales without it seeing her. But maybe, after seeing this dragon, she could finally get some answers from her mom. She knew some of the girls in the area had a Quinceanera celebration. Could it have something to do with that? A coming of age ritual? She decided she would ask her mom—after she had a better look at this dragon.

Her mother, however, had other ideas.

Hester Diamantine—her scales the color of diamonds frozen in ice and eyes burning with rage—screamed into the dry desert air behind her errant daughter. "Where on earth do you think you're going, young lady?"

"Mom!" Kylara responded, grasped for other words, and found none.

Her mom caught up to her extremely quickly. The young dragon forced a smile on her face but her mother showed far more teeth in her fury.

"Well?" Hester demanded. "What could possibly compel you to break my single most important rule?"

In the face of her mother's wrath, she didn't have an answer. She knew her mom would demand far more than, "I only wanted a peek." In an effort to preempt the inevitable lecture, she chose her only viable option. "I'm sorry, Mom."

"You'd better be, young lady. You're off our land, were flying so high everyone in the four-state area must have seen you, and when I catch up to you, I see another dragon who you seem to be approaching? Have you lost your mind?"

*No, I finally started using it,* Kylara wanted to say, but she didn't. Instead, she fell in behind Hester, caught her wake, and used it to glide home. Still, she couldn't help but glance at the other dragon with longing. If it was so bad to see the other dragon, why did she want to so badly?

## CHAPTER THREE

To call Kylara's home a cave was an insult. The back half of the house was built into the side of the mountain that towered at the center of their land, but that didn't make it feel like a cave. The back wall was the intermingled colors of the stone of the bedrock. The ceiling was peppered with skylights and solar panels.

Because of how the house was insulated by the mountain, the solar panels were able to produce more than enough power to fuel not only their aquaponic system that purified their water and grew much of their fresh food but whatever appliances or technological knickknacks they wanted. Even though it was only the two of them, the house was spacious enough to accommodate them both comfortably.

It was space that the young dragon desperately wanted right now. She had begged her mother to put in a home theater system complete with surround sound and all the latest game systems. Hester had allowed it only after she made her daughter crunch the numbers on how much electricity it would all require. If she wanted to use it, she had to hang her laundry on the line that day instead of using the dryer, but she didn't mind. When you had nothing to do, hanging laundry wasn't so bad. The theater room was where she wanted to vanish to now, but her mom had other ideas.

Her mother's demeanor suggested that she had no intention to allow her yearning for space to be fulfilled. She still wasn't speaking, but the posture of her wings was rigid and ready for combat. Her aura was a black box—utterly inscrutable. When she was like this, it meant she was pissed. Worst of all, she didn't lead Kylara directly to their house but instead, headed to a far corner of their land.

Kylara tried to prepare herself mentally for the inevitable eruption. Her mom was probably only buying time while she put her tirade into the proper sequence. Hester was mostly reasonable, but she certainly had a temper and her daughter had finally managed to break her most serious rule.

She merely wished she knew why. Growing up there, she had never honestly minded it. She had always had the freedom to roam their substantial piece of property and had two dogs, Telo and Jaro, and for a long time, that had been enough. But now, her mother would yell at her for breaking a rule she didn't even understand. It simply wasn't fair. She would be seventeen in less than a month. While she understood this was considered young for a dragon, she also knew that humans considered this to be close to the end of adolescence. She had waited and waited for Hester to explain her place in the world, but the explanation simply never came.

"Where are we going, Mom?" Kylara asked instead of all the questions she wanted the answers to.

"Here is fine." Her mother changed into her human form in mid-flight. A shower of diamond-colored shards eclipsed her dragon body before a woman somersaulted earthward. She landed on a pile of boulders, her feet planted squarely and her hands extended in a tai chi stance.

Kylara changed in the air and dropped to a nearby boulder.

Her landing wasn't quite as tight as her mother's, but she succeeded without having to take a step forward.

"You broke my most sacred rule today," Hester said. She didn't look at her and instead, closed her eyes and moved her body in slow, practiced motions.

"Why is it your most sacred rule?" the young dragon demanded. She hadn't meant to ask it but she was too frustrated to think before she spoke. She wanted answers.

"Now is not the time," her mom replied.

"Then, when?"

"When you're strong enough!"

Hester Diamantine leapt from her boulder into a graceful flip and extended a leg with such force that when Kylara dodged, the kick still broke the boulder she had been perched on in half.

"Mom!"

"Defend yourself!" the older dragon shouted and surged forward. Both hands— the normal one and the burned one with the missing finger—moved in a blur.

She blocked hastily, then again, and caught the third blow in an aikido hold and tumbled her mother away from her.

"Good. Faster!" Hester ordered.

It wasn't like she had a choice. The older dragon raced forward and used her insane strength to try to drive her daughter into the ground. They had trained together many times, but this was different. Why didn't she simply talk to her about what had happened? Would she use a duel as a pretext to punish her for her disobedience?

Well, she'd have to hit Kylara first if that was the case.

She dodged her mom's next strike. It struck the sand at their feet with such force that she wondered if Hester Diamantine had made glass out of the sand. Still, she could hold her own. She redirected the next two blows and swiped her adversary's feet out from under her. Hester had insisted that she learn aikido because it used an opponent's superior strength against them.

Her mom was undoubtedly stronger than she was, but with aikido, she could usually hold her own.

This time, however, the older dragon gave no quarter.

Hester moved so fast that her motions blurred. What strikes did land raised bruises instantly. It was a good thing she had her dragon healing power or her muscles might have given up under the onslaught.

Instead, she parried, dodged, and redirected the attacks when she could. It wasn't easy, but she recognized a sequence and was able to catch the final punch and hurl her mother into a boulder. Hester struck it with her right hand—the scarred one—and screamed in pain.

"Mom! I didn't mean to hurt your hand!"

"Then you're still a child. If an opponent has a weakness, use it."

"But you're my mom."

"What if I wasn't?"

Kylara didn't know what that was supposed to mean, but it was obviously a rhetorical question. Hester didn't wait for an answer but attacked with renewed ferocity.

The young dragon was no rookie, though. She dodged a kick, moved in close, and struck her opponent in the chest to rob her of oxygen. In almost the same motion, she spun behind her and got her in a headlock.

Never one to quit, Hester savaged her daughter's ribs with her elbows. The relentless battering continued with no sign of restraint.

Kylara didn't let her hold slacken in the least, not even when she felt a rib crack and the blows began to weaken. Only when her mom finally stopped her strikes did she relax.

The older dragon swung her head back and drove it into her daughter's face to draw a fountain of blood from her nose.

She released her adversary instinctively after the impact and wiped the blood away. Already, the capillaries in her nose had healed. She'd learned to ignore minor wounds a long time before.

"You pretended you had passed out," Kylara protested.

"Which you should not have fallen for. Still, you did well." Hester bowed to her daughter, launched skyward as she took her dragon form, and flew to the house, leaving the young dragon alone.

She was so confused. Did breaking her mom's number one rule mean they had to fight? They had sparred many times but never like that.

"What the hell is going on?" she asked as she kicked a rock with enough force to shatter it. Something had changed within her, although she didn't recognize it fully. She was done waiting for answers.

## CHAPTER FOUR

The young dragon landed in front of the house and changed into her human form. She went inside and found the living room empty and her mom in the kitchen.

"Kylara, sweetie, the beans are done. Can you please season them?" Hester asked without looking up from the fresh green chilies she sliced for salsa.

"Yeah, sure." She retrieved a wooden spoon and took out a spoonful of black beans. They needed to be salted rather than seasoned. Her mom had added oregano, thyme, and whatever herbs she'd found in the garden when she'd started cooking them but had neglected to add the salt because it made them take longer to cook, especially at this elevation. She now sprinkled a little salt in and decided they were delicious.

"Mom?"

"Yes, Kylara?" Her mom had moved on to tomatillos and a big pile of them sat on her cutting board. They had roasted them and a massive batch of green hatch chilies the day before. She knew from experience that even though Hester was making fresh salsa with the roasted tomatillos and peppers, both women would still pile their burritos high with roasted hatch chilies.

"Why can't I talk to other dragons?"

Hester didn't look up. Instead, she snatched a bunch of cilantro, rinsed it, and began to chop it, stems and all. She favored her scarred hand, which meant her daughter had hurt it in their duel. "It's my most important rule. You know that."

"But why?"

Her mother looked up, and she saw the fierceness in her eyes that she simply didn't know if she possessed. It wasn't only their dragon bodies that looked different. Hester Diamantine was a beautiful, imperious woman. Her face was all hard lines—high cheekbones, an angular jaw, a pointed chin, and eyes like flecks of ice.

She had the grace of a diamond but the presence of an iceberg. Her hair was silver and her fair skin was flecked with blemishes from too much time under the strong mountain sun. Kylara knew that some of those blemishes could be cleared with her dragon healing abilities, but their life there was a human one and humans aged, so Hester kept her imperfections. She thought they made her mother even more beautiful.

Kylara often felt as if she were the exact opposite of her cool-as-ice mom. Her skin was darker, a coppery shade that leaned to bronze after too much time in the sun compared to her mom's blemished ivory. Her hair was dark and straight, her eyes too big and too expressive. She shared Hester's athletic figure, but that was daily training, a healthy diet, and a dragon metabolism more than anything else.

Sometimes, she wondered what her dad looked like. She fingered the turquoise and silver amulet she wore around her neck—a family heirloom, her mother had said—and thought of him now. Did he look like her or was she a blend of the two and did not take after either?

"I'll tell you later," Hester said absentmindedly.

"Later when?"

"When I finish heating the tortillas! Honestly, Kylara, what has come over you?"

She knew that if she pushed any further, the tortillas might end up on the floor or all over the kitchen, so she let it drop.

Even though it had always been only the two of them, they still sat together for dinner every day. They spent considerable time together, in fact, since she was home-schooled and Hester was her only teacher, but their daily schedule fluctuated wildly. The morning of one day might be disassembling a water pump, while the next might be focused on the benefits of compost. Sometimes, they would spend days talking about specifics of dragon history, only to not broach the subject at all for months again.

But dinner was different. It was a time when they came together and shared food and their lives with each other. Even though Kylara was frustrated with her mom for not explaining herself, she still enjoyed sharing the meal with her, especially since they still had avocados for their burritos.

"How was your day?" she asked.

"Fine," Hester said as she added more salsa to the bitten-off end of her burrito. It was never spicy enough for her. When she didn't elaborate or ask her daughter about her day, her patience ran out.

"Mom, I'm sorry it looked like I was breaking your rule, but I only wanted to see the other dragon."

"Kylara, do you honestly expect me to believe that?" Hester set her burrito down, never a good sign.

"It's the truth. I've lived by your rules for my whole life but I need to know why. Why can't I talk to other dragons? I've never met one—not a single one. Why not? You used to be in Dragon SWAT and you worked with other dragons, but I can't even talk to one?"

"Kylara—"

"We spend time on dragon history and I've never heard

anything about dragons needing to keep their distance. When we watch the news, there are never any stories about young dragons entering society. I guess the Steel Dragon entered the dragon world later, but that was only because she didn't know she was a dragon."

"Kylara!"

"I simply don't understand! I want to follow your rules and I always have, but why? Is something wrong with me?" Tears had come to her eyes and she knew her aura was a hot mess, not that she often bothered to hide what she felt from her mother during dinner.

"No, Kylara, nothing is wrong with you," Hester said, although she said nothing more. She merely stared at her as if she was trying to decipher her, or hypnotize her, or dissect her, or—

"Mom!"

"Sorry. It's only... You've become such a beautiful young woman. I take it for granted, you know, how smart and hardworking you are. You've made me very proud, Kylara."

"Jesus, Mom, why are you talking like you're going to die?"

Her mother smiled but there were tears in her eyes. This time, her long stare didn't feel as hostile, merely incredibly sad. "It's not safe."

"I know it's not safe. All you've ever said is that it's not safe. It's the same as touching the electrical cables coming from the solar panels. But at least I know what will happen if I touch those. Why can't I meet a dragon? That's what I don't know. It's what I need to know."

"I intended to wait for your birthday, but it looks like my hand has been forced." Hester took a napkin and wiped her perfectly clean mouth. "I used to be in Dragon SWAT. This was years ago, before you were born. I worked with the Boston team for a long time—for decades. We dealt with all variety of threats to dragon kind. Dragons, of course, but rogue mages, disgruntled dwarves, irate pixies, and even regular humans sometimes."

"Mom, I know all that. You told me all your SWAT stories before I was ten years old. And you usually call them pernicious pixies."

"You need to stop interrupting if you want this story," her mother said, stood from the table, and walked to the huge windows that made one wall of their home in the mountain. She sighed and her shoulders rose and fell heavily as she looked out across the rich purples, reds, and oranges of the landscape in the setting sun.

Kylara all but inhaled the rest of her burrito, wiped her mouth and hands hurriedly —her mom was ruthless when it came to getting stains on the furniture—and hopped over the back of the couch to cozy up for the story.

The older dragon stared out at the setting sun until the red disc touched a mountain in the west. Finally, she turned to Kylara. "There's someone out there hunting for me. Someone very bad."

"You mean looking for you?"

"I meant what I said, Kylara, and I was serious about you not interrupting either."

She mimed zipping her lips shut and flashed the smile that usually placated her mother.

"When I said someone is hunting me, that's what I meant," Hester said. "They eliminated my two partners a long time ago and they would have killed me too if I hadn't bought this land and holed up here in the guise of a human."

"But you always said that Tormentus—"

"Was as tough as dragons could be, yes." Hester didn't reprimand her this time. "That's what's so troubling, to be honest. You know that when you"—she paused for a long moment—"came into my life, it changed my priorities. I had already had doubts about Dragon SWAT after losing Lara. No one there cared about her, simply because she was a mage. She was more than that to me—so much more—and with her gone, you were that much more important. I had put in for retirement and planned to try to find something administrative, but then Tormentus was murdered.

"I know you want to ask how but don't bother. I don't know. Someone beat the hell out of him until his dragon power began to fade, then they stabbed him or shot him in the heart. The autopsy couldn't tell us any more than that. Believe me, Rubonus and I went over it a dozen times. We couldn't even determine if it was a mage, a dragon, or a human. At the time, of course, the idea of a human doing something like that was absurd. But with the dragon bullets those mages were making that the Steel Dragon exposed, a human could have done it. We didn't know that then, of course, or else I would have tried to find a more isolated piece of land."

*More isolated than this wasteland?* Kylara wanted to scream, but she held her tongue.

"Rubonus took the loss of Tormentus hard. He threw himself into searching for his killer and wound up dead on a wild goose chase. It was the same damn thing—his healing power was overwhelmed before his heart was stabbed or shot or something.

"When Rubonus was killed, I knew I had to get off the grid. I had already bought this land and did all the paperwork like I was a human who had been gifted money from a dragon—not an unusual thing at all at the time, although now, of course, with the Steel Dragon, things are different. I kept us here to keep us safe. Now do you understand?"

"Yes… Well, mostly. I want to," Kylara blurted. "But why do I have to stay hidden? And who would want you dead after all these years?"

"I have a hunch it has something to do with one case or another that I worked on when I was still on the force."

"And you think they still are mad at you about it? This had to happen at least twenty years ago, right?"

"Not quite."

"Still, if it's not twenty, even fifteen years is a long time. Whoever this person was has probably forgotten all about you by now."

"Oh, Kylara, my sweet, young Kylara." Hester smiled and the flecks of ice in her eyes melted with warmth. "Fifteen years or even a hundred are nothing to a dragon. Nothing at all. They live for millennia. I have refused to return to countries for decades over a bad cup of coffee. I understand that to you, it feels like a lifetime, but—"

"It is my lifetime, mom."

"Your life is exactly why you can't be seen by other dragons. If someone finds out that dragons have been hiding out here instead of a crotchety old woman and her daughter, people will start to ask questions. If dragons ask the questions, it will only be a matter of time before they arrive here to ask about you."

*But why would they care about me at all? You were on dragon SWAT, not me!* The young dragon bit the words back and they remained unspoken. She knew such a callous statement would only infuriate her mother. Instead, she thanked her for explaining the rule and went off to take a shower in recycled water.

After her shower, she checked on her mom before she went to bed. Hester Diamantine continued to stare out across the desert as if her dragon sight might finally locate the hunter who was out there waiting to pounce.

# CHAPTER FIVE

Despite going to bed before her mom, Kylara woke the next morning to an empty house. It wasn't unusual for her. She fixed a pot of coffee—which her mother considered a valuable and necessary commodity—sweetened it with agave nectar, and added fresh goat's milk from Gertrude, one of their nanny goats. Armed with her beverage, she settled in a chair to watch the world wake up.

The desert was most active in the early hours of the day. Birds in colors of gray, brown, and tan flew from cactus to scrub, looking for unsuspecting insects. What plants were capable of blooming were in the process of closing their flowers for the day to protect them from the desert heat. A band of coyotes moved down the mountainside, oblivious to the predator hiding in a girl's body behind a pane of glass built into the mountain. Her stomach grumbled, even though she didn't particularly like coyote.

She checked the fridge but found nothing she wanted—more goat's milk and cereal in the pantry. There was a good supply of vegetables in their aquaponic garden, but after the duel her mom had subjected her to the day before, she wanted meat. A quick peek in the garage revealed that Hester had taken the Jeep to town, probably for exactly that.

Despite being dragons, they lived the illusion that they were humans. They spent considerable time training as dragons in the center of their land, where—according to numbers that her mother had made her crunch time and time again—they were far enough away from anyone else that they wouldn't be seen. Whenever they left the property, they did so by Jeep and made sure to not flex their dragon strength or show any inhuman speed. Hester was so committed to the farce that Kylara had seen her ask men to help her load furniture into the back of their vehicle that she knew she could have picked up effortlessly with one hand.

In the kitchen, she found a note warning her to not leave or else.

She scowled with annoyance. Her mom had told her why she wanted her to stay hidden. Couldn't she trust her to listen to her? Yes, she still had questions, but it wasn't like she would simply throw their whole life away when she was finally starting to get the answers she had wanted for so long. She felt like she spent so much time putting herself in her mom's shoes, but it seemed like Hester never did the same for her. The unfairness of it rankled. She trusted her mother so why didn't she trust her in return?

Kylara's stomach answered with a loud grumble. She grimaced and poured herself a bowl of cereal, added raisins and goat's milk, and ate. It didn't satisfy her in the least. Knowing her mom, she'd be gone until well past lunch. She didn't make the trip into town for only one or two things. She'd fill the Jeep with food and likely stop at a hardware store to get a new gasket for the pump that had given them trouble.

An hour later, her stomach grumbled again. Not only was she hungry, but she was also bored.

Movement beyond the window caught her attention and she glimpsed a deer move across the mountainside. She hurried outside before she thought about it. There wasn't anything wrong with a little hunting. They had gone hunting hundreds of times. It was necessary to maintain the illusion that only two human women lived out there. Otherwise, the amount of meat they would have had to purchase would certainly raise a few eyebrows.

Her mom had said to not leave, but surely she had meant the property and not the house? She was sure the caution was warranted, but this property had kept her safe for all this time. As long as she didn't fly too high, she would be fine.

Kylara changed to her dragon body and pushed off the mountainside. She flapped her wings in the cool air to drive upward as it was too early for any thermals over the desert yet. Once she was about thirty feet up, she banked and headed around the mountain their house was built into and to the north side of the property. The southern half of their land was dry desert scrub, a landscape carved by water that was rarely present. Boulders towered over what plants struggled to survive. It was beautiful in a timeless, hostile kind of way, but she much preferred the other side.

The north gave way to mountains, most of them taller than the one where they lived. In the higher altitude, pine and oak trees flourished. The ravines between the mountains ran with snowmelt most of the year and if one knew where to look, there were pockets of ferns, flowers, and a hundred other kinds of life there.

Sometimes, Kylara wondered if the plants felt like she did—trapped in this mountainous oasis. She was thankful that she had such a beautiful place to live and was sure the flowers would be too, but she also longed to see the wider world. If her mom ever let her leave, would she flourish in a new habitat or, like a mountain flower brought into the desert, would she desiccate into nothingness in a world far more hostile than she ever could have imagined?

Such musings slid from her mind the moment she saw the outline of a deer move in the woods below. As soon her shadow crossed over the animal, it bounded deeper into the forest but its retreat encouraged others to do the same. Where a moment before there had only been one deer, there was now half a dozen.

She followed them and flew so low that her tail jostled needles and pinecones from the tops of the trees. The young dragon didn't want to eat the females, not with fawns that looked like they might still be in need of milk and an education, nor did she want to take the male she had first seen. He had a massive rack of horns and was solidly built, the kind of buck they wanted to father the deer that lived in their property. Instead, she focused on a young male, a six-pointer who looked close to being forced out on his own.

Once she had chosen her target, the hunt was over. She simply waited for a gap in the pine trees, tucked her wings, and splayed her talons like a golden eagle before she plunged to the forest floor. The deer was dead before it knew what had happened. The others bolted away, both too wise and too stupid to pay their fallen comrade any last respects.

Her stomach grumbled at the taste of fresh blood and she lunched heartily. By the time she left the carcass, little was left besides bone and a bit of viscera. She wasn't one for organ meat, but Hester had taught the importance of not wasting many times. It was a law of life in the desert, so she ate the liver, lungs, and kidneys. She would have taken them home for her mom, but she had left so little of the deer intact that it would make more sense to catch another that they could butcher and eat in their human forms.

She took flight again, feeling sluggish and lazy with her full stomach. Before too long, she found a different herd of deer and had begun the process of deciding if she wanted to capture another young buck or one of the older does when her shadow spooked the animals into the deeper woods.

Except it wasn't her shadow, she realized suddenly. She knew how to watch her shadow and how to use it. That could only mean one thing. She glanced up and saw another dragon gliding above her.

"Ahh!" she shouted involuntarily, veered into a pine tree, and knocked it—and almost herself—to the ground. "Crap!"

Kylara pumped her wings to get above the treetops and increase her speed.

"Are you all right?" the other dragon shouted from above, loud enough to send a flock of birds that had been hiding in the pine trees flapping into the morning sky.

She made no answer and simply flew faster, thinking about her mother's warning. It registered somewhat alarmingly that she had never seen another dragon but now, in less than twenty-four hours, she had seen two, and one of them was deep inside their property. This couldn't be a coincidence. Her mom had been right.

"Excuse me, miss. I only want to talk!" the dragon called. He had a gentle voice, so unlike Hester's and most of the people who lived in this hostile desert landscape.

But, she reasoned, killers could have kind voices.

The young dragon wasn't sure what to do, though. This intruder had seen her, but that didn't mean he knew who she was or where she lived. Immediately, she corrected her course. She had subconsciously flown around the mountain to return to her house, but she realized now that she couldn't do that. If she could shake him off, he—and he did sound like a he—might think she was merely passing through. But if she led him to her house, he would know where she lived. If he wanted to hurt her mom or was working for someone who did, that was deadly information.

"Miss! I don't mean you any harm, honestly." His aura said the same thing but Hester had taught her that experienced dragons could use their aura to lie as effectively as they could use their words.

Kylara stole another glance at the dragon. He was still there and continued to follow her. She had to concede that he didn't look particularly experienced. He looked young to her eyes, although admittedly, she didn't have any experience with estimating the age of other dragons.

His scales were uniform in color—a light gold—with a ridge of spines, horns, and wing ribs that were a richer color like antiqued gold. He had no mustache, tendrils, or horns sprouting from the spaces near his lips or eyebrows like many older dragons did, which made him look somewhat baby-faced, but in a good way. She also noticed his broad chest and well-defined muscles beneath his golden scales in his arms and legs.

He didn't look like a killer to her. Honestly, he looked young, curious, and maybe a little lonely, exactly like her.

She wanted to talk to him to find out his name and what he was doing there, flying over her property, but her mom's warning from the night before would not leave her mind either. If there truly was a hunter or group of hunters who had targeted Hester, was it inconceivable that they would use a young dragon to try to trick her? All her history classes told her that dragons wouldn't hesitate to use any tool available to them.

That meant she had to treat this handsome young dragon as a threat. Which meant she had to get away. But how?

# CHAPTER SIX

Kylara tried to increase speed, but she knew she wouldn't be able to simply outrun the other dragon and return home. Right now, she was above a pine forest, but she knew that as soon as she descended into the desert, the view went on practically forever. If this dragon was within a few miles of her, he'd be able to see her. That was simply life out there. It was never fair for the hunted.

She couldn't outrun him, but up there in the mountain range she knew so well, flying above forests and ravines she had spent her entire life exploring, she might not have to.

"Who are you?" the dragon asked from the sky above her. "Do you live around here?"

"Go away!" Kylara shouted in response and turned away from the direction she'd originally chosen to fly over the tops of the pine trees. To the other dragon's eyes, it must have looked like she was traveling above the top of a forest on a plain up in the mountains, but she knew better. The treetops were all the same height but that was only because as the ground at the base of their trunks sloped downwards, the trunks grew taller and taller as they had more access to the water from the mountain stream that flowed down the hidden ravine.

"I only want to talk, truly," the golden dragon assured her.

He sounded so genuine but she couldn't turn her back on everything her mother had said. She had to treat him like a threat. At the very least, he was trespassing and his intentions could be far worse than that, of course.

She remained low above the pine forest, waited, and counted the distance. Her gaze searched for an old tree struck by lightning a decade before that marked the edge of the ravine.

Finally, she saw it.

Kylara tucked her wings and folded them completely against her sides. She dove into the ravine that had been carved out of the red rock over millennia and plunged into a deep pool marked by the old lightning-blasted tree.

She burst out of the water, bounded off a boulder in a practiced motion she had perfected long before, spread her wings, and followed the ravine downstream.

The golden dragon dove after her but miscalculated his dive and splashed into the pool in an ungraceful splash that resembled that of a whale more closely than it did the cannonball of a human.

Kylara couldn't help but giggle as he pulled himself out of the pond and squirted water from his dragon nostrils.

Unfortunately, he didn't give up. He located her before she went around the next bend in the ravine and continued the pursuit.

Little did he know how poorly that choice would go for him.

She took a deep breath and focused on the path ahead of her. This particular part of the ravine was what her mother called the Straits. She had used it to train her daughter's agility in flight and it was a demanding teacher.

As soon as she rounded the first bend, a massive boulder like a stalactite from a cave that once swallowed the sky itself jutted from the center of the stream. Instinct screamed at her to go wide around it, but experience told her to do exactly the opposite. If she loosened her posture at all, she would impact with the far wall. She had to stay tight and go on the inside of the boulder, even though it felt like she would collide with it.

As expected, she negotiated the obstacle with ease. She had made this turn dozens of times before and she succeeded yet again. Although, exactly like every other time she had accomplished the difficult maneuver, she couldn't restrain a whoop of excitement when the boulder brushed the coppery spines on her back,

She immediately had to change direction as the river below was forced through a tiny space between two rock walls. It was so tight that Kylara had to turn on her side to fit through the chasm. Her left wingtip dipped into the rapids below while her right wing barely protruded beyond the top.

Flying sideways, she peeked back to see the golden dragon round the bend with the boulder. His instincts betrayed him and he loosened his posture. She prepared a grin as he hurtled toward the far wall.

The expected collision never materialized. Instead, he twisted at the last moment and scrabbled along the far wall before he jumped out over the river and spread his wings again. He approached the chasm that would force him to either fly above it or go sideways through it.

This was another trick of course. He could simply fly over it, but if he did, he'd never reach the sinkhole at the end in time.

Kylara had already reached it. Once more, she tucked her wings and hoped she had got her speed and velocity right as there was no space to spread her wings to adjust. Thankfully, her instincts remained finely honed. She followed the waterfall into a hole in the earth and spread her wings before she splashed into the pool at the bottom.

To her shock, the golden dragon followed her. She saw him

fall with the water and hurtle toward the pool, screaming with delight until he splashed into the pool.

This pool, however, wasn't deep like the other, mainly due to the clusters of jagged rocks at its bottom. She had never successfully splashed into this body of water without being hurt. The only way to navigate this passage was to avoid entering the pool.

Kylara—no longer being pursued—flew low over the now subterranean river. It wasn't dark down there as light streamed in with the waterfall, and the river emerged into another ravine a few hundred yards ahead. She looked back again, satisfied that she'd lost her pursuer, but the gold dragon burst from the water and flapped his wings to close the distance between them.

That was when she began to worry. She knew this land better than anyone so how could this stranger keep up? Did that mean he was an assassin?

"Woo-hoo! I haven't flown like this in ages!" the dragon shouted and his words echoed off the walls of the subterranean river, his delight obvious.

Kylara turned to the route in front of her. She had one more chance to escape him, and it would only work if he thought he was close to catching up to her. Her plan made, she accelerated but not so much that the gap between them didn't continue to shrink.

She emerged into daylight in the next part of the Straits. Here, the rock walls were even closer together but instead of a straight line, they formed a tight switch-back. Kylara swooped left and right and only flapped her wings at the moments when she knew she wouldn't hit the barriers on either side. It hadn't been easy, but with practice and a willingness to learn from broken bones and her dragon healing power, she had mastered this passage.

A crash from behind her told her that her experience had finally paid off.

"Ahhh!" The dragon screamed, tried to claw his way out, and only exacerbated the rockslide he had already started.

Rather than continuing through the Straits, she elevated and fled. She glanced back only once to confirm that her pursuer had been stopped. He was buried beneath an avalanche of his creation. Only a clawed arm, his tail, and a damaged wing jutted from the pile of rock. His body and the debris blocked the flow of the river, so downstream began to dry up as the water behind the blockage grew deeper and deeper, a pool of water that might last until the next rainstorm or for the next thousand years.

Kylara waited for the golden dragon to move or evidence even a twitch. She expected him to break free but he didn't. He lay still as the water behind him grew deeper until it started to trickle over and through the pile of boulders that buried him. Even the cold water of the snowmelt river didn't wake him, and she worried despite her mom's voice in her head telling her to go home without delay.

The young dragon didn't know what to do. The gold dragon didn't move at all. What if he was hurt too badly to dig himself out? Her intention had been to shake him, not kill him. He might already be dead but if he was, what risk was there in checking? And if he wasn't, she couldn't simply let him drown. Sure, he might be an assassin, but he certainly didn't seem like one. Her indecision was almost painful. If she left him there to die, she would feel terrible, but to save him would break her mother's number one rule in a big way. If he was what Hester suspected, saving his life could very well doom theirs.

Still, she didn't think he was an assassin. He seemed young and lonely, exactly like her. She couldn't leave him to die.

Her mind made up, she wheeled sharply and returned to him.

She transformed into her human form and landed on top of the rockpile that had buried him with a graceful front flip.

It seemed logical to dig his head out first. One of his horns had been snapped in half from a falling boulder and one of his nostrils was rimmed with blood. She put a hand near his nose and felt for his breath. He still had one. Good. He wasn't dead. With the broken horn, he somehow looked even more handsome.

Next, she dug out his mangled wing. It had been broken in the avalanche but wasn't anything so severe that dragon healing wouldn't mend it. She stretched it out all the same and made sure the bones lay straight so they'd mend properly. This wasn't much of an issue with a physiology that could transform from winged, fire-breathing beast to bipedal mammal, but it might save him some pain.

Finally, she cleared the rubble from his other arm and legs. With him now exposed, she looked at him again. He was very young. If he was older than her, it couldn't be by much. Even down there in the dappled light of the sun that filtered through the trees at the top of the ravine, his scales sparkled and glowed. Not one of them was damaged or scarred and those that had been scraped in the fall were already healing to their former immaculate perfection.

Still, he didn't move, and she broke a few boulders to allow the water to flow past him so it wouldn't pool around his head and drown him. This was something that Kylara, being a desert girl, had a strange fascination with. It was a contradiction that deserts were dry because nowhere on earth was it so obvious that water had carved the landscape. That was what her mother said anyway. The ravine they were in was carved from water, and the boulders the gold dragon had dislodged would settle wherever the next flood placed them. Kylara enjoyed anticipating the way water moved.

A few minutes later with a few boulders crushed, she was finished. The stream wouldn't drown the golden dragon and she could now escape without being seen.

She froze when she realized that his eyes were wide open and that he watched her work. His golden gaze seemed to focus on the silver-and-turquoise pendant she always wore and which now dangled out from her shirt.

Immediately, she launched out of the ravine with her dragon strength, transformed, and took flight.

"Thank you!" he shouted.

She didn't understand why such a polite and simple phrase haunted her for the rest of her flight home.

# CHAPTER SEVEN

Kylara reached her home without the other dragon reappearing above the horizon. Even so, she was careful to fly well past the obscured dwelling, changed to her human form, and jogged home. It was a little paranoid, perhaps, but she was reasonably certain that no dragon would have managed to track her.

Her mom had always made it very clear how little most dragons valued their human forms. The Steel Dragon was an anomaly in this regard, and they both knew that she owed her rise to the global superpower she had become to her skills in her human form. Plus, this way, the young dragon had time to think.

She ran across the hardpacked earth of the desert, thinking about the dragon she'd encountered. It was a relief that she had managed to leave him behind, but her concern was that as soon as his wing healed, he'd resume searching for her. Was he the same dragon she had seen on the horizon the day before? It seemed logical that he was. But did that mean anything? Whether it was the same dragon or not, it didn't answer any questions about him. Who was he and what had he wanted?

The young dragon arrived home sweaty and out of breath despite her dragon speed and strength.

She went inside, still not sure about everything that had happened. Had she screwed everything up by being seen? Had she been a fool to let the dragon live? Would her mom have killed him? Kylara hoped not.

With a sigh, she stripped out of her sweaty clothes, moved to the shower, and was about to turn the water on when her dragon hearing caught the sound of a vehicle engine coming up the mountain road. It was her mom's Jeep, not unusual in itself, but from the engine and the rattle of the suspension, it sounded like Hester raced up the narrow road.

Thoughts of a shower abandoned, Kylara quickly threw on a clean change of clothes and went to the floor to ceiling windows that made up one wall of her home.

It was her mom and her Jeep traveled at such speed that the dust it had kicked up still hung in the air beyond the last ridge. The young dragon had lived there for her entire life and had never seen her kick up a dust plume like that. For some reason, that completely terrified her.

Something was very wrong. Had she found out something about the gold dragon? But how was that possible? Kylara clenched her teeth. She knew that if anyone could have someone learned about the clandestine chase, it would be Hester Diamantine.

The vehicle raced up the last stretch of road and stopped in front of the house with a flurry and spray of gravel and dust as it slid to a halt.

"Mom?" Kylara asked as she pulled her shoes on and ran out front.

"Get in the car, Kylara. Now!" her mom shouted as she popped the hood, cursed as she burned her fingers on the radiator, and dumped coolant inside the poor Jeep. It had a leak—a small one—that the woman had been planning to fix this weekend.

"Okay, let me grab a bag!" Her mom had warned her about

this happening one day. She didn't have anything packed but she knew exactly what she'd take. As she turned to go inside—she knew exactly what she wanted—she felt a flash of rage from her mother.

"There's no time to pack, dammit! Get in the fucking car!"

"But Mom, I have an emergency supply bag ready. I only need to cram in some clothes, photos, my journal, and my laptop. It'll only take—"

"All those things can be replaced, Kylara. People can't. Get in the car!" Hester had already slammed the hood shut and topped up the gas tank somewhat messily from one of the tanks of gas she always kept in the garage. She put the other tank in the back of the Jeep and got in the driver seat.

"Is this about the golden dragon?" her daughter demanded, thinking about the chase she had barely escaped. "Because I swear I did not mean for that to happen. I was hunting and he appeared out of nowhere."

"What are you talking about?" Her mother's already pale face blanched even more under her hat.

"There was a dragon up in the mountains. I tried to give him the slip but ended up trapping him in an avalanche in the Straits. He…he's not dead. And he saw my human form."

"No, Kylara, this isn't about that," Hester took a deep breath. It did nothing to calm her aura. "It sounds like you did fine, sweetie, truly. Using the Straits to trap a dragon was clever."

"Do you honestly think so?"

"Yes, but dammit, Kylara, we don't have time. Get in the Jeep."

Kylara, more scared now than when she had simply thought she'd broken the rules, obeyed without protest.

Hester buckled up and she did the same. Her mom turned the key, the vehicle sputtered to life, and they raced down the mountain through the faint wisps of the dust cloud the vehicle had made on her way up.

"The hunter I told you about last night?" her mother shouted over the roar of the engine and the protests of the suspension on the bumpy road. "He's found my scent. I don't know if he knows exactly where we live or if he only has our general location, but we need to run." She braked crazily and turned up a road that led deeper into the mountains.

"Shouldn't we take our dragon forms then? We won't have to stick to roads that way."

The road they were now driving on was so treacherous it made the last one seem like a paved interstate.

"No. We need to appear to be humans for as long as possible. We can always take our dragon form later if we need to but hopefully, we won't have to. The hunter will be looking for a dragon. With luck, they won't notice a mom and her daughter."

Kylara nodded. This was all too much. Yesterday, a dragon had seen her. Today, one had spoken to her. And now, they had to flee?

She already felt like they were in danger, but when they crested the first hilltop the little road took them over, she turned back and saw they were facing something far worse than her most dire imaginings.

Coming up the mountain road from the town, she saw what appeared to be a storm of flames.

Even more terrifying, there seemed to be a face in the center of it—one of fire and fury and that looked frighteningly hungry.

## CHAPTER EIGHT

"Mom! Mom, the scrub's on fire!" Kylara didn't know how to explain that she had seen a face in the flames, especially since it was gone now.

Hester lifted her foot off the accelerator for long enough to look in the rearview mirror. Mother and daughter both saw the flames form into what could only be described as a vortex of fire, jump across the gravel driveway that served as a firebreak, and sweep into the house.

The young dragon fought the urge to scream. She wanted to shout, transform into her diamond-crusted dragon body, and extinguish the flames, but what her mom said made her blood run cold.

"He knew where we lived."

It was such a simple statement but she said it as if the fire currently ravaging their home had burned it down ten years before rather than in that moment.

Kylara remained silent as the blazing vortex dissipated into a hundred tiny fires. From their angle on the top of the hill, she could see into their home through the wall of windows. The fires flared to life and devoured everything. She didn't know how else to think of it. The conflagration started in the living room, but a burst of sparks from the couch sent embers to the kitchen, up the stairs to the bedrooms, into the garage, and out into the aquaponic system. What was worse was that in every single place a spark touched, flames caught as if the entire house had been soaked in gasoline.

"Mom, we have a sprinkler system. Why isn't it working?" Even as Kylara asked the question, flames came together to create another swirling vortex. This one seemed to form an arm that ended in fingers that wrapped themselves around the exposed pipes of the sprinkler system and ripped it loose.

"Because it's not a normal fire," Hester said before she accelerated down the other side of the hill to block their home from sight.

"What do you mean it's not normal fire?" Kylara demanded. "Mom? What did you mean by that?"

An explosion detonated behind them. The blaze had probably found their propane tank and made short work of it. That meant the entire house was gone, or if it wasn't, it would be in another few short minutes.

"Mom, what was that?"

Hester Diamantine did not answer her daughter. Instead, she kept her gaze fixed on the road and her foot on the accelerator, forcing the Jeep through holes in the road and across a washboard surface that hadn't been graded in years.

Kylara—unable to help herself—twisted in her seat to see a great plume of smoke and ash rise from where their house had been. It climbed even higher as more of their clothing, possessions, and the frame of the house itself turned to smoke and ash. As it swirled above the devastation of their home, she thought for the second time that she saw a face.

It wasn't the features of a man or an animal but of something elemental. There was a hole for a mouth and two more for eyes, but the proportions wouldn't have looked natural anywhere else. Not that they looked natural on a spinning pillar of smoke and ash. Nothing looked particularly natural about that formation.

"Mom, I think it's going away," she said with a sigh of relief as the column seemed to collapse out of sight behind the hill.

"Let's hope so," Hester said. Her jaw was clenched—a habit her daughter had learned from her—and her hands squeezed the steering wheel of the Jeep so tightly that her knuckles sprouted diamonds. "If we can stay out of its line of sight, we should be able to reach Santa Fe."

"Wait, what are you talking about? Line of sight?" the young dragon demanded. She honestly didn't want to believe that the face she had seen was anything but a trick of the mind caused by heat, fear, and stress.

"Shut up and listen, Kylara," her mother snapped. "You need to get to Santa Fe."

"What do you mean I need to? We're going together."

The woman looked in the rearview mirror and shook her head. Kylara jerked her head to look over her shoulder and saw that the flames now crested the hill and pursued the old vehicle along the rough road.

"Santa Fe has the closest Steel Guard station. You must make it to a Steel Guard station."

"Mom, we'll go together. It's only a brush fire. You put one out when I was a kid."

"I did nothing of the sort," her mother snapped. "Now, take the wheel."

Kylara did as she was told. She knew her mom well enough to know that if Hester told her to take the wheel, it meant she wouldn't touch it again. As soon as she complied, the older dragon pulled her legs onto her seat and put one behind her daughter.

"What are you doing?"

"What the fuck do you think I'm doing? We're trading places, girl. We've done this a hundred times. Now hurry up. We're losing speed."

She nodded and fought to keep her terror and tears at bay as she scooted into the driver's position. With her butt planted in the seat, she thrust her foot on the gas and locked her gaze on the road.

"Mom, what is happening?"

"We're under attack, Kylara." Hester's full attention was on the flames that raced over the hill behind them. She sounded like she had answered as an afterthought. "You need to drive as fast as possible without wrecking the Jeep. You can do this."

"Mom, please tell me what the fuck is going on and stop acting like I'm going to leave you out here."

"Kylara, language!" Hester snapped and followed it with a rueful chuckle. "Oh, who gives a shit? Now's not the time for manners, I guess."

The young dragon didn't point out that her mother had also cursed or that she cursed way more than her daughter ever did. All she said was, "Mom!" and knew she would get the gist of her protest.

"That fire is gaining on us. I can't allow it to catch up to the Jeep."

"I'm driving as fast as I can!" she replied.

"You need to get to a Steel Guard station. They'll protect you. They can keep you safe."

"Mom, you keep me safe."

"And I'll try to for a while longer. You have to promise that you'll keep driving until you reach the Steel Guard."

"No, Mom! Not unless you tell me what you intend to do and not unless you stop acting like you can't simply come with me."

"I can't save both of us, Kylara. I always knew that."

"Mom, I'm sick and tired of you protecting me. We can face whatever this is together." She meant it, even though looking in the rearview mirror filled her with fear. The flames had begun to catch up. They moved across the parched desert landscape like a wave sweeping across water but only ash, smoke, and charred earth were in their wake.

"I made mistakes, Kylara. I should have been more careful but I won't let my mistakes cost you. You're the best thing I've ever done with my life, girl, and I will not let this monster get you."

"But, Mom, it's coming after you, not me. You said so yourself —that this was an old case that went bad."

A pulse of her mother's aura told her that her mother did not think that the blaze was focused on her. She was afraid that this hunter, or flame mage, or monster of fire, or whatever controlled this force of destruction had targeted her daughter.

Before she could ask what exactly she was thinking about, Hester looked her in the eye. "Promise me, Kylara. Promise me you won't stop. Take yourself and your necklace to the Steel Guard. Promise me this."

"Yes, fine, Mom. I promise."

"Good girl." Satisfied, Hester Diamantine opened her door and launched from the vehicle.

She turned into her dragon form before she even landed. Two pumps of her wings kicked up swirling dervishes of sand and she raced to fight the fire.

Kylara kept her hands on the wheel and her foot on the accelerator. Her mother could do this. She had seen her battle a wildfire before. When she was a girl—perhaps five or six years old—a truck had overheated and the driver, not being from the desert, had pulled off the road and into the brush. The heat from the vehicle had ignited the dried vegetation and the fire was driven by the wind toward the Diamantine residence.

It was the only time the older dragon had ever taken her dragon form anywhere near the edge of the property. The blaze had gained speed and swept uphill and across the brush. Hester, in her dragon body, had climbed to the top of the ridge, and—to young Kylara's horror—set the ground in front of the fire on fire.

The young dragon had screamed, convinced that her dragon mother had finally lost her dragon mind. But it soon became obvious what her mom's intention had been. Dragon fire was hot and powerful, and the blast she had unleashed on the desert scrub not only ignited it but burned quickly through the woody stems. Where a wide swathe of fuel had existed, in the next moment there was a barren landscape, as impossible for a fire to cross as it would be for a fish.

The dragon seemed to try to do the same thing now. Before she came anywhere near the wall of fire, she blasted the ground behind the Jeep, swooped low, and cut the path of the blaze with fire of her own. She doubled back and seared the ground again with such heat—Kylara knew from experience—that some of the desert sand would turn to glass.

This should have stopped the forward motion of the fire, but it didn't.

Instead, the flames seemed to come together and move to the left of the road, where the vegetation was denser as it was clustered around an old arroyo. Hester changed direction in mid-flight and tried to sear the ground in front of this new direction the fire had taken.

Her daughter watched all this in the rearview mirror as she tried to keep her gaze on the now almost nonexistent road and continued to drive up the mountain.

Her mother succeeded and the fire appeared to be all but snuffed out until the conflagration moved to the other side of the road again. Seen through the rearview mirror, it looked like a great lump of flame was forced through all the little smoldering fires that the fire had left in its wake like a rabbit forced through a rattlesnake. On the other side of the road where the vegetation had yet to be burned by this monster of hungry fire, the flames blazed to life again.

The older dragon tried to catch up. There was still considerable distance between Kylara and the flames, but now that the plan to create a firebreak had failed, Hester tried desperately to slow the inferno any way she could. She blasted the ground in front of it, but it wasn't the same well-aimed, careful blast of fire she had used before. The flames simply moved across it and gobbled what traces of plant life she had failed to incinerate.

Finally, the conflagration retaliated.

Hester swooped in for another strafe across the landscape when the fire once again formed a swirling vortex of flame and smoke. This time, the fiery tornado twisted off the ground and hurled the dragon from the sky.

She struck the ground hard enough to make an impact crater, but she didn't stop the fight. Instead, she whipped her tail around and righted herself as another wave of fire rolled into her. She blocked it with her wings and burned the membrane that connected the bones as she did so. Her scales were diamond, however, and she was a tough old dragon. She seared the base of the next wave that came at her and managed to take away the root of the fire tornado.

"Come on, Mom!" Kylara shouted from her position most of the way up the mountain. She now approached the pine forest that grew at higher elevations. The road would be better there, but she also knew that pine trees were equally as flammable as desert scrub. To a fire that seemed to be able to hunt, it would probably be an advantage.

She desperately wanted to turn back but what could she do? Her mom had never taught her how to fight like this. She'd most likely never seen the need. Would her efforts be able to turn the tide of battle?

When she looked into the rearview mirror again, she realized that she would not. Hester dodged as the spirit of the flames or the mage or dragon who controlled them tried to batter her with blow after blow after blow. The young dragon's vision blurred as her eyes flooded with tears. She wanted to help and desperately wanted to be able to do something, but her mom's final words raced repeatedly through her head.

She had to get to the Steel Guard station. That was what she wanted her to do. That was why she had told her to keep driving and why she faced a beast made of fire.

Ignoring her instincts in favor of this last instruction from her mother, Kylara gunned the engine to push the Jeep up the hill and raced into the pine forest. The road was certainly better there—a bonus because she could barely see it through tears she shed for her mom whom she had left alone in a battle for her life that she didn't see how she could possibly survive, let alone win.

# CHAPTER NINE

"Come on…only a little farther…" Kylara begged the Jeep as she pressed her foot on the gas. In response, a cloud of foul-smelling white smoke began to pour from the edges of the hood. When she looked in her rearview mirror, she saw nothing. She hadn't seen anything but smoke behind her for a long time and now, even that was gone, although it seemed a less threatening version of the fire's heat had taken up residence under her hood. With a scowl, she checked the gauge on the dash and saw that the car was indeed trying to tell her that it was near death.

She had stopped once to pour more gas in the tank and refill the radiator. The leak must have been exacerbated by her flight because when she'd checked, it had been bone-dry. The damage had been done, but she had still filled it and urged the vehicle forward. It had rumbled through the pine forest and to an actual paved road on the other side of the mountain. She had practically coasted the entire way down the mountain, for which the Jeep—and she—had been thankful.

The next three hours had been stressful. She tried to keep it moving as fast as possible without overheating while she checked the rearview mirror constantly for signs of either the fire monster or her mother and cried until she'd run out of tears. Hester never appeared, which she knew was a bad sign.

Fights didn't take that long. They simply didn't. And if her mom had defeated her opponent—was it even something that could be defeated? She honestly didn't know—she would have caught up with her daughter. There was only one Steel Guard station in New Mexico and it was in Santa Fe. There wasn't anywhere else for her to go.

Something under the vehicle shuddered as if to remind her that it had already gone quite far enough.

Kylara didn't stop to look, even though it felt like one of the tires had finally gone flat. Instinctively, she knew that if she turned the engine off, it would never start again. She pushed onward and coaxed it along the freeway as the skyline of Santa Fe began to resolve itself on the dusty horizon.

Her teeth gritted in a mixture of fear and determination, she drove for another three miles—although it took as long as the last thirty miles had—before she pulled into a gas station to try to fix the vehicle again.

All it took was a single circuit around the Jeep to see that there was no way to fix it. One of the tires was flat, exactly as she'd suspected, and all of them were full of so many cactus thorns that it was a miracle only the one had deflated. Without a doubt, another pothole might very well do them all in.

Part of the suspension also hung loosely beneath the vehicle, never a good sign. At least it wasn't leaking any fluids, but the white smoke that hissed from the hood was a reminder that there were no fluids to be leaked.

Kylara took a deep breath, tried to both remember everything her mom had taught her about automobile maintenance and also to not think about Hester too much, and opened the hood. A great billowing cloud of smoke escaped eagerly into the desert air. The engine reeked of burnt rubber and damaged metal. If the engine wasn't a brick, it was on its way to solidifying into one as it cooled.

"Car trouble?"

She turned to where a man leaned out of the window of a blue pick-up truck with a roof that had faded to the color of the metal beneath it a long time before. He wore a black suit that was trimmed with silver and a black hat with a silver band, and tattoos crept out past his collar and onto his hands. To her—whose knowledge of American culture was confined to small-town stereotypes and what she saw on TVs or movies—he looked like he should be driving a chromed lowrider, not the beat-up old country-mobile. To say he looked out of place in the vehicle was an understatement. He had stubbly cheeks and a friendly enough smile, though.

"Gee, are you a mechanic or something?" she asked sarcastically.

"Not at all, young lady. Not at all," the man said. "My knowledge of automobiles starts with the steering wheel and ends at filling the gas tank. But even to my untrained eyes, it seems like your Jeep needs to be put out of its misery."

Kylara sighed heavily. "You could say that." She kicked one of its still inflated tires. Between her dragon strength and the already compromised suspension system, it was enough to knock the wheel off. The Jeep collapsed with what—to her ears—sounded like relief.

"I didn't mean it literally," the tattooed man said.

"Yeah, well, I guess I can walk the rest of the way to the Steel Guard station." What she wanted to do was go into the gas station and soak in one of the baths of ice that most establishments in the area placed strategically and filled with ice and cheap beer. But she was alive and free because of her mom. She had been raised better than to squander what she had been given, even if all she wanted was to see her fly overhead.

"You don't need to walk, Little Miss. I'm headed in that direction. If you don't mind a little conversation—the radio out here don't work worth a damn—I'd be happy to give you a lift."

She scrutinized him carefully. Despite his tattoos and odd black-and-silver suit, he seemed nice enough. While she knew she shouldn't trust strangers, she also knew she could kill the man with a single punch or turn into a dragon if he proved to be stronger than he seemed. He wasn't a dragon. She would be able to sense some level of aura if he was. A mage perhaps? That would certainly fit with the tattoos.

"I know where the station is," she said and brandished her phone as a maps app loaded on her screen. "If you take any wrong turns, I know aikido and will choke you quite happily."

The man chuckled. "Are you serious? You just kicked a Jeep to death and still feel like you need to threaten me? Scout's honor, I'll take you directly there. If you suspect any funny business, please try to not bruise my face when you keep your promise."

Kylara looked at her vehicle and the smoke that issued from it in the desert sun. "I guess I can't leave that there."

"Sure you can," the man said. "Give me a minute, all right?"

Before she could respond, he climbed out of his truck and hurried inside the gas station. She felt a gust of air conditioning from the vehicle and was too tempted to wait outside. Instead, she climbed in, closed the door behind her, and pointed all the fans at her face. Unfortunately, this did little except spread her already ripe body odor around the cab, so when the tattooed man returned, he would enter a fully saturated zone of teenage funk.

While she waited, she looked around. There were few paper maps of New Mexico, plus one of Colorado, Texas, and Utah. There was some kind of bathrobe or something folded up under the seat. Behind the robe, she found a handgun. This wasn't all that unusual in New Mexico but was something she certainly wanted to be aware of.

She glanced over her shoulder and saw that the man was still inside, so she opened the glove box. Inside, she found a strangely dainty pair of handcuffs—some kind of sex thing? She promised herself to remain doubly aware of the man's actions—and a heavy metal coin with a dragon printed on one side and a woman's face on the other. She could almost recognize the woman—an actress perhaps?—but she heard the man whoop as he came out of the gas station. Quickly, she closed the glovebox and leaned back in the seat.

He climbed in, a curious look on his face that might have bordered on suspicion if she knew him better, then thrust a fistful of bills and an ice-cold sports drink into her hands.

"What's this for?" she asked and her eyes widened at the cash. It looked like it was close to a hundred bucks. It wasn't much for a girl all alone in the world, but it was much more than she'd had. She opened the bottle and drank greedily from it. The blue flavor was awful but right now, it was the best drink she had ever had.

"For the Jeep. I sold it to the fella working in there for a hundred bucks. I probably could have got a little more if I had taken the time to haggle, but if he said no and called my bluff... well, it's not like you can take it with you, is it? I bought you a drink because you looked like you needed it. Are you ready?" He grinned as if he had taken her out for lunch instead of sold her only possession.

Still, there wasn't anything she could do with a broken down Jeep. If she was at home, she could have fixed it—maybe—but with no money and no tools, it was purely wishful thinking. "You could have bought yourself a drink too."

"Ah, I wouldn't dream of stealing a kid's cash. Do you have a bag or anything you need or you ready to buckle up and hit the road?"

"I have everything I need." Kyalara felt her phone in one pocket and her ninety-eight dollars and forty-five cents in the other. She hadn't even taken a wallet. Her clothes—clean when her getaway had begun—were now soaked with sweat and dirty with both dust and ash. It was almost too much to process. She took a deep breath and tried to fight back a fresh wave of tears.

"Hey, now, don't get all upset over a sports drink and a bad car deal. You need to keep those fluids in ya, all right?"

"Yeah, I know." She sniffed and wiped her eyes. After a deep breath, she was under control again.

"I do have a question or two for you," the man said and studied her out of the corner of his eye after he had driven a few miles down the road.

"Sure," Kylara said. They should be at the Steel Guard station in fifteen minutes and she assumed a little conversation would not hurt.

"What's your name?"

"I...uh..." She didn't know if she should use a fake one or not.

"Never mind, never mind. I didn't realize I'd picked up a fugitive," he said and waved her awkwardness away. "Mine's Tully, by the way. Alexander Tully. I tell people to call me Alex but everyone always simply calls me Tully."

"It's nice to meet you, Tully," she said and he grinned.

"And you're sure you want to go to the Steel Guard station?" he asked. "They only recently finished building it. The damn thing looks like a concrete blister on the edge of town—no pool, no cable TV, no nothing."

"You know about the Steel Guard?" she asked.

"Well, yeah. Doesn't everyone?" he replied, his gaze on the road.

"I guess so, yeah," Kylara agreed. "It's probably hard to ignore the face of a new justice system that incorporates all the sentient species on the planet."

"Sometimes, I think they bit off more than they could chew," he said, fiddled with the radio, and found only static.

"The Steel Dragon is a hero!" she blurted. "She stood up to dragon kind and helped remake the world as a more just place."

He nodded as if conceding a point to a political rival. "Yeah, that's how Kristen started it, but I can't say they exactly solved the issue of justice overnight. You know that Dragon SWAT still exists, right? With the Steel Guard, we merely got more police, not less. Plus, most of the crap they stick their snouts into around here is simply regular, person-on-person crime."

"What gives you the right to call The Steel Dragon by her first name?" she demanded. Hester Diamantine had not skimped on the lessons of respect and trashing a dragon using their first name was high on her "don't you dare do this, Kylara," list.

Tully chuckled amicably. "I'm merely saying it's only been a year since Lady Steel—first of her name, long may she reign—has been in power. They recently opened the base here so they're gaining steam, but they have a long way to go before they're a unifying force for the planet that can make justice equal for all."

"Well, I guess so," she muttered. She hadn't thought about it before, but she decided that made sense. Dragons had needed their own police force for hundreds of years because they didn't all follow their rules. Hester Diamantine was a testimony to that truth. The fact that Kristen Hall had come along and told the dragons to be nice to the mages, pixies, and dwarves didn't mean they would all simply obey.

"I wish her luck," Tully said and raised an eyebrow at her silence. "Don't get me wrong, I wish their whole damn organization the best of luck. In fact, I'd go so far as to say I hope all the detectives get a raise in the near future. I'm only saying that change takes time."

"Right, yeah," Kylara said. She had envisioned something like the clips she had seen of the Steel Dragon's battles in which mages and soldiers armed with dragon-slaying bullets rode on the backs of dragons into battle. But of course, there wouldn't be all that out there in the middle of nowhere or in a new branch that had barely opened.

"There it is," the man said and pointed to a building that

resembled a concrete blister coming out of the desert with unpleasant accuracy.

Her hopes dropped further. It wasn't even very big. Her house in the mountain had been larger than this.

"Are you sure about this, kid?" he asked.

"Yeah. What other choice do I have?"

"You could tell me what you're running from and I could tell you if those guys can help. If it's a man who made you run down out of the mountain—and I mean a regular old man with a dick and a drinking problem—it might be better to tell your friend Tully and not file an official report. I don't like men like that, Little Miss."

"No," she said and cringed at what he thought she might have been through. "It's nothing like that." But thinking such thoughts made it clear that the Steel Guard was the only place that could help her. "If you could drop me off, that would be great. And look, you can keep the cash for your trouble. Also, I'd appreciate it if you didn't tell anyone about me."

"That Jeep of yours will tell a story back there." Tully pulled to a stop in front of the concrete dome.

"Yeah, well, I'd appreciate it if you didn't," Kylara said and offered a fifty-dollar bill to him as she slid out of the vehicle.

"I don't want your money."

"And I don't want you to talk about me," she replied, tossed the fifty on the seat, and slammed the door.

The man half-smiled and half-sneered and watched her go inside. Only when she had activated the intercom and was allowed to enter the building did he drive away in a great cloud of dust.

Kylara found herself in what seemed to be an airlock between the two sets of doors, one that led back to the desert and one that led into the structure.

"Look into the camera and state your name and purpose, please," a garbled voice said.

Kylara looked up and saw a camera mounted in the corner. "My name is Kylara and I'm running from..." It was too insane to say a fire beast, right? "I'm here for help."

"Help with what?" the garbled voice asked.

"My home was burned down and I think that...uh, something is chasing me."

"Please open the door after the buzzer sounds," the garbled voice replied, although it sounded more cheerful than it did before.

The buzzer sounded, Kylara waited, and when it stopped, she opened the door. She entered a blessedly cool circular room. In the center was a huge circular desk surrounded by plexiglass on all sides. Except it wasn't only plexiglass, she realized because it shimmered faintly. Was it a magic shield of some kind? The only other door from the circular room was to a bathroom with a *man/woman/dragon/dwarf/pixie/all genders* sign on it that took up way too much space.

A perky young woman with blonde pigtails was seated behind the desk and looked completely too small in comparison to the huge piece of furniture.

"You must be Kylara. We spoke over the intercom. My name is Jenny Spats. You can call me Jenny, or Miss Spats, or Jenny Spats. How can I be of service to you and your magical community today?" She giggled in a way that made Kylara want to test the magic spells protecting her.

"Hi...Jenny," she said. "I think someone or something magical is after me. Can I speak to a detective or something?"

"Of course, sweetheart. Of course!" The young woman beamed. "It'll be only a few minutes. Our detective just got in and he always needs his coffee." She rolled her eyes like this was an inside joke that the two of them had shared many times. "In the meantime, feel free to freshen up in the bathroom. I see you have a sports drink, dee-lish! But if you want water or a soda pop or anything at all while you wait, just ask, mkay?"

"Right," she said. She looked at the ring of chairs lining the outside of the circular room, then at Jenny's wide-eyed, smiling face that would be inescapable in this room, and chose the bathroom. The woman swiveled her chair to follow her with her gaze as she moved through the room.

She was too dehydrated to need to go, but it was better than waiting outside where the young receptionist would no doubt continue to stare at her. A look in the mirror told her why Tully had been so quick to help and probably why Jenny had let her in.

Her Jeep drive had left her unbelievably dirty. Except for where her tears had made streaks down her cheeks, her face was a mask of dust and ash. Her clothes were equally as filthy, and there was a large tear in the shoulder of her shirt that must have happened when she switched places with her mom. She couldn't do anything about that, but she washed her face, wet her hair, and pulled it into a tight ponytail with a hairband she somehow still had on her wrist. Finally, she returned to wait in the lobby.

Kylara chose a position where she could see the clock on the wall. She didn't want to waste her phone's battery since she didn't have a charger.

"Did you make your mind up about that drink, Kylara?" Jenny asked.

"No, thanks. I'm good. Can you maybe tell the detective to hurry?"

"Oh, I did while you were in the restroom."

"Thanks."

"You are most welcome." The woman beamed.

After five minutes, Kylara cleared her throat.

"Oh! The detective will see you now," the receptionist said.

"But how can...you've sat there this whole time." Jenny hadn't picked her phone up or typed anything on her computer. All she'd done was try to spin a pen on her thumb and catch it. She had tried maybe a hundred times and with no success.

"Huh?" Jenny asked.

Footsteps interrupted the conversation and the detective opened a door that had been cleverly hidden in the desk and stepped out from what the young dragon assumed was a stairway. She gaped when she realized he wore a black suit trimmed with silver, a black hat with a silver band, and had tattoos on his hands and neck.

"Tully?" she blurted.

"Detective Tully, Miss Kylara, but yes. Are you ready to tell me what happened?"

"But…you didn't say you were a detective."

"Didn't you see my badge and cuffs in the glove compartment?"

She remembered the weird coin with the dragon and the woman's face and suddenly realized why she had recognized the face. It belonged to Kristen Hall, the Steel Dragon. "You said the Steel Guard was a tiny organization with no budget."

"What can I say?" The man grinned. "I could use a raise. Now, can you tell me what forced you to flee over the mountains and what you were doing so far from home?"

"I… How do you know I'm far from home?"

"The cactus thorns in the tires of your Jeep belong to a variety that only grows in higher elevations. Now, go ahead and start at the beginning. What happened to you?"

Kylara hesitated, not sure what to say. Could she trust him with who she was? She decided she had already trusted him before she had known he was a detective and reminded herself that her mom had sent her to the Steel Guard. It wasn't like Hester had sent her to a police station. She had sent her to an organization known for working with far stranger situations.

"Oh, just a minute, Miss Kylara," Tully said and flicked his wrist toward Jenny's desk. A pen and notepad elevated and came to hover in front of him. "Let's start with your name," he said as if he hadn't summoned a freaking pen and paper and made them levitate.

"You're a mage?" she asked and remembered to close her mouth.

"Of course. Didn't the tattoos give it away?" He looked amused. "Now, full name?"

"My name is Kylara Diamantine, my world was taken from me, and I think someone is trying to kill me."

"And why do you think that?" the detective asked as his pen scribbled notes without him touching it.

Now suitably impressed that the people there weren't normal, she told him what had happened. She explained that she had grown up in the mountains and that her mom, Hester Diamantine—the detective seemed to recognize the last name—had raced to their remote mountain home and ordered her into the Jeep. Without being asked, she told him her mother was a dragon and that she had battled some type of thinking fire after she instructed her daughter to go to the Steel Guard for help.

Detective Tully nodded and listened as he took his magic notes. He asked a few questions about the logistics of the story— where the house was, how much land she saw burned, and a few other details. Finally, her story told, he thanked her, excused himself politely, and said he needed to validate her story. He sent his little notepad down the stairs and asked Jenny for a drink.

"Did you ask Jenny for anything?" he asked with a grin.

"She hasn't," the woman said as if the suspense was killing her.

"No— Look, will you do anything?"

"You have a point. Jenny! Sandwiches please! Don't skimp on the hatch chilies. Do you want a sandwich?"

Kylara's stomach grumbled in reply.

Tully grinned. "You like hatch chilies? What am I talking about? You're a dragon from New Mexico so you gotta like hatch chilies. Jenny, don't skimp on her chilies either."

"Yes, sir." Jenny made an odd little salute and went downstairs.

While they waited, he rambled on about the building and how

she was safe there. From what she understood, another couple of floors existed below ground. The building had been built in this way to make it a safe house against attacks—dragon, magical, and pedestrian. Which was all fine and good, except the clock kept ticking and her mother still had not appeared.

The sandwiches arrived. Kylara wanted to yell at the woman for taking forever but they were toasted and the aroma was overpowering, so she ate first.

Her gaze shifted constantly to the clock. When an hour had passed with no answers and Tully rambled on about how difficult it was to police pixies, she finally snapped.

She stood and clenched her fists at her size. "I demand that you do something. My mother's life might in danger!"

"Would a drink help?" Jenny asked.

"No!" she screamed. "You are all supposed to do something!"

"Miss Kylara—"

"And stop calling me that! It's simply Kylara."

"Sure, Kylara, no problem. Let me see…" Tully's pen scribbled something on a piece of paper on Jenny's desk and he sent the paper below.

A note pad immediately appeared and settled in his hands.

"I should have been more clear," he said. "You merely seemed so interested in pixie politics that I—"

"Tell me what that thing was."

"Right. Of course," he said and flipped through the notebook. "Your story was prioritized as a top-level threat. We sent a team of two dragons and a mage to investigate." He flipped the pages of the notebook again. "The house was where you said it would be but, uh…"

"But what?"

"Well, Kylara, I'm sorry, but it's been razed to the ground…er, into the mountain. It would appear that the fire burned it all to nothing."

She nodded and wiped what felt like the thousandth tear away. "I heard the explosion."

"They confirmed the fire too. It looks like it followed the road for quite a distance but never reached the pine forest you told me about."

"And what about my mom?"

Tully flipped to the next page, and the next. He flipped to the beginning and checked again. "I'm so sorry. They could find no sign of your mother at all."

CHAPTER TEN

The next morning, for the first time in Kylara's seventeen years of life, she woke up to a different ceiling.

She rubbed her eyes, blinked, and rubbed them again, but the inset panels of fluorescent lights refused to transform into her familiar ceiling fan. She sighed and stuck her foot over the edge of the bed to touch the cold concrete floor. Bed was a generous word. This was more like a metal frame bolted to the wall with a halfway passable mattress and sheets that she wished had been used at least once. She had cooked potatoes with less starch than them.

The night before, Tully had taken her below and into the bowels of the Steel Guard station. It was bigger down there, although still all concentric circles. He had said it was for her protection, and after a day spent running from a fricking fire monster, she had believed him. Now, she saw the room for what it was—a cell.

To prove this hypothesis, she slid out of bed, crept to the door, and peeked out. A guard stood in the hallway wearing the same silver-and-black uniform Tully had worn, minus the hat. He smiled and nodded at her, but she darted into her room again.

She had been told to ask him for breakfast, but she knew that was mostly to keep her inside the station and make sure she remained where she was.

What was most frustrating about the situation, she thought as she plopped onto the bed, was that even if there was no guard watching her, she didn't know where she was supposed to go. Her home was gone and her mother was missing. She refused to think her mom was dead. The few people in the town near her burned home who even knew she existed didn't count as friends and would only ask questions if she arrived asking for sanctuary instead of shopping for groceries, car parts, or a replacement water pump.

She had never met another dragon—well, except for the striking young one she had escaped the other day. Tully had already grilled her about her family, which she knew nothing about. It was one of the handful of conversation topics her mother simply refused to engage in.

And where was her mom? Kylara didn't want to even entertain the notion that Hester Diamantine, former agent for Dragon SWAT, was dead. But if she wasn't, where was she? She could not imagine a fire stopping the dragon. Like her, she had diamond scales. The blaze had seemed intelligent and dangerous, but couldn't her mother have simply flown a mile up into the sky and escaped the sources of fuel the fire had seemed tied to?

And then there was the fact that she had lived with her mom in their house in the mountain for most of her life and had never so much as seen another dragon. Now, she had seen two and been attacked by something that might very well be controlled by a third. Had she been the one to lead the hunter her mother had feared to them? Had she unwittingly unburied an agent who had then burned her home to the ground and taken her mom from her?

Even if she hadn't, Kylara knew that she was only alive and free—well, she wasn't exactly free, currently, but she had been—

because Hester had gone back to fight the fire so she could escape. More than anything else, that made her ache with guilt. Her mother might be alive if she had been a better daughter and a better warrior and if she had trained harder and mastered her powers at a higher level.

Unable to even sit any longer, she threw herself back onto her bed and let herself weep. She had spent many a night in the Diamantine residence crying but rarely did she let herself be loud enough for Hester to hear her. Now, exactly like she had before in her room, she stifled her sobs as tears streaked down her face.

A while later—ten minutes? An hour? She honestly didn't know—a knock came at the door.

Kylara sniffed her tears back and wiped the streaks from her face. "Whoever it is, you can come in."

She expected the guard so was a little surprised when a woman with red curly hair entered the room instead. "Hi," the stranger said and walked quietly to stand next to the bed. Or, more accurately, she came to stand next to the prison cot she currently occupied. "Can I sit?"

"Knock yourself out." The young dragon sniffed. "It's not like it's my bed anyway." She took a deep breath and tried to pull herself together. This was probably another round of questions. Was it the fourth or the fifth? She felt as if she had already told them everything she could. The last round of questioning had been especially frustrating because she had not been able to even begin to answer.

The woman sat and she rolled over to look at her and recognized her immediately. It was Kristen Hall, the Steel Dragon herself!

Kylara sat bolt upright, hopped out of bed, and bowed to her visitor. Or was she supposed to have curtsied? Her mom had taught her dragon formalities but only as theory. Meeting another dragon—and not any dragon but the Steel Dragon—had her completely befuddled about what to do.

"Welcome, Lady Steel—or wait, you prefer Lady Hall, right? I think I read that on a fan-blog."

Kristen Hall—the leader of the dragon world and the person who had done more for mage rights than anyone else on the planet—laughed.

Immediately, the young dragon felt her face flush. "Please accept my apology for my lack of hospitality and manners, my lady."

"Please, don't worry about it." The Steel Dragon smiled. "I don't go for all that formality. I wasn't raised in the dragon world. You can call me Kristen, although I guess you would know that if you read fan-blogs."

"Did I… I didn't say that, did I?" Kylara felt like all the blood now rushed to her face. It was odd how a body part so close to the brain could still deprive it of so much blood.

"You don't need to feel embarrassed or anything. Detective Tully briefed me on everything you've been through, and I'm here to help. I know you've endured a rough twenty-four hours but I'm here to start making things better. Now, they tell me you've denied yourself breakfast. What else can I do for you besides make you eat?"

Kylara felt her heart leap in her chest. "Can you help me get my mother back?"

Kristen looked away, her jaw tight. When she turned back to her, she had a hopeful smile and an aura to match. The young dragon could tell they were both fake but she appreciated the effort.

"We will do everything we can to bring her back to you," she said with steel in her voice. "Honestly, right now, we don't have many clues to work with, but I have some of my best people scouring the site where your mother fought this… You described it as a fire beast?"

"Yes, ma'am. Or…well, not quite. It didn't have a body or

anything like that. But I saw a face in it and it could make limbs and control them."

"I see." Kristen nodded and patted the bed next to her in an invitation for her to sit again. She complied and slumped with obvious dejection. It didn't take a master detective from Dragon SWAT to see that the Steel Dragon had never seen anything quite like this before.

"Are you sure you can find my mom?" Kylara asked hesitantly.

"It may take time, but our mission at the Steel Guard is to make sure that justice is achieved for everyone. We are taking this attack very seriously and treating it as a threat to regional peace. I can promise you that we will find answers."

"Thank you," she said and hoped she sounded like she meant it.

"You don't exactly seem comforted," Kristen said.

She smiled at that. This must be the "disregard for social rules" she had read about in the Steel Dragon so many times. "Well…if I can, I want to help."

"You can't go back there right now," Kristen stated firmly. "We don't know if you, your mom, or both of you were the target. Also, you're a minor, so that won't happen. Sorry, but these are some of the perks of being the leader of the Global Dragon Council."

"Right, yeah. Well, I assumed you would say that," Kylara conceded.

What she did not admit was how proud the little sparkle she saw in Kristen's eye made her feel.

"If you worked that out, I know you have something else to ask."

"I guess… I guess I don't know what to do now," she confessed. "I can't go home. I don't want to stay here—no offense—so what options do I have?"

Her visitor rubbed her chin and nodded. "Well, it seems like you don't have much family. Is that right? This whole situation would be much simpler if you have a nice, rich uncle out there."

"No, no family. Mom never talked about them. Did you...find something?"

Kristen shook her head. "We know she didn't have any other children. There's a second cousin on the continent but honestly, the guy doesn't have a great track record, and given that you've never heard of him doesn't exactly encourage me to send you there."

"Where do you want to send me?" she grouched and didn't realize until she had said it that she had sassed the single most powerful being on the entire planet.

Her visitor chuckled. "I'm so sorry. I had hoped this would go better than it has."

Kylara looked at Kristen, who was smiling although her eyes looked pained and her aura began to show cracks as well. "I don't know what losing a mom is like, but I do know what it can feel like to have your world turned upside down and taken away from you. When I first discovered my powers, I wished I had someone to teach me."

She snorted. "Yeah. I wouldn't mind learning how to defeat a thinking fire."

"What if I told you I can help you learn exactly that?" the woman asked.

"What do you mean?"

"Well, so much has changed in the last year, as you probably know. One thing you might not know about, though, is that I have launched a school. Or, more precisely, I took what used to be a school for dragons and turned it into a school for dragons and mages. Since both have special powers that need to be trained, a facility built for one will work well for both—I hope. This year's class will be the first that mixes mages with the dragons already attending, so it will be an interesting and...er, potentially challenging year. But it would also give you an environment in which to study and learn more about yourself and your powers as a dragon." She beamed her winning smile at her.

Kylara wished she could feel as optimistic as Kristen seemed, but a boarding school? "I don't know. My mom's curriculum was extensive. I don't want to sound ungrateful, but I already know how to use my dragon form fine."

"I've noticed that." The Steel Dragon's smile didn't falter. "Was it your mom who taught you to control your aura so well?"

That question caught her by surprise. "Uh…I guess? I'm not doing anything with my aura right now, though."

"It shows. You're extremely hard to read for a dragon, especially a young one."

"Umm…thanks? To be honest, Mom never focused on it much and never bothered doing much deception with hers. I could tell when she was very angry and stuff like that, and I know it's common to use auras to trick people, but I'm not trying to trick you right now or anything like that."

"That's good to know." Kristen chuckled. "But I truly am impressed. Your aura is barely detectable. In fact, if I wasn't looking for it, I don't think I would have known you had an aura at all."

Something lingered in the Steel Dragon's eyes—an unasked question or an unspoken theory—but before Kylara could decide if she wanted to press her on it, the look was gone.

"So, what about it?" her visitor asked. "If you go, you can learn much more about your aura and how to use it. Plus, well…I know that when I first started, I was desperate to push myself to learn more about self-defense. At the academy, you'll also learn how best to defend yourself against various forms of attack and how to use your dragon body and powers to retaliate if anything like what took your mom comes after you. Best of all, it's a safe environment with powerful dragons and mages watching over it. You'll be safe there."

"Until you find my mom?"

"Exactly." Kristen nodded. "Once we find her, of course, you'll be free to do whatever your family thinks is best. Who knows? You might want to stay, at least until your mom rebuilds your home."

Kylara nodded, unsure what to do. It sounded good. If she was honest, it sounded great. A whole school filled with people like her? Actual young people instead of only her mother? The thought prompted a fresh pang of guilt and made her feel wretched for even considering abandoning the search for her mom.

"Look, I know it's not ideal," the Steel Dragon said and placed a hand on her thigh. "If I had my way, we'd already have caught whoever did this. But, from what we have so far, this will take some time. I will keep you posted as best we can, but maybe learning at this school would be good for you and help to keep your mind off of the search. Also…well, I probably shouldn't say this, but many of the students there are from dragon society. They could use a new face to shake them up. Not that I'm giving you permission to cause trouble." Her aura said otherwise.

The young dragon didn't know how committed the Steel Guard was to this search. Tully certainly didn't seem sure of his chances, but maybe she could learn something at this school to help her find her mom. It seemed more likely than learning anything in this station outside of Santa Fe.

"Where is it?" Kylara asked

"That's the best thing. It's here in New Mexico."

"Oh. Well then, yeah. Sure." That changed everything. It meant that as soon as she learned how to track, she could go find her mom, whether the Steel Guard wanted her to or not.

# CHAPTER ELEVEN

It took a few hours to fly to the new school although it was surprisingly close to Kylara's house—well, in mountainous desert terms anyway. The academy nestled on a plain in a valley between two mountains a few hundred miles away.

Kristen flew with her the entire way, as did two other dragons who were not introduced. It felt wonderful to fly over the landscape instead of simply hugging the ground to fly only in the area in the very center of their land. She loved flying. There was something spectacular about taking to the skies, and now that she could go somewhere besides back to her home, it was even more magical.

Although, of course, she would have much preferred to simply go home and find her mom waiting for her.

"We had a vote to rename it recently," Kristen said, perhaps sensing her mind start to swirl into depression. "Welcome to the Lumos School for Magic and Powers."

"After Lumos! I read about him. He was a hero from the last war." Kylara couldn't help but feel excited to talk about a legend. "A golden dragon who never tried to accumulate much wealth.

He had light powers, right? He fought the Masked One and died trying to...uh, protect you..."

"Right." It was obvious that the wounds were still fresh, even though Lumos had been dead for over a year. Not only that, after reading so much about the Steel Dragon, it was so weird to talk to her about it in person.

"I'm sorry for your loss," Kylara said, perhaps a little belatedly.

"It's fine." Kristen steeled herself. "Lumos knew what he was getting into and would have been proud to know that dragons like yourself will learn in the same school as mages. I do miss him, though."

The young dragon, unsure of what to say, flew on toward the valley between the two mountains.

From their elevated vantage point, the campus was breathtakingly beautiful. Despite being in the desert, the valley and both sides of the mountains that surrounded the school were lush with greenery. Mesquite trees and cactus were in evidence, of course, but also oaks, maples, and cottonwoods that all stood majestically in fields of green lawn that looked especially vibrant after flying over the red and brown of the desert soil and faded greens of the desert plants.

Three main halls dominated the center of the valley. They were made of whitish brick, had beautiful roofs covered in red tile, and so many windows that Kylara had no doubt that the building had been built long before the convenience of air conditioning changed the look of architecture.

"The students call that the U," Kristen said when she noticed her gaze. "Two of those are academic buildings and the other is for administration, teacher offices, a clinic, and that kind of thing."

"And what are those other buildings behind them?" she asked. "More classrooms?"

A half-dozen long, low structures extended out like the spines in a fan. They had domed roofs and made her think of greenhouses.

"Housing," her companion answered. "For the students. The school is remote, as you can tell, so all the students live here while they attend. I hope you'll find the accommodations adequate."

"It seems like a ton of space. How many students go to the... uh, Lumos school?"

"We have about a hundred dragons. Or maybe I should say that the school normally has about a hundred dragons, at least for the last couple of centuries. Starting this year, two dozen mages have been admitted as well."

"Oh, Okay... It's only—"

"Yeah, I know. It seems like almost too much space for a hundred and twenty students." Kristen chuckled. "But it's because the dorms are built for dragons. For indoor classes, you'll be expected to attend in your human form, but many of the students prefer to sleep in their dragon form rather than their human form, so the buildings were constructed for their comfort. Do you have a preference?"

"Uh, yeah. I spend most of my time in my human form."

"That's no problem. I'll make sure you get a room that doesn't feel like a cavern. We have space for you to be comfortable. Beyond the dorms, there are also some training fields in the back, and that's about it for the tour. Are you ready to meet our headmaster?"

"Uh...sure?" In all honesty, she wasn't. Kylara was used to spending all her time with her mom and not socializing with anyone else at all. She had already talked to more people in the last few days than she had in the last year. It was exhausting to meet so many new people, but it was also exhilarating.

"If you need time—"

"No. No, I'm fine. I'd love to meet him." She tried to make herself believe it.

"Excellent." Kristen tucked her wings and spiraled down to the lawn in the center of the U. "She's not a him, though."

Kylara followed her lead and made a slow, circling descent to the center of the U. She transformed seconds before she landed, shed some of her momentum by tucking into a tight flip, and settled on the lush grass. Even through her shoes, she could tell it was the softest thing she had ever stepped on.

"Very nice. Very nice!" an old woman tittered as she walked down the steps from the central building of the U. For a moment, Kylara thought the librarian had escaped or perhaps she was an old housekeeper the Steel Dragon hadn't had the heart to let go. But when her guide ran to the woman and embraced her in a long hug, she realized that this was the headmaster.

"Oh, Amythist, it's been far too long," Kristen said, released the old woman, and held her at arm's length. "How is it that you haven't aged a day?"

"Maybe because I already look like I'm a thousand years old." Amythist smiled a wrinkled smile.

"If I find out it's because you have some special tea blend that you've been holding out on, I will not be pleased," the Steel Dragon said.

"If you want a cup of tea, all you have to do is ask." The old woman smiled.

"I would love one—oh, but where are my manners." She gestured for Kylara to approach with a waggle of her fingers.

The young dragon complied shyly. She had never met another dragon before she had met Kristen, and now she was meeting *the* Amythist? The fan blogs made it sound like she was practically the reason why Kristen was able to defeat the Masked One.

"Amythist, this Kylara Diamantine. She grew up in the area and will attend while we try to locate her mother. Kylara, this is Amythist, our new headmaster. She is in charge of all students and staff and as an elder dragon, she's not to be trifled with." Kristen threw an arm around the old dragon when she said it.

Kylara didn't understand if that meant she was joking or that since they were friends, trifling with her would be like messing with the Steel Dragon herself.

"Oh, hush, Kristen. You make me sound like I'll put the poor girl in detention for looking at me wrong. I assure you, dear, I don't bite, not in this body anyway." She winked and Kylara caught a glimpse of the dragon who hid inside the form of this little old lady.

"It's nice to meet you, Lady Amythist." She curtsied.

"Oh! Such manners! I like this one already. Diamantine, you said? I've heard of your mother. She used to serve on Dragon SWAT, correct? I didn't know she would raise her daughter better than many of our more...prestigious families." There was something in the way she said "prestigious" that made Kylara suspect that she cared very little for it. "Was it she who taught you how to change into your human form in midair and land like that?"

"Yes, ma'am."

"Well, it's too bad she's not here, then. I would love to have her whip some of our cadets into shape. Too many of them think the human body is not worth training."

"My mother always taught me to think of what I could do as a human before I took my dragon shape."

"A wise woman, indeed," Amythist said. "But come in, come in. Of course, I have tea for you, Kristen, although it's not my brew. The plants that grow here are quite different than what thrived in my garden in Michigan. Tell me, Kylara, if you're from the area, do you know anything around here that makes a decent cup?"

Was this her first quiz? "Well, there's always Navajo tea," she said quickly.

"I'm not familiar with it." The old woman looked intrigued.

"It's a yellow aster, also sometimes called greenthread. You can use the flowers and leaves to make a tea that's an anti-inflammatory, although it tastes terrible if you don't sweeten it with honey or agave nectar."

"Oh, Kristen, why didn't you tell me you would bring someone so refreshing?" Amythist beamed.

Kylara smiled. She liked the headmaster. There was something about the dragon masquerading as a little old lady that she trusted. It didn't hurt that Kristen trusted her too and that the young student knew something about her backstory.

They entered the central building of the U, where long tiled floors were flanked with display cases filled with everything from reconstructed skeletons to artifacts from humans living in the region. Between the displays were posters of student research projects. Kylara read a few as they walked toward Amythist's office. *The Use of Dragon Flame in Industrial Processes* sounded vaguely interesting, but *Storm Dragons and Irrigation* explained how the campus could be so green.

Amythist stopped at a door with a window of milky glass and her name on the front—*Amythist Skyjewel.* She opened it and led them into a cluttered mess. Bundles of drying herbs hung from the ceiling and potted plants crowded for space near the window at the back of the room. The desk was strewn with papers, seed packets, and more dried leaves.

"Pardon the mess." She winked. "But there are perks to being headmaster, of course, one of which is that no one can tell me to clean my office. Kristen, would you mind heating the water while I have a chat with young Kylara here? I already put some tea in the pot."

While Kristen busied herself with the tea, Amythist sank into the chair behind her desk and motioned for her new student to sit as well.

"Now, I know you've been through a fair amount, but I'd like to ask you some questions so I can understand your level of education. If you don't know the answer to something, simply tell me. If you guess right, you'll end up in far more difficult classes which will do considerably less for you. Understand?"

"Yes, ma'am."

What followed was what she thought of as a 'round the world' of academic questions. Amythist asked first about the basics of math, science, and world geography, but moved quickly into dragon biology, dragon history, and magic theory. Kylara found most of it easy, but she couldn't even begin to guess at the magic theory.

It was one topic her mom had never liked to talk about. She knew that Hester had been quite close to Lara, a mage who had worked with her during her days at Dragon SWAT. While she seldom mentioned her, the young dragon knew that losing the woman had hurt more than losing anyone else. It also didn't take a genius to realize that her name included Lara's name. It was an honor that she knew most dragons would never give to a mage.

Thinking about her mom made her sink into her depression once more, so much so that she didn't catch one of Amythist's questions until the old dragon cleared her throat and drew her attention back to the present.

"Are you all right, my dear?" the headmaster asked and gestured for her to take a sip of the tea that cooled in front of her.

Kylara took the cup and sighed. "Yeah—no? I don't know. It's only…so much. I had never even met a dragon besides my mom a few days ago. Now, I'm being enrolled in dragon school by the Steel Dragon and talking to Amythist Skyjewel. And I'm grateful, I truly am, but I can't stop thinking about my mom and that… that monster that took her. What if it comes here? What if everyone will be in danger because of me?"

"I understand how difficult it is to not know where our loved ones are, I do," Amythist said. "But you don't need to worry about anything happening here. Our professors are all mages or dragons."

"Plus, the student body is tough too," Kristen joked.

"Which is not something that young Kylara needs to worry about." The old woman scolded the Steel Dragon like she was little more than a student herself. "Because our staff will handle any threat. As for your mom, Kristen was indomitable before she was head of the Dragon Council and leader of the Steel Guard. With her resources, I'm sure it will only be a matter of time before they find her."

"It is a top priority," Kristen said firmly. "In fact, if you're ready, Kylara, I should leave and return to the investigation before I have to attend to more Council business. Are you all right?"

"Yeah. Yeah, I guess so. But promise me you'll tell me if you find anything about my mom. Even if it's bad news," She held the Steel Dragon's gaze, which might have been the scariest thing she ever did.

The woman seemed to weigh the words heavily before she nodded. "I will, if that's what you want."

"It is." She didn't let her words or expression falter.

"Okay then. We'll keep you up to date. But please understand that these investigations can get very dark before the light makes everything clear."

Kylara nodded. "I understand." Her words emerged far more meekly than she would have liked, but Kristen seemed to accept them without question.

"Now, I'll bid you two farewell. I'll keep an eye on your progress, Kylara. I'm very interested to see what a dragon whose parents didn't go to this school will make of it."

"Thank you, ma'am."

"Don't worry, I don't bite either."

Once Kristen left, Amythist politely continued her assessment of Kylara's education. After a few more minutes of questions, she deemed the education that Hester had given her daughter to be quite adequate.

Seeming satisfied with Kylara's answers, the headmaster

nodded once, then seemed to gather herself up, her eyes growing ever so slightly fiercer. Just enough that one seeing Amythist like this would never question the hidden power behind her frail-looking form.

"Now, there won't be any problems from you about dragons and mages, training together, will there?" Amythist said. Her tone remained polite as ever, but there was steel sheathed beneath the words.

Ky scrambled for a good answer. It hadn't even occurred to her, although it should have. She'd read about the enmity between dragons and mages, learned all the history. But her mother had always stressed that the two should be equal in rights and respect. "What...?"

"Because we will not have such behavior in the Lumos School," Amythist went on. "We are building a better future in this place, one where dragons and mages work together as equals, and all sentient beings are worthy of respect."

"That's what my mother always said," Kylara replied.

Amythist stopped speaking. The steel in her eyes turned to a twinkle of amusement in a flash. She let out a chuckle. "I'm a bit inspired by the subject. You see, it was only such a goal that would allow Kristen to coax me back out of retirement. But it is a noble endeavor, one which does all our people honor."

"I agree," Ky replied. She'd read of the horrors that happened during the Mage Wars. Besides, Kristen Hall was something of a hero for her. "I always rooted for the Steel Dragon, ma'am."

Amythist laughed aloud and relaxed her posture. "Did you, now?"

"Well, that's enough of that, then. Now for the fun part," The headmaster leaned over her messy desk. "Let's talk about your dragon powers. What abilities do you have? Do you have your mother's diamond scales?"

"Yes, ma'am, I do," she admitted.

"That's hardly surprising. Traits like that often follow from parent to child. And what else?"

"Well, I can transform into a dragon and back into a human, obviously. In my dragon form, I can fly and breathe fire and my scales are diamond-encrusted as I said."

"Very good. That's all very good for a dragon your age. Tell me, can you control which parts of your body become diamond?"

"Not so much. My mom could but I haven't mastered that yet."

"Well, at least there's something this school can do for you then. And what about diamond powers in your human form? That would be a trick that would make you tougher than the Steel Dragon herself."

She shook her head. "My mom could never do that, but she tried to learn how once we started following the Steel Dragon's exploits."

Amythist nodded as if this was all to be expected. "And what about your aura?"

"That's one area in which I lack somewhat. I could tell when my mom was mad but not much else."

"Did she focus on teaching you how to shield it?" the old lady asked.

"Not really."

"That's odd. Your aura is very closed off as if you're shielding it exceptionally well."

"I wish I could tell you more." Kylara felt like she was failing this quiz.

"Oh, it's a small matter, my dear. There must be some facet of your dragon powers that is affecting your aura. It's likely that your mother had a similar trait and passed it on to you either genetically or through her training style. In any event, we'll discover it in due course. Now, do you have any questions for me?"

"Only one..."

"Please."

"Will it be possible for me to learn how to track a dragon?"

Amythist stiffened. She took a sip of tea, went to set it down, took another sip, and finally answered. "I know you feel like you have to do something for your mother, but you already have. You made it here like she wanted, correct?"

"I guess so, yeah."

"Which means that when Kristen and her team find her, it's you she will have to thank. You may feel like you should be out there, scouring the desert, but no dragon has the skills needed to find your mother. That's the work of a mage, and Kristen employs the very best. It may seem odd, but the very best thing you can do for your mom right now is to continue the education she started for you. It was something that was very important to you both."

Kylara nodded. She didn't like the answer but saw the wisdom in it. At least for now.

"If there's nothing else, I have arranged for you to have a tour of our campus."

"A tour sounds good," she admitted. Maybe focusing on the academy would help alleviate her guilt—or at least make her forget about it for a few minutes.

"Excellent." Amythist pressed a call button on her desk and a minute later, a young man about Kylara's age knocked on the door. He had sandy hair with brilliant gold highlights and eyes that shimmered. She had no doubt that he was a dragon—she had seen enough clips of dragons on TV and the Internet to recognize the posture immediately. There was something in the way a dragon held themselves. Now that she thought about it, though, she realized Kristen hadn't had it but this guy did. Not that it looked bad on him.

"Kylara, this is Samuel. Samuel, Kylara. When I told him we had a young lady joining us, he volunteered to take you on a tour."

"Greetings, Lady Diamantine." Samuel bowed deeply. "I must say, you look familiar. Have we met?"

"I don't think so, no," she said and tried not to blush at his devilish grin.

"It must merely be your beauty, then."

"Oh, goodness, Samuel. Save it for later," Amythist chided him. "The girl's only just got here."

"It's all right," Kylara said. "It's very nice to meet you, Samuel." She curtsied to the headmaster and her guide led her from the office and out to the school grounds.

# CHAPTER TWELVE

"Right this way, Lady Kylara," Samuel said and gestured down the hallway.

"You don't have to call me that," she said, flattered that he saw her as a lady but also not ready for dragon formality.

"You got it, Ky," he said with a wink. "You can call me Sam." He set off briskly and she fell into step beside him.

"The ground floor is mainly the administrative areas. If you have a problem with your schedule, this is the place to complain about it." He chuckled at his joke but she didn't. Her mother had never even pretended like she had a choice in what she would learn. The idea of a school letting students choose their curriculum seemed...foolish.

"Do you complain often?" she asked.

Sam glanced at her out of the corner of his eye. "Only when I have a sympathetic audience, so I'll try to keep it to a minimum."

"That would be great, thanks." She couldn't help but smile. Was she flirting? She had seen enough movies to think that she was.

He seemed to think so too because he smiled even more broadly. "The ground floor also has a health clinic, the library, a movie theater that only plays boring combat footage and documentaries, and probably other things I've forgotten. The top floor is all the teacher offices. The headmaster is the only professor who has her office on the ground floor."

"It seems huge," Kylara commented. "I never imagined a library could be inside this building."

"Well, that's the point of spatial magic, right?"

"Huh?"

"Spatial magic? Like, space distortion or whatever?"

"I'm sorry, I don't know much about magic."

"Yeah, no kidding." Sam laughed but it didn't feel mean-spirited to her. "Spatial magic changes the size of things. It makes this building bigger on the inside than the outside."

"That's possible? I thought it was merely theory!" she blurted.

He grinned. "Of course it's possible. We're living in it right now. I could show you all the offices upstairs but it would take forever. Plus, you won't need to go to the second floor unless you're failing and need help in office hours, or if you get detention."

"Do you ever have to go to the second floor?" Kylara asked.

"Maybe once or twice," he confessed.

"Because you failed or got in trouble?"

"Yes," he said frankly, then opened a door to the outside and led her out before she could ask which one he had agreed to.

They walked across the U toward one of the two buildings that framed the central green. "All your indoor classes will be in one of these two buildings," he explained. "Emerald Hall tends to be more hands-on lessons, while Lumos Hall is more academic, but honestly, with the new names and the mages starting this year, all that will change."

"What do you think of the new names?" Kylara asked, hoping to sound innocent. Kristen had said that some of the dragons there weren't too keen on the changes.

"Are you kidding? I love them! You've heard about what those guys did in the war, right?"

"I have."

"So then you know how kickass they both are. Or...were, I guess." They stopped in front of a life-size statue of a golden dragon with a long mustache and smiling eyes. "He was my great-great-great grandfather," Sam said proudly, his gaze fixed on the gleaming golden statue. "We didn't get together all that often, so I sometimes still forget that he's..."

"No longer with us?" Kylara suggested.

"Yeah. That works. Still. I'm proud of him. He led a life of honor and died a warrior's death."

"You're not sad to have lost him?"

"Of course I am." His eyes were a little moist. She wished she was better with auras so she could sense what he truly felt. "But he lived for thousands of years. I think if I have a run that good, I might as well end it fighting for justice too."

"I suppose so, yeah," Kylara agreed. She was starting to like Sam. He was handsome, clever, and had a sense of honor—the kind of dragon her mom would have liked, Kylara thought.

"The dorms are behind Old Main. That's where we'll stop the tour so you can get settled and shower or do your nails or whatever girls do."

"Right, Sam, I've been here an hour already so I need to do my nails."

He laughed. "You're not like other dragons, Kylara."

They held each other's gaze for a moment, and something stirred in her stomach. It felt remarkably like yucca moths trying to escape.

"I wondered if you wanted to see the training fields first, though," Sam said and ruined the moment in possibly the most awkward way possible.

"Sure."

"They're tucked back there. Can you change into your dragon form at will yet? It'll be faster if we can fly."

"Yeah, I love to fly!" Without hesitation, she launched and transformed into her dragon shape. She pumped her wings, flexed her diamond scales, and spun to look at him, wondering why he hadn't transformed yet too.

He was still on the ground, his jaw agape and his eyes wide with shock. "I knew I'd met you."

"What are you talking about?" Kylara asked.

"You were filthy last time. And your hair was down. That's why I didn't recognize you."

"Sam, I've never met a dragon before. I assure you that whoever you're talking about is—"

Her words cut off when he transformed into the golden dragon she had left buried in the canyon on her land.

"You're the trespasser," she shouted as he pumped his golden wings to join her in the sky.

"Trespasser? I was simply flying. You're the one who almost killed me!"

"Killed you? I saved your life. If I hadn't unburied you, you might have drowned."

"Okay, sure, but I was only buried because you flew away from me instead of talking."

"So because a girl doesn't want to talk to you, that gives you the right to pursue her?" Kylara could not believe that she had begun to like this guy.

"I only wanted to say hello. What's wrong with that?"

"You said hello. That doesn't mean I had to say anything in return."

"And here I thought you were well-mannered," Samuel said.

"Well-mannered? Honestly? Did you approve of my manners when I dug you up from your clumsy crash?"

"I only crashed because you knew those switchbacks and I didn't."

"I knew them because they were my land. You weren't supposed to be there."

"What does it matter if a dragon flew overhead?" Sam snorted.

"It matters because after you left, a firestorm with a grudge against my mom burned our house to nothing. I barely escaped with my life. She didn't." Kylara realized when she said it that she shouldn't have. If he was working for the hunter, she'd given her identity away, and if he truly didn't know anything about it, there was no point in blaming him.

"Ky...I'm sorry. I didn't realize... I promise you I didn't have anything to do with—what did you say? A firestorm with a grudge?"

"You know what? Let's forget it, okay? Will you show me the training fields or what?"

"Right this way, my lady," he replied, but the humor was gone from his voice.

They flew over a stretch of forest before they reached another long area of open space a little lower in the valley.

"Where is everyone?" Kylara asked. If she had access to a place where she could train and spar with other dragons at her leisure, she imagined she'd be there all the time.

"They're empty right now. Classes won't start for a couple more days," Sam said almost robotically. "Once classes begin, this is where dragons and now mages can practice their powers outside without fear of burning the school buildings down."

"That's handy," she conceded.

"I suppose so, yes," he said. She thought he was offended because she had implicated him in what had happened to her land and her mom. Did that mean he was offended because he had no part in it, or was he acting guilty because he was?

"Can you take me to the dorms now or are there cliffs in the way?" She made an attempt at humor and assumed that either way, it was better to seem friendly to him.

"Is that supposed to be a joke about my accident?" he asked, obviously affronted.

"What? No. Okay, yeah, it was, but it's no big deal. I used to do the same thing in the Straits all the time when I was little."

"Great. So now your childhood self is tougher than me?"

Kylara sighed, not sure how flirting could have crashed and burned and devolved so quickly—until she remembered that crashing and burning were literally involved.

They flew to the dorms in silence. She tried to think of something to say but ultimately came up with nothing.

Samuel broke the silence but not with warm words. "You'll be in the second dorm from the right. It's for female dragons who prefer their human forms. That's what you like, right?"

"Sorry. It seems like you stopped caring what I liked."

He groaned—a petulant, annoying sound—before he asked if she needed anything else.

She didn't, so he nodded and flew away. Kylara headed toward the dorms and tried to clear her head but instead, she thought about Sam. He was plainly pissed that she had implicated him in what had happened on her land, and maybe that was fair. Except he ignored the fact that her home had burned down and her mom was missing. Hester had always said men would get angry at women for failing to sympathize with them, while they failed to empathize themselves.

But she suspected there was more to it as well. Samuel had seemed embarrassed that he had crashed and taken that out on her, even though it was unfair. She had never cared much about her aura powers but now, she wanted them more than ever before. Maybe she'd have a window into his heart if she did—not that she cared.

She was still trying to convince herself that she didn't care when she landed in front of the dorms and stepped inside.

# CHAPTER THIRTEEN

Kylara pushed the door to the dorm open and found herself in the midpoint of a long, two-story structure. A hallway ran in each direction with more doors opening from the hall and stairs to the second floor at each end. Directly across the hall from the entrance was an open door.

A voice issued from there. "Just a minute! My toes..."

Not sure what to make of that, she looked around the space she was in. The building seemed pleasant. It wasn't opulent like mansions on TV but clean, sturdy, and well lit. A bulletin board hung on one wall of the room she was in with posters advertising various clubs, performances, and organizations. She felt like it was the first normal place she'd been in since her flight from her home.

A minute later, a woman came out into the hallway. "Hi! Ruby Firedrake," she said and proffered a hand. Kylara took it but pulled back immediately.

"Oh, sorry," Ruby said. "I had heated my skin to make my nail polish dry faster. Are you all right?"

"Yeah, I'm fine, thanks," she said. "I'm Kylara by the way. Kylara Diamantine."

Ruby smiled. The girl was young but older than Kylara—in her mid-twenties, at least, although she was a bad judge of age since most faces she knew were from TV, which of course used actors to play whatever ages the directors wanted. She had a big poof of red hair and eyes the color of her first name.

"I'm your dorm supervisor and a dragon, obviously. Or I guess it's not obvious anymore, now that there are mages here too, but yeah, I am a dragon."

"Me too," she said helpfully.

"Diamantine, you said, right? Do you prefer a human-sized room?"

"Yes, please."

"Me too. Follow me." As they walked, Ruby went over the rules. They seemed standard to her. No drugs, no alcohol, and no sleepovers. No boys after hours. Public spaces were to be kept clean and they would be forced to clean their bedrooms if any insects appeared. It seemed scorpions had been a problem in the past.

"Here we are." Her guide unlocked a door to a room on the ground floor and gave her a key. "Oh, I forgot to ask who is coming with your belongings. If you can give me their name, I'll let them in so they can drop them all off."

"Oh...um, thanks, but I don't have any."

Ruby turned an even brighter shade of crimson. "Oh, my goodness, I am so sorry. I should have been more sensitive. Headmaster Amythist told me about your home being destroyed and I'm... If there's anything I can do, please let me know."

"Thanks. A toothbrush would be great, actually."

"Oh, you poor thing." the girl tutted. "I'll have a toothbrush by the time you're back, all right? I'll find you fresh clothing too and you can let me know if there are any other odds and ends."

"I'm sure I can get them at the campus store or whatever." She didn't want to be a burden before she'd even settled in and was too used to looking out for herself and her mom.

"No, honestly, I'd love to. When I took this job, I thought I'd help students, but most of the dragons here are so rich, it's more of an issue to make them get rid of stuff. I'd be happy to help."

"That's very nice of you," Kylara admitted and suddenly became all too aware that she only had ninety-eight dollars to her name.

"Now, while I go find a toothbrush, maybe you should get some food. Are you hungry?"

Finally, a question that didn't feel like a trick. She responded with an emphatic, "Yes!"

"Excellent. You came to the right dorm. The dragon sleepers tend to prefer their food raw—not that there's anything wrong with eating fresh meat—but here, we have what I call real food," Ruby explained as she led her from the dorm to the central spine of the buildings that, when seen from above, had looked like a fan.

They entered and Kylara paused to gape at the most gorgeous room she had ever seen. It was massive, with marble floors and big round wooden tables positioned throughout. Chandeliers hung from the ceiling, and the smell of a hundred different kinds of food hung in the air.

"The kitchens are in the back behind the food. It's buffet-style, so serve yourself and take your dishes and silverware back there when you're finished. There's always a wicked spread at mealtimes, but if you're not a total jerk to the mages who work the kitchens, you can usually get a snack between meals too. Breakfast is from seven to eight, lunch from eleven thirty to twelve thirty, and dinner starts at six and runs until eight or nine."

"It's amazing."

"I think so too," her companion agreed. "And the pantries are worth checking out too, but right now—well, I can hear your stomach grumbling. I'll leave you to it, all right?"

"Thanks, Ruby."

"No problem. And I'll have that toothbrush for you when you're done."

Before Kylara could thank her, she hurried to the dorm, her toenails sparkling in the afternoon sun.

A glance at the elaborate clock on the wall showed that it was twelve twenty. If she hurried, she could still get lunch.

She moved through the dining hall, past tables mostly cleared —although some students had left their mess behind—and to a bank of steaming platters of food.

It was a feast unlike any she had ever seen. Growing up with her mom, food had been about nutrition, calories, and ease of prep, in that order. Flavor was mostly an afterthought. Sure, they seasoned their pots of beans and put spicy peppers on their food, but the thing was that they ate beans almost every day. They'd kill a deer and eat it until it was gone. What dishes they did cook were made to last for a week of leftovers.

In the buffet in front of her, Kylara saw a dozen foods she'd never seen let alone eaten. She helped herself first to some kind of steamed crab legs. Besides these, every type of bread she could imagine was available, along with vegetables that had been roasted, braised, sautéed, and boiled. Individual sauces were on offer near a salad bar with ingredients she couldn't even name.

She helped herself to all of it, stacking one plate with nothing but crab's legs and another with everything else. With a plate in each hand, she scanned the dining hall for somewhere to sit.

It was mostly empty, no doubt because the lunch hour was almost over and because most of the students hadn't arrived on campus yet, but a few groups of kids were still seated and eating.

Kylara considered going to a table and introducing herself. *Hi, my name is Kylara. For some reason, my mom kept my existence hidden from the world but now, I'm here because it turns out she was right and was eaten by a fire monster. No, I've never eaten crab's legs before. Is it that obvious?*

Instead, she smirked, found a clean table, and sat on her own.

She ate alone and enjoyed the food immensely. Hunger took precedence and she ate with gusto, slowing her pace only when she came to the crab's legs. Once she discovered how to crack them open—she used her hand and dragon strength rather than the tools she saw another young dragon in human form use a few tables over—she decided they were delicious.

She took her plates to a counter for dirty dishes, wiped her table, and returned to her dorm. Without a doubt, almost all the food had been imported. None of that grew in the desert. Was this how most dragons were accustomed to eating? Did they enjoy a life of opulence that Hester had denied her daughter? Maybe that was why her mom kept her away from the rest of the dragon world. She didn't want her to become spoiled or privileged.

But no, the face in the fire was a reminder that her mother's paranoia had been justified.

Kylara returned to her utterly empty dorm room and sighed. True to her word, Ruby had acquired a toothbrush. It was the only thing in the room that gave any indication that someone lived there. Two beds were made with more starchy sheets and uncomfortable-looking pillows, and two bare desks and two empty wardrobes provided the only furniture. She assumed that meant she might have a roommate but seeing the empty room reminded her that not only did she not have any possessions, but she also had no friends.

She slumped onto the bed and tried to focus on how full she was. Eventually, her mind wandered to her grief, her loneliness, and her failure to help her mother, and she cried herself to sleep, her sobs echoing off the walls of the empty room.

# CHAPTER FOURTEEN

Kylara woke to the sound of banging on the door. Visions of the fire monster flashed before her eyes as she scrambled out of bed. She only realized once she was standing that a beast like that wouldn't knock. The door flung open and a dragon girl who looked about her age stood in the doorway.

"Oh. My. Goodness. Roomies!" The girl squealed and before she could even wipe the sleep from her eyes to take a good look at her, she was wrapped in a hug, held at arm's length, then hugged again.

"My name is Tanya Fastwing and I can already tell we will be the best of friends. I don't know when you expect your luggage to arrive, but mine is here already so I'll start unpacking and we can go from there, okay?"

"Uh...okay," she responded.

Tanya turned and her perfectly curled twin blonde pigtails bounced energetically. "Tony! You can start unloading. Yes, now. Yes, she's here. It's fine, Tony." The girl turned to her and rolled her eyes as she spoke in a low tone. "Tony is absolutely wonderful. He's served my family for years, but he refuses to get a hearing aid. He thinks he can fix his hearing with magic." She shook her head as she moved into their room.

Her blue-and-white dress looked like something out of a movie from the golden age of Hollywood. Kylara also realized that she held a parasol, of all things. She had only a moment to take all this in, though, before giant trunks—four of them—floated into the room. She yelped with surprise.

"Is there a problem?" Tanya's perfect brow furrowed. "Oh, my goodness. I didn't ask for your name! I'm so sorry. Once I start talking, I simply don't stop. My mom says it's a real problem and there I go again!" Her awkward laughter settled into a smile. "What is your name?"

"Kylara Diamantine and I was merely surprised. I've never seen floating luggage before."

"It's Tony. Doesn't your mage have telekinetic powers? My goodness. How do they get anything done?"

"My family doesn't have a mage," she said. "I thought that no dragons did since the Steel Dragon."

"Oh, we stopped making Tony wear his bracelet as soon as we could, but he's, like—how old are you, Tony?" Tanya shouted down the hall. "He's, like, ninety-one. We couldn't simply fire him, although I do wish he'd stay at home and rest."

"I don't need rest. I need to stay fit," Tony said, a tiny old man with a back as curved as the edge of Tanya's parasol.

"Whatever you say, Tony." The girl flourished her fingers to show him where to put her chests.

"If there's nothing else, my lady."

"Go get some hearing aids."

"What?"

Tanya put her hands on her hips as her face reddened. "I said to go get some—wait. You did that on purpose, didn't you?"

The old mage cackled and wandered away down the hallway. She ignored his exit and began to organize her wardrobe. Kylara felt a stab of fear when she saw more dresses and more matching parasols.

"So, tell me about yourself. What's your special power?" Her roommate made it sound like they had been having a conversation this whole time. It was hard to resist her.

"My scales are lined with diamonds." She saw no point in deception at this point.

"Cool! Very cool! I bet you hear this all the time, but if you could do that in your human form, you'd be like the Steel Dragon."

"Yeah, you're right. I—"

"I don't have any special powers at all, can you believe that?" Tanya interrupted. "For hundreds of years, this school has only been for special dragons, but now the Steel Dragon is in power and I get to come here. Well...I guess it's the Lumos school now, but still, that counts. Are you excited about the semester?"

"Not really," Kylara hadn't even had time to process thinking about classes, schedules, and everything else. She had been focused on her mom and how much her life had changed.

"Oh, you should be. You have nothing to worry about. Diamond powers should make you an ace in the duels."

"Duels?"

"It's an elective but you should take it," the girl said.

"What electives will you take?" she asked and dug deep for school language she'd learned from TV.

"I don't get to take any." Tanya leaned in conspiratorially. "I'm kind of on probation. Can you believe that? Ever since the Steel Dragon learned light powers, dragons have tried to expand their abilities. They've had no success yet, but the thought is that it might be possible for a younger dragon to do so. That's why I'm here. I'm supposed to learn to control my 'inner magic,' whatever that means, so I can gain a special power."

"That sounds cool."

"I agree," Tanya responded enthusiastically. "But I'm also nervous. Like, if I fail, will they cancel the program completely? The hopes of every vanilla dragon in the entire world are resting on my shoulders." Her laughter was loud and nervous. "What am I saying? It'll be fine."

"I'm sure you can work something out." Kylara tried to sound supportive.

"Thanks. I sure do hope so." A little sigh punctuated the statement and she could tell exactly how nervous the girl was about developing a new ability.

"So, where are you from?" she asked, hoping to change the subject from something that seemed to be stressful for her new roommate.

"Los Angeles and oh, my goodness, I already miss it. Like, did you see the buffet here? The avocados were as hard as rocks." A peel of laughter followed. "I knew I was supposed to be roughing it or whatever, but that seems a little much. And then there were the crab's legs. Who do they think they're fooling? They were undoubtedly frozen."

Kylara nodded and hoped her fingers no longer smelled like crab meat. "Were there many dragons in Los Angeles?"

Tanya darted her a you-can't-be serious-look. "Uh...yes? We have all the Hollywood dragons there, plus all those who want to get with human movie stars, which is *a lot*. I never went in for all that, of course, but still, when my parents threw parties, we'd normally have to turn dragons away there were so many. Where are you from? Are you from one of the more isolated communities?"

"Yeah...you could say that," Kylara decided she had to be from the world's most isolated community of dragons—a community of two.

"I'm sorry, did I say something wrong?" the girl asked. "It's hard to tell because your aura is so closed off but seriously, if I said something rude you can simply tell me. I do this all the time. I meet a cool new person and talk and talk and suddenly, instead of a friend, I have another person who thinks I'm merely a stupid ditz from LA. I didn't mean to brag or anything. I don't even know any Hollywood dragons. Honestly. My sister met Hubert Radiance once, but she said he was a total goon and—"

"I've never met a dragon before!" Kylara blurted.

"That's what I was saying," Tanya said. "I've never met a famous one either."

"No. I'd never met a dragon before yesterday. You're maybe the fifth dragon I've ever talked to in my whole life."

"No. Burning. Way."

She was relieved. Her roommate seemed excited. She had been worried she would treat her like some kind of a freak.

Tanya sat on Kylara's bed and patted the mattress excitedly for her to join her. "How is that even possible? You have to tell me everything. Is your mom in a cult or something?"

A tear came to her eye at the mention of her mother. She wiped it away but not quickly enough that the other girl didn't notice. "Okay, so first, you need to tell me what happened to your mom."

"That's why I'm here," she explained. "I grew up not far from here and spent my whole life with only my mom. I've talked to a few humans but never a dragon. It was against the rules, to be honest."

"Oh, my goodness, that sounds horrible."

She smiled. "It wasn't that bad. Mom took training very seriously, but it was all right."

"So why the waterworks?"

Kylara couldn't help but smile. "A few days ago, we were attacked. She was...taken, I guess, by some kind of fire creature. What's crazy is that I don't think I would be here if she was still all right. And I want her to be all right, but I also don't understand why I was never allowed to meet another dragon."

"Moms. They always have reasons," Tanya said matter of factly.

"I guess so."

"So what happened after she was taken by this fire monster?" the girl asked.

"I reached the Steel Guard station and told them. The Steel Dragon said she'll solve it, and I should come here in the meantime."

"You've met her?"

Kylara nodded.

Tanya leaned in conspiratorially "Between you and me, my dad doesn't like her very much." Then, in her regular voice, she said, "My mom and I love her, though, and of course, getting that dumb bracelet off Tony was for the best. You shouldn't worry if Kristen Hall is on the case. She'll find your mom, Ky. That's simply who she is."

"That's what everyone keeps saying."

"Well, everyone is right. In the meantime, we both need to focus on school and making sure you don't stick out like a total nerd."

"Huh?"

"Ky, I love you, I already totally do, but I can tell you're not exactly from around here. Or...maybe I can tell you are from around here and that's the problem. Either way, we need each other."

"For what?"

"I need you to teach me how to use weird powers, and you need me to teach you how to not be a total spazz when talking to other dragons. Also, if your home was attacked, it sounds like you need clothes, and lucky for you, I didn't listen to my mom and brought too much. You can borrow anything you want until we get a chance to take you shopping."

"Do you mean that?" Kylara asked.

"Of course, roomie. Well, except the parasols. They're my

signature look and with your complexion, you hardly need them."

"That's honestly not a problem," she said before she had a look at Tanya's trunks and saw that elaborate dresses were unequivocally her roommate's new aesthetic. For the time being, it seemed, they would be hers as well.

# CHAPTER FIFTEEN

Classes began a few days later and Kylara was lost in the whirl-wind of her first school year ever. She had done well in her interview with Amythist, so she had been placed out of some classes. Her schedule only had five—a blessing, given how overwhelming it all felt compared to simply learning whatever her mom wanted to teach her for a few weeks at a time.

She took classes on Magical Theory—a new requirement for all dragons this year—Practical Dragon Powers, Dragon and Human History—another new class required by the headmaster at the Steel Dragon's insistence—as well as a Geography of Dragons class and Dragon Law. The latter was almost painfully boring, even though the professor started each lesson by telling the students how important this particular one would be.

On top of all this, she tried to learn people's names, seem normal, and get used to wearing clothes other than jeans, t-shirts, and flannels. Currently, she wore a yellow dress with a pattern of tiny white flowers in the fabric. It went past her knees but left her arms, back, and an uncomfortable amount of her chest exposed.

Tanya assured her that she looked "absolutely divine, like the picture of spring itself," but she associated spring with flurries of snow and flushes of rugged wildflowers, so she didn't get the reference. Still, she loved how her roommate would braid her hair and lend her jewelry to match, although she never removed the silver-and-turquoise necklace her mom had given her, no matter how much Tanya complained that the colors conflicted with her outfit.

That particular morning, she had already endured Dragon Law and was currently en route to her second class of the day, Dragon and Human History.

She arrived, sat somewhere in the middle, and saved a seat for Tanya. The girl was the only thing interesting about the class. She arrived moments before the bell rang, wearing a white dress with long sleeves and a silver belt that appeared to be made of tiny chains and looked utterly impractical.

Her friend sat beside her and smiled. "What kind of mage propaganda will the prof lay on us today?"

"It's not propaganda," Kylara explained for possibly the hundredth time. "You've only ever heard the dragon side of things. He's merely presenting what it was like to be a mage during the first two wars."

"Even though he wasn't there?" Her friend raised an eyebrow at their tattooed professor.

"Of course he wasn't there. Mages don't live as long as we do. That's why the letters are so important."

Tanya flinched. She didn't enjoy reading the historical documents any more than Kylara did. "Still, I wish he would brighten these lectures up with demonstrations of something."

She understood. Her mom had done a decent job of presenting both sides and making it interesting. In fact, listening to Hester describe decisive battles had always been a highlight of her education, especially when she made her practice some of the more famous dragon attacks.

In contrast, the next fifty minutes were spent trying to stay awake while the professor somehow made the siege of a castle in which fifty mages held off fifty dragons for fifty days boring. Maybe it was that he said the word fifty at least fifty times? She didn't know, but when he dismissed the class, she was thankful to still be awake.

The two girls shared their third class of the day as well—Magical Theory. This one was much less boring to Kylara but far more confusing.

Their professor was a middle-aged woman with long hair that was shaved on both sides of her head. Every inch of her skin was tattooed except her face, and that looked like it would be lost to ink soon. Already, swirls and geometric patterns pushed into the professor's cheeks from the designs on the sides of her head.

"As we've discussed, there are distinct categories of magic," Professor Sharra said. "Who remembers what they are?"

The hands of the four mages in the class raised so fast that some of the papers on their desks rustled.

The professor looked past them to the twenty or so disinterested dragons. "Anyone?" She checked the roster. "Kylara Diamantine, please name one of the categories."

Kylara straightened, searched for an answer, and came up with only one. "There's fire magic."

Their lecturer nodded. "That's right, although it's exceptionally rare for mages to be able to do much with fire. There are exceptions, of course, Neal Havington being the most infamous example."

"He made a fire tornado that ripped through Detroit to try to hurt the Steel Dragon, right?" she asked.

"Very good, Kylara, although the tornado wasn't his doing but the work of a storm dragon."

"Would a fire mage be able to make a fire monster?" she blurted.

"A fire...monster?" Professor Shara paused and turned to look at her. It felt like all the points and edges of her tattoos were directed at the young dragon.

"Yes, ma'am. That is...can a mage make fire do their bidding even if they're not nearby? Can they give it a mind of its own?"

The mage's brows furrowed and blurred the tattoos on her forehead together. "There are legends of such techniques, but that's far beyond the scope of this class. Plus, most of you already have access to fire magic in your dragon forms. We won't go into it much here."

The four mage students wilted.

"The other types of magic are much more common." The professor gained momentum now and tried to move away from the off-topic conversation. "Light magic is especially pervasive and almost all mages can use it."

"But we're not mages," a male dragon with perfect hair said. "We're dragons." His eyes gleamed as he looked at the mages.

"Which is precisely why we'll all attempt to make our hands glow today." Professor Sharra continued as if the student had set her up for this transition. "The Steel Dragon unlocked that ability, so we hope some of the bright minds of the future will be able to as well." She smiled and made it clear that she thought the chances of any of the dragons unlocking this ability were remote. "We'll move into some of the other elements later. The headmaster herself will teach the unit on telekinetic manipulation but today, we'll focus on making our hands glow."

The mage instructed the dragons to look inside themselves and try to find sources of mental blocks. They were to then push past these and in doing so, to unlock their inner magic. Kylara's main mental block was her missing mom, and she didn't see how making her hands glow would do a damn thing about that, so she didn't exactly make much progress.

Not that any of the other dragons fared any better. The mages were all novices—that was why they were in this class with the dragons—but they still managed to make their hands glow and a couple of them even created spheres of light that they tossed to each other over their dragon classmates' heads toward the end of class.

Kylara produced no light at all, but doing the exercises made her feel weird—like there was a river inside her that had been dammed up by an avalanche long before. It was a frustrating, unsatisfying feeling, and she wondered if it had something to do with why her aura powers also seemed so restrained compared to everyone else's.

After Magical Theory was lunch, which was usually a high-light of the day.

Despite having completely different backgrounds, the two roommates were becoming fast friends, and lunch was one of the times when they were able to build their budding relationship. Tanya loved to watch her try new foods, and given that her previous diet had consisted of beans, fresh meat, and vegetables from their aquaponic system, there were so many new foods to try.

"Oh, my goodness, sashimi!" The other girl beamed and stacked her plate high with tiny filets of raw fish. "You will need soy sauce, some of that wasabi stuff if you like spicy food, and a bowl of rice. You never get full only by eating the fish."

Kylara nodded and stacked her plate with the same assortment of filets as her friend. They found an empty table and began to eat. She discovered quickly that the wasabi was not what had been promised.

"I thought you said this was spicy." She coughed. "It feels like someone fire-blasted my nostrils."

"Oh, my goodness, Kylara, seriously? It's refreshing. Way better than those hatch chilies you dump on everything."

"Hatch chilies are good," she retorted. "This is terrible. And the texture of the fish is slimy."

"It's better in California where it's fresh," Tanya conceded. "But I don't know...I think it's good. But you're right that I've had better. There is one place that when we have break, I would love to—oh, my goodness, Kylara, don't look now but you're being watched." The last was said in the excited, breathless whisper the girl used when discussing anything resembling gossip.

She took a deep breath, waited a moment, and turned to peek where Tanya had been looking. Samuel sat two tables over and stared at her. She raised an eyebrow at him, which broke his gaze and forced him to return to eating a bowl of noodles that she envied when she turned to her plate of cold, flaccid, raw fish.

"Kylara, tell me everything. Who is the dreamboat with the golden hair and why is he staring at you and not me?"

Kylara sighed. "That's Samuel. He's the great-grandson or something of Lumos."

"Oh, my goodness, he's related to *the* Lumos? Kylara this is huge! He can't keep his eyes off you."

"That's because he's mad at me."

"You have been here a week and already, handsome boys related to famous dragons are mad at you? I think the wrong one of us has been giving the culture lessons."

"He's only mad at me because I caught him trespassing on my mom's land," she explained.

"I thought you said you had only ever met maybe five dragons before." The girl couldn't keep her gaze off Samuel.

"Yeah, well, he's one of them. I outmaneuvered him and he got caught under a pile of rocks."

Her friend broke out into a giggle so loud that most of the cafeteria stopped their conversation to look at the source of the outburst. She reddened, and even with Kylara's extremely limited aura powers, she could sense her embarrassment.

The groups in the cafeteria had barely begun to resume their conversations when Kylara felt a hand land on her shoulder so firmly that it knocked her chair onto its two back legs.

She bolted out of her seat and spun behind her assailant before she even thought about it. A moment later, they were both on the ground, one of her legs was across his neck, and the other on his chest. Her ankles locked together and the offending arm stretched between her legs, locked in an arm-bar.

The cafeteria broke into whoops and cheers and the voices of young adults screamed, "Fight, fight, fight!" It was an odd contrast to the marble floors and ornately carved tables that filled the space they were in.

"Yeah, good one," the boy said. He had a pockmarked face and slicked-down black hair that she could tell she had thoroughly mussed. "I only want to say hi, but I'm glad you could show us all that you spend too much time in your human body." It almost sounded like a joke but his anger seeped through. "Can you let me go now? It was a good trick, but the servants haven't cleaned the floor yet and your little friend spilled soy sauce when she laughed like a hyena."

"Sure, sorry," Kylara said and released his arm. "I'm a little on edge right now. I didn't mean to overreact."

"It's not a problem," he said, pushed to his feet, and brushed himself off. He wore a black suit and a black shirt, but no tie. "I'd be on guard too if I knew the people near me wouldn't watch my back."

"I'm sorry?" Kylara glanced at Tanya, who scowled at the boy before she focused on him again. "I don't understand."

"I'm Karl Midnight." He extended his hand. She looked at her friend's scowling face and didn't take his hand.

"And is there a reason you told me that after you tried to touch me?" Kylara asked, unsure why the other girl looked so uncomfortable but certain that Karl Midnight seemed to be the source of her discomfort.

Karl smirked. "Most girls like the Midnight touch."

"Yeah, well, I'm not most girls," she replied.

"Fair enough." Karl seemed to take that as a challenge. "No worries, by the way. I get it. You're in a new place with new faces and it's easy to be on guard. Plus, it probably doesn't help that no one has given you a proper welcome yet."

Kylara couldn't help but glance at Samuel when Midnight said that. He frowned at their exchange—as if it had anything to do with him.

The other boy didn't notice where she was looking, only when her gaze returned to him. "You're welcome to join me and my friends at our table if you like. We've all been here for a few semesters so we can help you understand how things are supposed to work around here."

"What do you think, Tanya?" she asked her roommate.

The girl bit at her lip. "I don't know, Ky."

"Oh, hey, good answer," Midnight sneered at her.

"What is that supposed to mean?" Kylara asked.

"She mumbled something and then said no, which is what she's supposed to say. I wasn't inviting a powerless dragon to our table, exactly like powerless dragons shouldn't be allowed at this school at all."

"The Lumos School is for all dragons and mages," she said slowly and smiled at Tanya.

"The Steel Dragon has the right to change the name but not our history," Midnight explained sourly. "This academy is for dragons with powers—dragons like yourself, Kylara. I heard you say in our Practical Dragon Powers class that you have diamond scales. You ought to hang out with dragons like yourself. These powerless ones are simply runts and you never know, it might be catching."

"I am already hanging out with dragons like myself," she responded and finally fully understood what this asshole was—a bigot. "Tanya has never let me put her in an armbar. She's not as slow as you are."

"Wait, what?"

"I also don't like to hang out with dragons who eat flies. You might want to close that maw of yours. A bug might fly in there."

"You're making a mistake, Diamantine," Midnight sputtered.

"My only mistake was not realizing what you were sooner. You're one of those assholes who doesn't bus his tray, right? You think mages are here to take care of you and that you have a natural right to be an asshole to everyone."

"I am a Midnight dragon! I have the right to be whatever I want," he roared in response.

To which the entire cafeteria responded with laughter.

"I couldn't have said it better myself," Kylara said. "Now, what are you still doing in my face? Midnight, right? Shouldn't you be under a rock in the dark with your kind?"

"See you in class, Diamantine." He turned on his heel and marched out, pausing only to knock the trays of food at his table onto the floor.

"That was cool of you Ky. Like, super cool," Tanya said and stared at her plate.

"It's no problem," she said. "I guess the movies weren't lying. There truly is one of those at every school. He shouldn't mess with you anymore."

"Yeah... I'm sure he'll learn his lesson," the girl replied but she avoided eye contact.

Kylara turned to watch Midnight storm out but in doing, so she noticed Samuel watching her. She thought she saw the hint of a smile on his face before he turned away.

# CHAPTER SIXTEEN

After lunch was Practical Dragon Powers. It was Kylara's longest class at two full hours and the one she had thought she would be most comfortable in, thanks to hours and hours of training with her mom. The class wasn't perfect, though. One of the things she didn't like about it was that Tanya wasn't in it.

"Well, I'm off to Advanced Mage Powers." Her roommate sighed. "If I can't make a ball of light, I don't know how I'm supposed to master wind powers or magic portals, but here we go."

"You can do this, Tanya." She tried to remain optimistic. "Just think, if you can make this work, you'll be part of history."

"I hope I'm not that boring," the girl quipped before they parted ways.

If the truth be told, Kylara wished she didn't have to take the class either. At first, she thought it would be cool. She had imagined dragon duels, wing attacks, and new ways to breathe fire, but it turned out this class was designed primarily to increase a dragon's control of their unique abilities. The class she wanted was dueling, but it seemed Practical Dragon Powers was the pre-req.

The thing was, Kylara could already turn her scales to diamond. She told herself she could learn how to turn the diamond off but was there a point in doing that? It certainly didn't seem worth two hours of every day for the next three months.

Although it appeared their instructor was perfectly content with not letting the dragons practice their unique powers.

"Did I hear a message saying that this class would be late?" the professor demanded so loudly that she could hear him as she hurried to class. "Because when I said one o'clock, that is what I meant."

The Practical Dragon Powers instructor was a silver dragon named Kor Silverspine, although everyone called him the Silver Bullet and not only behind his back. He sat in the middle of one of the training fields, his silver body marred with tons of little scars. Kylara knew that dragons didn't scar easily—which made her mom's burned hand all the more remarkable—and it meant that he had seen some intense combat.

"Sorry I'm late, professor," she said and landed land in front of him.

Before she could move, a silver spine punctured her claw and pinned her to the ground.

"Were you sleeping in my class?" Silverspine roared.

"What? No. I mean, no, sir!" she responded and ripped the spine out of her hand with her dragon teeth. The name "Silver Bullet" came from his power to create and throw barrages of silver darts from his body—a power the new headmaster didn't seem to have any problem with him using on the students.

"Because I thought I made it very clear that I am not to be called professor, instructor, mommy, or any of that other nonsense. Call me Silver Bullet until the time you stop getting hit by them."

She nodded and listened to a few variations on the speech as a few more dragons arrived, each greeted with the same barb in the foot. Kor made no effort to be charming.

"Today, we'll focus on your human forms," the Silver Bullet snapped. "A well-honed body is one of the keys to getting magic to flow more easily through it, so we'll start with honing. One hour of the exercises we did yesterday. Human form!"

"But the human form is weak." It was Karl Midnight. Kylara hadn't seen him arrive so he must have been early to avoid getting a boo-boo.

"Then make it stronger, Midnight!" The instructor brooked no argument.

An hour of extreme physical exercise followed until the whole class was exhausted. Kor knew how to push dragons past their usual limits of strength and speed, so it was a sweaty and tired Kylara who listened to the instructions for the next exercise.

"Two of you worms will fly to the top of each of these pedestals," their instructor shouted as his mage assistants stacked two twenty-foot-tall pedestals using chunks of marble. "Everyone else will sit outside the square and watch what our first two combatants do so they don't make the same stupid mistakes. The only rule is to stay on the pedestal. If you fall or fly off, you lose. Questions?"

Samuel raised his hand.

"Great, we have our first volunteer." Kor beamed like a coyote that had caught a jackrabbit. "Anyone else?"

No one fell for the trick this time, so he flicked a silver spine that stuck into the ground in front of a red dragon Kylara thought was named Larissa.

She didn't look eager to have been selected but she winged up to the pedestal and landed atop it.

"Now, have at it!" the Silver Bullet yelled.

Samuel, with a smirk so wide only a dragon's mouth could have managed, whipped his long, serpentine dragon tail out.

Unfortunately, it couldn't bridge the distance.

"Will you try to take a bite out of her next, you worm?" The Silver Bullet laughed. "It's a powers class, you dolt. Use them!"

Karl led the rest of the students in laughing at Samuel's expense.

Larissa whipped her tail around her front claws and the top of the pedestal. Anchored in place, she took a deep breath and launched a blast of fire at her opponent. Her aim was true, and there was no way he could dodge while staying on the platform, so he tucked his head inside a wing and weathered the attack.

Kylara—not for the first time—wished she had made a friend in this class so she could ask if Larissa could do more than blast fire. As it was, it seemed the girl was indeed skilled in combustible breath. She unleashed a wave of flame, a ball of it, and a series of tiny spheres that burst against Samuel's skin and looked particularly painful.

He deflected it all from his post, and the next time she paused to fill her lungs, he returned fire with an attack of his own.

It wasn't fire that came from Samuel's mouth, but light. The beam was so bright it made him hard to look at. Kylara closed her eyes and turned away, only to discover that afterimages were burned into her eyelids.

Despite its potency, it didn't knock Larissa from her pillar. She continued her attack but mostly blinded, and it was easy to tell by the sound that she could no longer aim. The rest of her fire strikes went wide.

Samuel frowned and lashed his tail at her, maybe in an attempt to make her flinch and fall, but she was blinded so she didn't even notice.

In the next moment, he began to groan. A moment later, all the dragons around Kylara moaned in pain as well like all their tails had severed. She decided she could vaguely feel something, but she seemed to suffer far less than everyone else.

Especially Sam who, with a sigh of depression, tumbled from the pillar of stacked stone.

As soon as he landed, the students began to straighten as if whatever cloud had passed over their souls had evaporated into the sky.

The Silver Bullet clapped, even as tears ran down his cheeks. "Well, how about that? The first fight of the year wasn't a complete and total embarrassment for all parties. Larissa, you're more than welcome to call me Kor after a display of aural powers like that."

"I don't understand," Kylara said and he turned on her like she was a dog who had learned to speak.

"Was Samuel able to defeat Larissa using only his physical powers?"

"No, sir," she replied.

"Were Larissa's mental powers weaker or did they give her the win?"

"They gave her the win, sir."

The Silver Bullet turned to face the rest of the class. "Remember, you need to be aware of both physical and mental powers. Both can impact a fight. Many a battle can be won before the combat even starts. Larissa, we'll work on focusing your aura power so you don't have to make your comrades in arms depressed every time you need to get out of a tight situation, that clear?"

"Yes, sir, er...Kor." She didn't exactly sound elated to be on a first-name basis with the dragon turned drill sergeant.

"Very good. Next!" The Silver Bullet scanned the crowd. His gaze found Kylara. "It looks like your brain or your scales were too dense to get affected, Diamantine. Get up there!" he ordered and she begrudgingly obeyed. "Who else?" he demanded.

From her position atop the pedestal, she was able to see Karl Midnight shove another dragon forward, although it seemed like the Silver Bullet didn't notice his action. He took the step forward as volunteering and yelled at the blue dragon to get on the damn pedestal.

She tried to keep her balance as she awaited her first battle nervously.

# CHAPTER SEVENTEEN

Kylara tried to stabilize herself on the pedestal. It was barely large enough for all four of her dragon feet, so she planted them and wound her tail around her legs. She felt like a cat perched on top of a stool, not exactly a terrifying draconic specter of destruction.

The blue dragon pumped his wings, elevated, and circled before he came in to land. While he did so, she tried to decide what kind of powers he might have based on the color of his scales.

They were dark-blue but mottled like brush strokes or clouds heavy with rain. Maybe he had ice powers? Or could breathe water? She knew there were many different dragon powers and that scales didn't necessarily correlate with what they were. Or maybe they did but it wasn't always obvious at first glance what the scales indicated. That meant she needed to be ready for almost anything.

Of course, there wasn't much she could do to get ready. Her scales were always edged with diamonds. There was nothing she could do to augment her already extremely tough and durable armor. She wished she knew something that could do damage over distance besides fire-breathing, but she assumed that if this combat came down to two dragons blasting flames at each other, her scales would give her the edge.

She glanced at Kor for some kind of clue. He had given her power away when he'd ordered her up there so her opponent already knew she had unusually hard scales. Would their instructor give her the same advantage by revealing what the blue dragon could do?

It certainly did not appear that he intended to do any such thing. She wouldn't ask, either. She was too sure of her skills to do that, but he volunteered no information. The Silver Bullet stood in his human form, his arms folded and a scowl on his face that only barely revealed his eagerness to see the coming combat.

Kylara knew that she could "turtle up" as her mom had called it. She could roll up, present only her back to her opponent, and make herself almost invulnerable. While she didn't know how that would help her win, maybe it would encourage the other dragon to give up from boredom.

Her adversary finished his circuit around the area and landed on the pedestal across from her.

They stared at one another, waiting for the other to make the first move.

"Burn her, Tempest!" Karl Midnight shouted.

The blue dragon acted immediately and launched fire at her. She'd had extensive practice with her fire breath and unleashed an equal and opposite force to stop the assault. Her opponent stopped his attack, crouched low on his pedestal, and shot a fireball at her.

She batted it away with her tail and it streaked into the sky where it ran out of power and turned into harmless smoke. Tempest released another fireball followed quickly by another. Kylara blocked the first, then curled like a turtle to block the second.

"Hey, no fair!" her adversary complained.

"Her power is her diamond scales," Kor shouted. "She's using them. What are you doing?"

He snarled, inhaled a great breath of air, and blasted a huge spout of flame that completely enveloped her in flames. When he was finished and out of breath, she poked her head out from her tightly wrapped diamond scaled defense.

"I'm not a marshmallow. You can't expect to burn my outside and melt my inside."

Tempest roared and when he did, it began to drizzle. Kylara looked into the sky from beneath her diamond-encrusted wings and tail. It was odd that it was raining, given that there were no clouds in the sky. Was this Tempest's power? Drizzle? It seemed like someone had a less offense-oriented ability than her scales. This would be a battle for the ages in that it would last for ages.

But there was more to Tempest than merely a little rain. He sat on his pedestal, flapped his wings, and breathed deeply. He was summoning magic. She could feel it building inside him. More and more of his inner energy burned and crackled within like a cloud growing over the ocean. Finally, when his magic seemed at its peak, he flicked his tail high above his head. Lightning streaked from the sky, struck his tail, and moved through his body and out his mouth.

Kylara had enough time to see all this before she ducked her head inside her diamond-powered turtle defense.

She expected the lightning to maybe tingle or perhaps make her wings feel like they fell asleep, so it came as quite a shock when instead, it hurt.

The reality was a powerful lesson. She had thought that she was safe against almost all dragon attacks. Her mom had made it sound like her dragon scales had gotten her out of most situations—except when her hand had been burned, of course. But now, within a minute of entering her first battle, she had discovered that other dragons could hurt her.

Tempest roared and another bolt of lightning sizzled, struck his tail, and seared through him and into Kylara.

This one hurt even more, and she yelped in pain when it struck.

This emboldened her adversary, who began to build his magic as he had before but faster now as if he sensed his opponent's defeat.

She unraveled from her turtle defense and blasted a great plume of fire at him. A gust of wind surged at the wrong moment for her and took away the brunt of her attack. His wings—slick with rain—were enough to nullify any damage the fire might have done to him.

He didn't wait for her to try anything else and flicked his tail three times. Three more bolts of lightning careened from the sky to strike his tail. Although each of them struck him a split-second apart, they combined into one fearsome assault inside him. A bolt of lightning unlike any she had ever seen pounded into her chest.

Kylara screamed in pain as she dug her diamond-tipped claws into the pedestal. She would not lose! Not against one of Midnight's cronies and not at her first chance to prove to this school that she wasn't merely some sob story from the desert.

Tempest roared—the blast had probably been designed to be a finishing blow—and called for more lightning. This time, it struck one of his horns and he redirected it through a claw and out into her chest. She held on tightly as a corner of the pedestal started to crumble beneath her.

Kor stepped forward and waved his arms. It looked like he was trying to call the end of the duel, but no one could hear him. The cracks of thunder from the lightning strike still echoed in the canyon. Kylara couldn't hear anything except the sounds of her opponent's fury.

The blue dragon roared so loudly that the rain was blasted away and evaporated almost instantly.

For a moment, she dared to think his energy was spent, but

then she saw that the raindrops hadn't disappeared and instead, condensed into clouds that now swirled in the sky above him. A great gust of wind rushed in from all directions at once. It began to swirl around the two combatants and the mass above them grew darker and heavier as the bottom of the cloud was drawn into the swirling winds.

It wasn't only lightning that Tempest could control, then, but the weather itself.

Kylara dug her claws deeper to anchor herself in place as the wind grew in strength and speed, but her adversary had other plans and blasted her continuously with lightning.

The dragons below were silent, their eyes wide and mouths agape as this school-sanctioned duel grew into something far worse. The only person not frozen in place was Kor, who yelled and gestured wildly with his arms, but he could not be heard over the wind or the echoes of thunder.

She knew she was about to lose. The harsh truth was that she was on the proverbial ropes and merely did everything she could to hold on and prolong this duel a little longer. Despite this awareness, however, she didn't feel helpless. She had an odd awareness of magic within her—so much that could almost touch it. The air was thick and potent with it.

If she could only take hold of it, maybe she could direct it. All she could think about was that she wanted to make the other dragon stop. She didn't care how and would do anything to make it happen, but it had to end. She had to win. There simply was no other option.

Kylara took a deep breath and suddenly, the magic inside her communed with her and listened to her commands.

Tempest seemed to sense something was wrong too. Rather than focus on his burgeoning tornado, he roared at the sky. The cloud above them, now so gray it was almost black, cracked and rumbled as lightning slashed within it and gained speed and strength before it made its final plunge to the dragon who had called it forth.

*Make him stop,* she demanded of the magic and somehow, it listened. It was as if she had tried to take hold of water and had suddenly found a vein of ice. Something surged within her and the magic was hers. It cracked from the sky and struck Tempest, but rather than redirecting the energy, he took the full force of the blast of electricity.

The pedestal beneath him exploded and hurled shards in every direction as his perch crumbled to nothing beneath his feet. Although he no longer seemed to be concerned about his pedestal. He flailed helplessly while electricity crackled and surged across his body from the lightning strike.

After another crack of thunder, Kylara felt her pedestal start to fall. She dug in with her diamond-tipped claws and refused to relinquish her position until Kor called the duel.

She landed heavily, still clinging to the pedestal, and when her head struck a chunk of marble from the other pillar with her already hanging on by only a thread, she passed out.

# CHAPTER EIGHTEEN

The first thing Kylara sensed when she returned to consciousness was the pedestal still clutched in her claws. The marble was cool beneath them, a comforting, reaffirming weight that told her she had done it. *You won.*

She opened her eyes and saw that although she was still on the dueling platform, it was no longer on the top of a pillar of marble pieces. Instead of being stacked neatly, the chunks of stone were now laid out in a line that led from where the duel had taken place to the platform she still clung to.

"Hold still, all right?" She twisted her head and saw Samuel standing behind her. His claws radiated golden light as he held them gently against her body. A warm energy radiated from them and it felt wonderful.

"How long was I out?" she demanded and looked around for the rest of the dragons. It seemed odd to feel the mixture of pain from the lightning strikes and pleasure from whatever the hell Samuel was doing while a group of other dragons stood nearby. She located them across the field, mostly in human form and clustered around the shape of the blue dragon who was still unconscious despite the verbal barrage from Kor.

"When I said 'hold still,' I guess what I meant was don't move or I might gore you with one of my claws," Samuel said and ignored her question. "I need another minute or so."

"What are you doing?" she asked but bit the words off. *Not that I'm complaining.*

"My light powers can heal," he explained. "I can pour light magic into another dragon and it essentially enhances their internal healing abilities. I simply need to finish...I don't know... fully charging you?"

Kylara let him complete his intervention. He moved his claws to each of the places where she had been struck by lightning. Her scales were unharmed but the flesh directly beneath them was red and blistered—or at least it was until he put his claws near it. Then, it mended itself without draining her quite so much.

"Thanks, Sam," she said when he had finished.

"You're welcome. Or I guess I should say we're even."

"Even?"

"You rescued me when I was trapped under those rocks. My wings were draining all my healing abilities even though they were in a position that would never have let them fully heal. If you hadn't dug me out, I would have starved to death trying to heal. The least I could do was return the favor."

"Well, even if you only did it to get even, thanks all the same." She smiled at him and he returned it nervously.

"It's cool. Honestly, Tempest is an asshole and I'm impressed that you beat him. I wouldn't want you to succumb to your wounds and cast doubt on your victory." His roguish grin appeared again. She couldn't help but like it.

"Wait, I won? What happened?"

Sam looked quizzically at her. "Frankly, I hoped you could tell me what happened. Do you have storm powers?"

Kylara shook her head. "Of course not. I would have used them if I did."

"That's the thing, though. It looked like you did use them. The bolt of lightning that struck Tempest and his pedestal was different than those he was redirecting. It was bigger and more like actual lightning than the bolts he threw."

"Maybe that's all it was," she ventured.

"Yeah. Maybe a bolt of lightning came out of a dragon-made storm in the middle of a duel to topple the dragon who had created the storm."

She laughed awkwardly to try to lighten the mood. Samuel didn't fall for it. "Are you sure you're not hiding anything? That blast knocked Tempest out cold."

"Is he all right?" she asked, suddenly horrified that she might have hurt a dragon without meaning to. Her heart sank and she finally scrambled off the pedestal and walked to where her opponent was still sprawled on the ground. She had to admit, despite being struck by lightning more times than she could count, she felt remarkably good. The golden dragon's healing powers were a resounding plus.

"He'll be fine," Sam said. "The mages are already working on him, and those who help in Practical Dragon Powers are always the best healers on campus. Well, the best besides me, that is."

Still, Kylara couldn't help but move closer to see what had happened to Tempest.

The dragons parted as she and Samuel approached, and she saw that the lightning had struck her opponent on the crown of his head. His entire head was blackened like a cartoon character who had looked up the tailpipe of an old automobile. One of his horns was cracked as well.

"Ah, our victor finally joins us!" Kor boomed when he saw her. "That was an excellent use of defense, although you should have listened to me when I called the duel as a draw."

"Thank you, Steel Bullet."

"You can call me Kor, kid. It was brave of you to come out of that diamond defense of yours. You probably wouldn't have gotten the storm dragon so worked up if you hadn't goaded him into overpowering himself."

"I…didn't overpower…myself," Tempest wheezed with one eye half-open. No other part of him had moved.

"You sure as hell did, you damn fool," the Steel Bullet raged at him. "I told you to stop the duel and take a draw, and what did you do? You pulled in the biggest damn storm the region's seen in ten years. The main reason we have a school out here and not in New York goddammed City is to maintain some discretion. Do you think human weathermen will miss that?" He pointed at the massive thunderhead that continued to drizzle on them.

"And then," he continued, not even slightly out of breath, "you get so hurt that our mages can't even tend to the clouds. Fool of a dragon if there ever was one."

"But I didn't get overwhelmed. I swear it—" Tempest coughed, but the mages hushed him and Kor had already turned his back to the loser of the duel.

"Since both pedestals were knocked down and our mages have to play doctor to the loser's boo-boos, you can all have the rest of the class off," the instructor stated.

A ragged cheer went up. Even to Kylara, who had only been in school for a week, there was something special about free time when one was supposed to be in class.

"Make sure you rest and eat well." the Silver Bullet grinned to reveal human teeth that were all completely silver. "Because tomorrow will be much harder than this cute little warm-up we had today."

Where before, the group had only managed a ragged little cheer, they showed true comradery now as they all groaned as one single, disgruntled class.

# CHAPTER NINETEEN

The next few weeks blended together. It was pleasant, most of the time. Kylara enjoyed her classes, even the boring ones, if only for the social connections. There was something delicious about gossiping, studying together for a test, or complaining about the cafeteria food, even though the last one was something she could never bring herself to do. Most of the dragons agreed that it was sub-par compared to what they were accustomed to but from her point of view, the meals were excellent.

She received one report from the Steel Dragon during those first few weeks, telling her that the fire on her property did indeed appear to be magically controlled because it had burned in a different direction than the predominant winds. That, of course, pissed the hell out of her because she already knew that the flames were controlled magically, thanks to the fricking face at their center.

The report made her anxious about her mother, although she had honestly never stopped worrying about her. The fire monster—as she thought of it—was huge and powerful. She knew that and could accept it, but could it have killed Hester? The answer that remained constantly in her heart was *Absolutely not.* Although that might have simply been because the Steel Dragon's team had yet to find her body. The young dragon knew her mother was tough but not invulnerable. Surely, if she was defeated, some of her diamond scales would be there to tell the story.

Which made Kylara want to go out and search, but she had learned nothing that would help her in this regard. Her aura powers remained stubbornly locked away, and no teacher gave any indication about how one could track a magic fire monster.

She tried to push the thoughts of her mother—and the associated guilt—from her mind as she donned another of Tanya's dresses.

Despite all the changes and frustrations in her life, she was extremely appreciative of the girl's friendship. Tanya was positive, never let the conversation fall into awkward silence, and was surprisingly empathetic given that she had grown up as part of a wealthy family in LA.

By dragon standards, her millionaire parents weren't much, however, since they didn't have unusual powers or a long, pedigreed history, so she understood what her roommate was going through as an outsider. Kylara knew she should be more thankful for the clothes as well but it was a little difficult when she had to waste time every day learning how to put a new dress on and have her friend fuss over her hair and jewelry.

It was thus a pleasant surprise when Ruby came knocking while Tanya was out.

"Ky, it's Ruby. Do you have an hour?"

She answered the door with a raised eyebrow. "I'm only studying, but yeah. Did you mean a minute?"

"I did not." The girl beamed. "I noticed you've borrowed clothes from Tanya but that doesn't mean I forgot about you. I finally got approval for a discretionary budget for you due to your financial hardship."

"I'm sorry, Ruby, English please?"

The girl's eyes sparkled. "We're going shopping!"

---

The flight to Tucson, Arizona, was pleasant, even though Kylara didn't strictly understand why they needed to cross state lines for clothes and decent shampoo.

"Because where we are in New Mexico doesn't have decent shampoo." Ruby laughed at her joke. "But seriously, we're so far in the middle of nowhere that it's practically the same amount of time to go to Tucson and it's a nicer flight."

She could at least agree with that. The landscape below was beautiful. Sage was in bloom and the smell mixed with the aroma of the pinon pine was intoxicating.

They arrived at the Tucson Mall, but rather than entering through the many banks of sliding doors, her guide took her to the top of the building.

A pang of nervousness knifed through her. This was not how the movies with malls she'd watched with her mom went—at least, not the ones that didn't involve flesh-eating zombies.

"Are we sneaking in or something?" she asked once they had both landed and taken their human shapes.

"What? Certainly not! Look down, for goodness sake."

Kylara didn't understand. They stood on the roof of the mall and below their feet was some kind of red-and-white painted image that looked very much like a "keep away" warning.

Ruby studied her and when she didn't get it, the girl laughed. "It's a dragon landing pad. In other words, the VIP entrance."

"VIP?" she asked as two men and three women emerged from a door on the roof. The men carried a canopy and brought it out to shield the dragons from the sun while the women held snacks, drinks, and a notebook.

"Welcome to the Tucson Mall," one of the women said like the two dragons were queens who had arrived at the greatest place on earth.

"Pretzel?"

"Coffee?"

"Foot massage?"

"Whole-body massage?"

"Yes, yes, God yes, but maybe later," Ruby shouted as the attendants put food and drinks in her hands.

"What brings you to our humble establishment today?" the women with the notebook asked. Her nametag simply said, *Sin.*

"My dear dragon friend needs new everything," the girl proclaimed. "New clothes, new shoes, new hair, new everything."

"That truly won't be necessary," Kylara mumbled. "I only need a few supplies."

"But of course, Lady…"

"Firedrake," Ruby responded.

Sin looked from one young woman to the other, not sure who was Firedrake, but Ruby darted Kylara a look that said to leave it at that.

"Lady Firedrake, simply tell us what type of provisions you desire and we will make it so. Nothing unnecessary."

"Okay, that sounds…fine, I guess," Kylara said.

"Right. Nothing unnecessary." Her companion's expression dripped with mischievousness.

"Now, style-wise," Sin said cheerfully. "Are we interested in updating the formal look or in something more casual?"

Sensing an opportunity to claw things back before they got out of control, she answered before Ruby could. "I had hoped for more casual clothes. Like…uh, jeans and athletic shoes and shirts, that kind of thing."

"Athletic shoes?" Her companion raised an eyebrow.

Kylara looked at her worn boots. "Yeah."

What followed was a whirlwind as overwhelming as the tornado that had almost hurled her off the battle pedestal a week before. They went to so many stores that she lost count. She had always thought shopping meant going places, finding things, trying them on, and deciding if they were worth the price.

With Sin, it was a much more streamlined process. The young dragon would look at something and if she seemed to even vaguely like it, the woman would snap and one of the other attendants would scramble to get one in her size. While Kylara hadn't given them any of her measurements, everything she tried on always fit perfectly. If she didn't like it, Sin would insult the garment and they would move on. If she gave any indication that she liked something she tried on, Ruby would send it to the counter and she would never see it again.

After five or six or seven stores, she began to worry about where all the stuff was going and what it would cost.

"You don't need to worry about that," her companion explained as she sipped her third virgin pina colada. "We haven't even come close to the ceiling of your budget. The Steel Dragon told the headmaster to provide for you, and she made sure to do exactly that."

"Yeah, but we don't need to be waited on like this."

"Do you want to deny Sin her job?" Ruby waggled her eyebrows.

Kylara slumped. "No, I guess not."

"Then onward. I bet you're right about having enough clothes and shoes now, so let's do your hair, your nails, and call it a day. Fair?"

"Fair."

It was a different young dragon who climbed to the top of the roof. Instead of a dress, she wore perfectly fitted jeans and lace-up sneakers. Her top was a t-shirt with a stylized dragon on the front that had been cut on the sides and tied back together. She thought it was somewhat silly—and not exactly durable—but Ruby insisted that it looked great on her and Sin constantly repeated, "Gorgeous, darling. Gorgeous."

Her hair wasn't much shorter, but her split ends were gone and the very bottom of her scalp was buzzed, so when she put her hair up into a ponytail, it revealed a design at the base of her neck. The hairdresser had also cut her bangs slightly, so when she put her hair up, strands now framed her face. She thought perhaps it got in the way, but she had to admit it suited her face.

On top of that, she had turquoise nails to match her necklace, freshly scrubbed and pampered feet—the woman doing the pedicure had never seen such calluses on such a young woman—and a few paperbacks that Ruby had seen her eyeing and bought without telling her.

"Admit it. You had fun."

Kylara snorted. "Yeah, I guess I did. I've never done anything like that before. But…uh, how do we get it all home?"

"It's already taken care of, Lady Firedrake," Sin said and gestured to two large, wrapped packages on the dragon landing pad.

"Thank you very much." Ruby bowed to their assistant. "And please tip yourselves ten percent above your usual fee."

"You honor us, my lady." The woman bowed and her assistants mirrored her.

The two dudes hooted and high-fived.

"Are you ready, Kylara?"

"Ready, Lady Firedrake."

They transformed into their dragon forms, snatched the parcels—Kylara only realized belatedly that both were for her—and returned to school.

After an uneventful journey, they arrived at the dorm and dragged the packages inside. They could both lift the loads easily with their dragon strength but they were still bulky, so the young dragon wasn't able to see into her room as she pushed her new clothes, shoes, and everything else inside.

"Are you good, Ky?"

"Oh, my goodness, yes, Ruby. Thank you! I can't wait to show Tanya."

"Awesome! If you need anything else, I'm down the hall."

"Of course. Thanks again, Ruby," she said and moved past her purchases and into her room. "Tanya? Tanya, you'll never believe this! Or...well, you will, but I went on a shopping spree. Tanya?"

Her roommate wasn't there, however. She wasn't in her bed or at her desk.

Desperate to share her new wardrobe with the person who had been more than willing to share hers, she went in search of her friend. She checked the cafeteria first, but she wasn't there. It wasn't a huge surprise, but when she also failed to find her in the library or gym, she began to get a little concerned.

Tanya didn't have any friends besides her. Even though she had been raised with dragons, she now attended a school for specials, which she was not. This made her more of an outcast than Kylara with her diamond scales, even though the girl understood dragon society and its rules far better than she did. In other words, she knew her friend wasn't off with another group of friends. So where was she?

Once outside, she vaulted skyward and took her dragon form, thinking that maybe Tanya was at one of the training fields. She flew over the woods between the classrooms and the fields. From that elevation, she could see that the fields were empty—no dragons and no Tanya.

She was on her way back when she noticed something she hadn't seen before. An area under a cottonwood tree was unusually dark as if the tree was absorbing the light or something. Kylara—already concerned about Tanya—couldn't help but investigate.

When she flew lower, she saw none other than Karl Midnight standing in the darkness. Little strands of shadow radiated from his dragon claws. It was those strands that created the pool of darkness.

Only it wasn't a pool, she realized with horror.

It was Tanya.

She was restrained by his shadow webs, and two other dragons—Tempest and a greenish one Kylara didn't know—laughed as they bound their captive with ropes to prevent her moving at all.

Furious, she dove toward the troublemakers.

# CHAPTER TWENTY

Kylara rocketed toward the three dragons who attacked her friend. She spun before landing and swatted Karl on the back of his head with her tail. He was in dragon form like her but focused on his dark threads instead of the diamond dragon and he sprawled from her attack.

The webs of blackness that had seeped from his claws evaporated the moment she pounded into him, but Tanya was still restrained by the ropes his two cronies had used in their human forms.

Karl rolled to his feet and placed himself between Kylara and Tanya. "Well, what do we have here? It looks like Diamantine got a little overzealous in wanting to drive this worthless lizard of a dragon out."

The other two bullies chuckled. She glared at them both and made it plain that if they transformed into their dragon bodies, she'd aim for them too.

"I aimed for you, moron."

"Moron?" he snapped and launched a tendril of blackness that coiled on the earth and snapped to her dragon wrist to bind her claw to the ground. "Then what does that make you? It must take a real idiot to be roped by a moron."

Kylara pulled at the tendril of darkness and discovered that it was stronger than she had expected. "You do realize that you called yourself a moron, right?"

"You're the one who doesn't know how to choose friends. I would think a pretty-faced nobody like yourself would jump at the opportunity to use this school to make real connections but instead, you hang around with Tanya no-name."

"It's better than having to talk to a weak-minded bigot like yourself. What do you two even see in him?" she asked Tempest and the girl who could turn into a green dragon. "Do your parents make you be nice to him or something?"

A shared look between the two of cronies told her that yes, there was more to this relationship than a shared interest in being shitheads.

"Dragons have always pranked each other here," Tempest said.

"Yeah," the green dragon agreed. "We didn't do anything to her that we wouldn't do in class."

Tanya tried to complain but the ropes they'd tied across her body kept her mouth shut.

"And using ropes to stake a dragon? That's a technique Kor approves of?"

"A real dragon would never have let herself get staked down." Karl sneered at the captive. "No dragon has been tied like this since the second Mage Rebellion. And the dragons who were caught were slaughtered."

"Are you threatening her life?" Kylara demanded as she tried and failed to pull free of the dark magic.

The cronies shared a concerned look. Not that they were concerned for Tanya. It might have simply been a shared look of, "Oh, I hadn't realized that we might get in trouble for this."

Karl laughed. "Why would I want to deal with the Steel Dragon's stupid little Steel Guard over this worthless reptile? We merely wanted Tanya to realize what her real place in the world is—which is not here, right, Esme?"

"My sister should be here instead of her," Esme said, although her words lacked the fury his possessed.

"Exactly," he agreed. "She should never have been admitted here at all. We're simply helping her find her way out."

"You'll stop all this crap right now," she growled. "Tanya leaves over my dead body."

"As you wish!" He flexed and nine more tendrils of dark rope erupted from his claws. They streaked across the space between them, hugged the earth, and threaded in and out of it like vines. She tried to leap into the air but her claw was still stuck to the ground. Thinking quickly, she flapped her wings and hovered awkwardly in place, but it was enough to ensure that most of the dark ropes missed.

But not all, unfortunately.

Three of the ten caught her hand that was still anchored to the ground and wound up her forearm. Once the tip of one of them reached her body, it divided into five more threads that spread out and around her wings. She tried to flap to break free, but when she brought her wings close to her body, the tendrils simply constricted, crushed the appendages against her, and forced her to fall.

As soon as her other limbs touched the dirt, Karl took hold of them. More threads of darkness entangled her, tightened, and pinned her limbs to the earth.

Kylara took a breath and blasted the magic with flames, but it didn't accomplish much. Two of the cords of darkness burned away but she knew from their class together that he didn't rely on any single thread. As long as he had one connection to his target, he could reinforce it and use it to make dozens more tendrils. Even though she burned away some of his leaders, she did nothing to end his attack.

"I would think you'd know from class that I know how to defend myself against fire," Midnight sneered.

"Then you should also know that there's nothing you can do to my diamond scales."

"You're right about that." He nodded. "Although of course, Tempest found a weakness, didn't he?"

"I don't know, Karl," his crony whined.

She would never know if he was genuinely uncomfortable or if that was merely a feint because as he spoke, Esme raked her side with claws enhanced with some kind of energy.

Kylara shouted and tried to pull away from the pain but couldn't, not with Midnight binding her. But he hadn't bound everything. She whipped her tail at Esme's dragon form, caught her across the chest, and left a long gash where her diamond spines connected with the green dragon.

"I thought you had her restrained!" the girl whined.

"I do now," Karl said, and more of the threads of darkness darted from the web to entangle Kylara and tie her tail to the ground.

She looked at the dark-scaled dragon. Even though he hadn't moved, she could still tell that he was under considerable strain. It demanded all his strength and concentration to keep her pinned, but he accomplished it despite that.

"Let me go and—"

"You'll what?" He fumed and flexed and the threads of blackness across her back tightened. She felt a knee buckle and she was dragged closer to the ground.

"For a dragon with powers, you sure do act like one without," Karl hissed. "First, the empty threats and now what? A pathetic attempt at a bribe? Honestly, this ought to be good. I heard about what happened to your little farm. What could you possibly offer me?"

Kylara ground her teeth, tried to come up with a retort, and failed. Midnight continued to tighten his hold on her and forced her earthward, inch by inch. Soon, she would be completely immobile. "I'd say self-respect but you're right, that would be impossible."

He roared and suddenly, all the threads across her back went taut and dragged her into the ground.

"Oh, wait a minute," he said as if he'd remembered that he was not a douchebag. "That stupid fucking necklace you always wear. You could give me that in exchange for no one having to see Tanya tied up like a suckling pig."

From the grunts that issued from her friend, it was quite obvious what she thought of all this—an emphatic, "Don't give this creep what he wants." But Kylara wasn't exactly paying attention to her friend. The pendent was special to her, the only thing she had of a long-gone father and now the only thing she had of her mother, but it was merely a possession. She would have traded it for Tanya's safety in an instant if another solution didn't seem to present itself.

As the threads pulled more tightly and she became more immobile, her fury grew. She was helpless and pissed because this was all her fault. Midnight was right. She knew exactly what he was capable of and should never have landed at all. The only reason she was stuck to the ground and bound by his stupid tendrils was because she had messed up. She knew for a fact her mom would be disappointed.

But as she struggled to move, she sensed something inside her that remained unbound. It felt like what the Silver Bullet called her inner magic. Now, it bubbled with rage, frothed with fear, and swirled within her in search of an escape.

Kylara simply let it do as it wanted.

She didn't know what to expect so wasn't surprised when Karl held his claws up to shield his face. Nor was she surprised when she saw all his shadow ropes puff into nothingness. That was, after all, precisely what she wanted.

Tempest and Esme shielded their eyes as if she had called

down the sun or something. After a moment, she realized what was happening. She was glowing.

Now that she realized what was going on, it seemed obvious and utterly bizarre. She knew for a fact that her mom didn't have glowing powers and neither did she. Yet Karl and his cronies lurched away and tried to protect their eyes, blinded by the light that poured from her diamond scales.

"We know you're around here, Samuel!" Tempest shouted.

"And we won't forget this!" Karl roared before he bounded away and tried to take flight. His two cronies misjudged his escape attempt as a rescue for them and caught hold of his tail. With their dragon strength and blindness, they grounded him and the three collided with one another and landed in a messy pile of humans and dragons all rubbing their eyes.

Kylara wasted no time. She sliced through the ropes that bound Tanya with her diamond claws and burned them away.

"Ky! My hero!" the girl shouted and scrambled to her feet from her place of captivity. "I didn't know you had light powers."

"I don't."

"Okay, not to be rude, but you do," her friend said and held her hand up. A shadow danced behind it that could only have appeared if the light source was Kylara herself.

"Can we talk about this later?" she asked.

"Of course, roomie." The girl beamed and followed her into the air to return to the dorm. They left Karl and his followers in the dirt, rubbing their eyes and even more confused than she currently felt.

# CHAPTER TWENTY-ONE

The two young dragons reached their room without incident. If Tanya was at risk of being thrown out because she had been captured in such a historically embarrassing way, they were lucky as no one saw their flight. Even Ruby Firedrake—whose room they snuck past easily given that the older girl sang softly to herself about turning the heat up—remained oblivious.

Once in their room, Tanya closed the door and put her back to it, slid to the floor, and landed on her butt. "Ky! I can't believe you did that for me."

"Stood up to Midnight? No problem."

"Seriously, Ky, I appreciate it. I...I mean, Karl was right. I should never have been trapped like that in the first place. It was very stupid of me."

"No, Tanya. Almost anyone can be overcome when facing three dragons. Those numbers even gave the Steel Dragon some trouble. Plus, they fought dirty. Why did they have those ropes to tether you? That's creepy and unexpected. It's no surprise that they trapped you. They would have done so to anyone."

"You're sweet to say so, Ky, truly, but I should have known when I went over to them. I was so stupid. I could see it was darker under that tree than it should have been, but what did I do? Did I show caution? No, I walked right in! It's exactly like my dad always says." She shook her head and hid her face behind her hands. When she removed them again, there were smudges near her eyes where she had messed her makeup.

"Why did you walk over to them?" Kylara asked. She didn't mean to sound rude but she couldn't help herself. Karl Midnight was such a piece of crap, she couldn't understand why Tanya would have even considered talking to him.

"Because Esme said she could teach me how to make my claws poison." She somehow slumped even lower.

"And you believed her?"

"I know it was stupid." Tanya moaned with humiliation and embarrassment. "But...well, I'm desperate! The mage classes have not helped and everyone knows it. And I thought that if I could learn a power—any power—maybe people would start to treat me better."

"Yeah, but poison claws?" Kylara wrinkled her nose at the thought. "All that can do is cause dragons extra pain. That's not the kind of power I would want."

"Well, that's easy for you to say," her roommate protested. "You have diamond scales and light powers. Why didn't you tell me that? It's incredible!"

"It's no big deal," she said. "I wanted to help you."

"No big deal? *No big deal?* Are you crazy? How could you even keep something like that a secret? If I had that power, I'd use it all the time. Can you make your hands glow like you told me that dreamboat Samuel did so he could heal you or is it only the blinding flash? Both are cool, of course!"

"Okay, for starters, Sam is not a dreamboat."

"Ky, I don't need to be able to read your aura to tell you that you're lying to yourself about him."

"Okay, look, putting Sam aside for a minute, I don't know how I made myself glow."

"It was you, then. Karl said Samuel was hiding but I know what I saw. Can you do it again? Like right now?"

"Can we not do this? I'm tired and I wanted to show you my new clothes."

"The jeans are too casual for me but I won't lie, they make your ass look great." Tanya perked up, successfully distracted. "The shirt is cool. I'm not into t-shirts in general but you pull it off. I love the turquoise fingernails as well, by the way. They look like diamond claws."

"You can borrow whatever you like—"

"You can pull it off since you have that homestead in the desert aesthetic going for you, but I'd never be caught dead in pants." The girl shook her head fervently. "Okay. We talked about your clothes. Now back to your magic freaking powers."

Kylara sighed. For a moment, she had thought that she had diverted the girl from the uncomfortable subject of exactly what the hell was happening to her but it seemed to have been wishful thinking. At least they weren't talking about Samuel anymore. "I don't know how I did it. I simply did."

"Well, can you do it again?"

"Why? Will you go talk to Midnight and his minions?"

"No, Ky, I mean can you do it right here in our room?"

"Oh, uh..." She couldn't think of a reason to not try, so she stuck her hand out like she had seen Samuel do and tried to make it glow.

Nothing happened and she shrugged.

"Did you reach for your inner magic?" her roommate asked and sounded way too much like Professor Sharra, their Magical Theory teacher.

Kylara sighed, closed her eyes, and tried to focus on her inner magic, whatever that meant. She thought back to what had happened when Tanya was in trouble and how she had felt a need inside her to do something to help someone who was in real danger. If she was honest, she had felt something similar when she had been on the pedestal across from Tempest.

But it wasn't reaching for inner magic that had saved her, not exactly. It was more like she had reached for a source of energy—magic, she assumed—that was all around her. Part of that energy went through her, but part of it went through everything. All she had done during those two confrontations was reach out to that river of energy and direct a little more of it through herself.

"Ky! Your hand is glowing!"

She opened her eyes and saw that her fingertips radiated light. She gasped and this, of course, made the light extinguish itself. "Whoops."

"Don't whoops me, Ky! Do it again."

Kylara took another deep breath and focused on channeling the energy to her fingertips again. Now that she had even a vague clue about what she was doing, it was easier. It was rather like turning into a dragon or blowing fire. She simply had to latch onto the already existing stream of energy long enough to let it pass through her. Or…no, maybe it was more like she had to jump in and go with the current, but that wasn't right either. It was like—

"You're doing it."

Once again, her fingers glowed unmistakably. This time, rather than a shocked reaction that shut the energy off, she continued to breathe evenly and let her "inner magic" flow with the "outer magic" she sensed all around her. Already, she could see those words were merely placeholders for the mind to grapple with while the soul or whatever you called the essence inside that didn't think so much as act took control.

As she breathed in and out, she was able to make her fingers glow brighter. The light worked from her fingertips and down her digits to her palm, where it brightened.

"Kylara, this is amazing!" At some point, Tanya had scrambled to her feet and now danced around the room in her excitement.

"You're using light powers exactly like the Steel Dragon. And you're my roommate! You can show me how to do it and I won't be expelled for being a failure to all of a dragon kind."

"I guess so...yeah," Kylara was dumbfounded. Where had this come from? She knew she hadn't been able to do it before because she had tried. The last few years had been spent all but worshipping Kristen Hall and her team of dragons. She knew about Lumos and his light abilities and had tried to activate those same powers during many a late night, to no avail. So what had changed?

"What else can you do, Kylara? Have you been holding out on me? Can you turn your skin to diamond in your human form? Because if you can, you should stop hiding it from me."

"No, I don't think so," she said, "But...well, I had a duel with Tempest."

"Oh, I heard about that." Her friend grinned. "Your skin was so tough you made him blast himself off his pedestal, right? A classic move, Ky."

"That's what I thought too, but I now wonder if it was me. Lightning is kind of like light, right? Maybe I did send that bolt of lightning from the sky."

The other girl stopped her dancing and began to pace as she rubbed her chin in thought. "Ugh...maybe? Tempest denies that he did it. Even I have heard him say he didn't lose control and I'm not even in that class, but I don't know, Kylara. Light and lightning powers don't go together. There are storm dragons and there are some, like Tempest, who can shoot lightning, but I've never heard of a storm dragon making light. Those are—what does Professor Sharra say?—different kinds of magic powers."

"But Professor Sharra was talking about mage powers, not dragon abilities. Maybe lightning and light are related for dragons."

Tanya's expression was enough to tell her that no, light and lightning were not related so it was pointless to insist.

Kylara swallowed awkwardly. "Do you think I have storm powers too, then?"

"You should use your inner magic to find out." Her roommate practically hopped in place. "If you have diamond skin, light powers, and the ability to control the weather, you can save your mom. You'd be more powerful than the Steel Dragon herself."

"I don't know about that," she said cautiously.

"Well, not now, but with practice, silly. Now try it."

She laughed. "Okay, you're right. If I can control the weather too, that would be freaking sweet, but maybe we should go outside? I don't think our room would look too great after a lightning strike."

"Oh, duh. You're right, of course. Let me grab a parasol and we can go." Tanya chose a pink one with red flower petals on it, but before the two girls could head out to a corner of campus to see what Kylara was capable of, a knock came at the door.

She could tell merely from the firmness of it that it was not Ruby who had come looking for them.

Tanya glanced at her and she shrugged and gestured for her to open it. The other girl did so, took three steps back, and all the color drained from her face while the energy faded from her step.

The headmaster of the school stood in the hallway.

"Well, good afternoon, ladies." Amythist smiled. "If you would please follow me, there's something I would very much like to discuss with the two of you."

The girls looked at each other and both swallowed hard.

"Is there a problem?" the old lady asked.

"No, ma'am," they said in unison and followed the headmaster across campus to her office.

# CHAPTER TWENTY-TWO

Amythist said nothing as she led the two young dragons through the green in the center of the U and into her office. "Would you please take a seat?" she asked as she poured tea for the three of them.

"Do you think it's poison?" Tanya whispered when the old woman turned her back to them to rummage around for honey.

"No way," Kylara whispered in response.

Amythist turned to them, the honey in hand, and settled into her chair. "I must inform you that there are three young dragons in the infirmary right now. They are being treated for blindness and what appears to be a sunburn on their skin. Would either of you like to tell me anything about that?"

Kylara's gaze lowered to the cup of tea in front of her. Suddenly, the idea of it being poison no longer seemed so farfetched. Although, truthfully, she felt like she had already been poisoned. A great big pit had formed in her stomach and filled slowly with dread. "I didn't mean to, ma'am. I don't even know how I did it."

"But you did do it?" Amythist pressed.

She nodded. "Yes. It was me. I was furious about what they

were doing to Tanya, and…well, maybe I overreacted. Does this mean I will be expelled?"

"Well, that all depends," the headmaster said with a wry expression. "What were they doing to Tanya?"

She looked at her roommate, unsure of what to say. Midnight had said the entire point of binding her with ropes was to prove she was unworthy and was no more powerful than a mage or a group of humans. She didn't want to expose her friend if she felt vulnerable.

Fortunately for her, Tanya had no such reservations. "Esme said she would show me how to make my claws venomous—which of course I would love to know since I have no powers—but it was a trap, ma'am. As soon as I got close enough, Karl Midnight used his creepy dark ropy things to bind me. Before I could break free, Tempest and Esme began to tie me to the ground. I would still be there if not for Kylara. If anyone should be punished, it should be me for being so naïve. She merely tried to help."

"Oh, don't be so melodramatic, Tanya." Amythist chuckled behind her cup of tea. "I won't punish you for trying to achieve the goals we have set for you. Although please, be more cautious in the future. Those three aren't…professors. You should know there's little to learn from them."

"Yes, ma'am. Of course, ma'am." The girl looked incredibly relieved.

"Now, as for the dragon who blinded the other three…."

Kylara lowered her head in shame. "I'm so sorry, ma'am. Truly. I didn't mean to take their vision away but…well, I accept whatever punishment you think I deserve."

"Given how their healing powers will have their vision restored soon enough, I don't think we need to send you to the gallows. It might already be back. When I checked on them, they could already see blobs so I don't think there will be any lasting effects. There's no need to worry."

She breathed easier when Amythist told her that. "It's good news ma'am. I didn't mean to hurt them and I'm glad it's not permanent." *Even if they were jerks.* She wisely didn't say that, however.

"However..." The old lady rose from her chair and began to pace behind her cluttered desk. It was a reminder of how powerful—and how short—the headmaster was. "This kind of feuding is not allowed on this campus. It is one tradition that we will keep and honor into the future. The Lumos School will be a safe place for dragons and mages of all levels to learn. If we have students who feel like they can solve these little tiffs with violence, this academy will no longer be the refuge it needs to be."

"But Kylara was only defending me," Tanya protested.

"And the only reason I won't punish you for interrupting your headmaster is that you're defending her," Amythist said sternly and the young dragon reddened.

"What will our punishment be, ma'am?" Kylara asked.

"I won't hand out punishments for defending your friend. Normally, I would make you two serve detention with the three who started this nonsense, but given that you already blinded them for the afternoon, I think they've been punished enough. This will serve as your first and final warning, though. If there are any more incidents like this, there will be consequences. Is that clear?"

"Yes, ma'am," they responded in unison.

"Very good. Tanya, you may go. Kylara, if you would stay a moment longer, that would be appreciated."

Tanya paled. "Ma'am, please, this was my fault. I deserve anything that Kylara does."

"Oh, do calm down, child. I won't eat your roommate, for goodness sake. Now, excuse us or I assure you, I will find a professor with something that needs scrubbing."

The young dragon nodded quickly and left the office, but she continued to glance over her shoulder at her friend until the door shut behind her.

Amythist's gaze came to rest on Kylara and a mischievous grin settled on the old dragon's wrinkled human face. "Well, she does talk a lot, doesn't she?"

She couldn't help but laugh at the juxtaposition. "I like it, ma'am. There are no awkward pauses while I'm with her."

"That's always pleasant, isn't it?" The headmaster settled into her chair, took a sip of her tea, and silence filled with the room.

Kylara didn't know if she was supposed to speak or wait quietly, or what. She tried to do the second while Amythist savored her tea and was about to do the first when the headmaster spoke.

"So, light powers. That is an interesting discovery. Or did you already have those and simply waited for the right time to reveal them like the Steel Dragon did?"

The young dragon hesitated, not sure what to make of being compared to Kristen Hall by someone who knew her. It was both flattering and frightening. "I don't think Karl Midnight is the same level of threat as the Masked One, ma'am. If I had known about having light powers, I certainly wouldn't have wasted my reveal on him."

The old dragon laughed so hard that she had to wipe tears from her eyes. "He is a little twerp, isn't he?"

"Ma'am!"

"Oh, never mind, never mind." Amythist waived her protestations away. "A headmaster isn't supposed to say those kinds of things about students. We mustn't play favorites, you know. So if you ever tell anyone that Karl is one of my least favorites, you will find yourself in detention."

"Yes, ma'am."

"These are the perks of being in charge." The old lady tittered. "Now, as for these new powers of yours... Can you do them now?"

"I can try." Kylara held her hand out as she had done with Tanya. She was nervous—far more so than she had been when hanging out with her best friend in their room—but after a minute or so of concentration, she was able to illuminate her fingertips like she had before.

"Very interesting. Yes, very interesting indeed. And you swear today was the first time you've ever used them?"

She nodded.

"And what of your mother? I know of Hester Diamantine and her diamond scales. Did she have powers beyond those? Did she ever claim to use her scales to 'reflect' the light or something like that?"

"No, ma'am. My mom only ever used her scales for defense or combat. She could breathe fire but she couldn't do anything with light."

"And your father?"

"I...I never met him." She moved her hands instinctively to her turquoise pendant without meaning to do so.

"I understand, my child. My father also remains an enigma, even after all these centuries. Do you have any idea where these powers came from? Did you make a breakthrough in Professor Sharra's class?"

Kylara snorted a laugh. "I wish! I mean...no, ma'am. Sometimes, I feel like something is happening when we go through the motions of the different forms of magic, but I've never made a ball of light there."

"I see. And what of your diamond powers? Have those evolved or changed since you've been here?"

"No, ma'am. I...ugh, this is a great school and everything but the Silver Bullet—that is Professor Kor...I mean—"

"Oh, calm down, I know who you're speaking of, child. There's no reason to get so upset about it. He hasn't helped you to unlock anything of yourself?"

"I don't think so, ma'am, no." She wondered if she should tell

Amythist about the lightning strike. Was it possible that she had, in fact, caused it to happen? She simply didn't know. While she had meant to stop Tempest, did that mean she had caused the strike? She simply didn't see how that was possible.

"Is there anything else you wish to tell me, Kylara?"

She recognized the expression on Amythist's face because she had seen it on her mom when she attempted to peel her daughter's aura away to find her feelings.

Kylara shook her head, knowing that her aura seemed to be consistently impregnable to dragons. "No, ma'am."

The headmaster held the girl's gaze for a while longer before she set her cup down and told her she could go. She knew the old dragon hadn't penetrated her aura, but she also knew that fact would make her seem all the more unusual.

As she returned to her dorm, she couldn't help but wonder what else would happen to her in the academy.

## CHAPTER TWENTY-THREE

Classes the next day were blessedly normal. After all the excitement of the fight and the visit to Amythist's office, the two friends wisely stayed indoors and did nothing more than take turns trying on Kylara's new clothes.

She felt worlds more comfortable in a pair of jeans, sneakers, and a cute sleeveless blouse than she had in Tanya's elaborate dresses. She might have preferred a t-shirt even more but her friend was aghast at the idea of her wearing something so pedestrian.

Still, disagreements about outfits were decidedly small potatoes when only the day before, your new best friend had been bound and gagged with magic ropes.

It was at lunch that she felt the first splinter fracture the calm of the morning.

The girls filled their plates with the day's special—chickens roasted in a hundred different flavors and biscuits, each loaded with different kinds of herbs, and a couple of exotic-looking salads on the side to make the meal seem more "international." Kylara thought the salads weren't that weird, but she was used to eating beet greens and sweet potato leaves from their homestead.

They sat and were about to tuck in—Tanya said she could eat the chicken with her hands because there were bones inside—when Karl Midnight, Tempest, and Esme walked past and glared openly at them.

"I can't believe they're flexing their aura like that here." Tanya scoffed and looked insulted.

Kylara couldn't exactly feel the details but she could sense that they were angry. Of course, that wasn't hard to miss on their faces. "They merely want everyone to know that they didn't lose."

The girls followed them with their gazes until they sat at a nearby table. Tempest and Esme focused on the task of devouring chicken, but Midnight continued to glance at the two friends. He would only turn away from them to whisper and hiss to the other two dragons, who would chuckle and stare vacantly at Kylara as they did so to remove any doubt about what exactly they were gossiping about.

"Ugh, I wish they would stop," Tanya whined. "Do you want to go to our room to eat or something?"

"Ruby said not to," she replied.

"I know, but I wish they would stop."

"Wait, I have an idea." She raised her hand, extended her fingers, and began to wiggle them.

"Your plan...is to wave nicely at them?" Her friend looked incredulous.

She didn't let the phony grin on her face falter, not even as she focused on letting her inner magic flow with the magic around her.

Karl Midnight, not a master of subtlety, glanced at her and saw that she was smiling and waving at him. He scowled and turned to his cronies. All three of them hunched together like vultures trying to devour roadkill, and their whispers continued furiously until they all turned to glare at her at once.

Their expressions melted away, however, when they noticed her glowing fingertips.

This time, when they returned to their huddle, their faces were pale, their voices silent, and their backs hunched.

"Ky! Stop. You'll give them a sunburn." Tanya said the last part loudly enough to carry across the cafeteria, which earned snickers from most of the tables. It seemed that what had happened to the young dragon wasn't the most carefully guarded secret, nor was the spectacular defeat Kylara had unleashed on Midnight.

"I think they'll leave us alone now," she said and wiped her forehead with a napkin to remove the sweat. Making her finger glow hadn't been easy.

"Ky, stop wiping yourself, for goodness sake. We're in public."

"What are you talking about? Who cares?"

"I don't know—maybe that extremely cute golden dragon, Samuel."

"Samuel is not cute."

"Well, whatever he is, he's walking up behind you right now."

She turned as Sam come to a stop and smiled awkwardly.

"Hey. Do you...uh, mind if I join you?"

"I...thought you...um, hated me for leaving you to die," she said.

Tanya laughed loudly enough to be heard throughout the cafeteria, so all gazes turned to look at him where he stood uncomfortably in front of Kylara.

"I...don't hate you." His gaze darted to all the other young dragons enjoying the gossip.

Tanya recovered from her outburst and flashed him a smile. "Of course you can sit with us." She gave Ky a sideways glance as she invited him to sit. There was no hint of a question in the look, though, more like a challenge. "A couple of dragons with light powers might be able to show me a thing or two."

Samuel sat and he scooted his wooden chair closer on the marble floor. It squeaked painfully. "Honestly, that was what I wanted to talk to you about. I've heard some parts of it through the rumor mill, but stories have a way of growing out of proportion."

"Many things grow in Kylara's presence," Tanya said coyly.

The young golden dragon looked like he wanted to die but he soldiered on. "I hoped I could hear about what happened directly from the hero of the day." He punctuated the statement with his award-winning smile and Kylara couldn't help but forget some of the past awkwardness.

Plus, there was the hero part. "Wait, hero of the day? I don't understand. We might have been expelled."

"Fat chance!" He laughed. "Karl and his goons have been cruising for trouble for ages. I'm sure I'm not the only one who is glad to see they finally bit off more than they could chew."

"I thought everyone liked them," Tanya murmured.

"No way," he said. "I'm sorry about you getting picked on but honestly, the fact that you're an enemy of those dweebs raises your status in my book."

"I didn't do anything," the girl confessed. "Kylara's the one who singlehandedly blinded three dragons."

"So that part is true?" Samuel asked.

"You don't seem surprised," Kylara said.

He smirked. "I saw you light your fingertips up so I'm not entirely shocked. Did you honestly blind them, though?"

She nodded. "I gave them sunburns too."

"That's so cool! I didn't know you had light powers. Why...uh, why didn't you tell me?"

"Because I didn't know about them until yesterday."

"How did you find out you had them?" he asked.

"I saw Tanya in trouble and went to help. Midnight had me tangled in those webby things of his, and I don't know—I simply reached out, as it were, and started to glow."

"Ky is making it sound like it was not utterly epic when in fact it was utterly epic," Tanya added.

"Wow, that's amazing." He nodded. "It's odd too, though."

"How's that?" Kylara asked.

"Well, light powers run in my family and they usually manifest early on. It's not unheard of for it to appear later, but it's rare. Normally, it goes with the golden scales, so it's almost a foregone conclusion."

"It's because Kylara is special," Tanya interjected.

"I'll say," he agreed. "But I've only heard of a few dragons having more than one power. It made me wonder...do you only have the two?"

She dropped the piece of chicken she had been eating. "Why... why do you ask that?"

"Well, when you dueled with Tempest and he was struck by that crazy bolt of lightning, I assumed he was lying so he didn't look like he lost control in front of everyone. But now, I'm starting to wonder... Think about it. He isn't exactly humble. I don't know why he would lie about a lightning strike like that, given how powerful it was. It seems you have light powers but do you lightning powers too?"

She shook her head. "No way. Honestly, I've never had any kind of storm or lightning powers and if I did, believe me, I would have found out. I grew up in the desert, remember? I can't tell you the number of times I went outside and prayed for rain, or danced for rain, or begged clouds to form. If I had storm powers, I would know about them."

"Sure. That makes sense..."

"But," Tanya added when he trailed off.

He smiled and tried to make it look like he hadn't intended to say exactly that. "But you said you never had light powers either and you most certainly do. It seems like something special is happening to you, Kylara."

"And what makes you think it's any of your business?" she snapped, not liking the way he looked at her. She also didn't like the fact that she only gained these special powers now that her mom was gone and her home was burned to nothing.

"It's not. You're right. I didn't mean to pry," Samuel said. "I'm curious, is all."

"Yeah, well, maybe you should be curious somewhere else."

"Of course." He put his silverware on his plate, wiped his area with a cloth napkin, and stood. "I apologize for offending you."

"It's fine," she grumbled but hoped her tone made it clear that it was not fine.

"But…well—and again, no pressure—if you want to see what else you can do with light or if you ever want someone to train with, I'd be happy to help you. After all, light powers are my special ability."

With a cordial bow, he excused himself, took his plate to kitchen, and moved to the cafeteria exit.

"You didn't need to scare him off like that, Ky," Tanya said. "He's not exactly unpleasant to look at."

"I guess you're right," she mumbled. But it wasn't his looks that made her watch him leave but his offer to help her explore her new powers. She wondered what could motivate him to help train her. Part of her wanted the experience of training with another dragon, but she also wondered why her mom had refused to let her do exactly that for her entire life.

# CHAPTER TWENTY-FOUR

If Kor had heard anything about an unsanctioned dragon duel taking place on his campus, it seemed his solution to the problem was to force the students to train even harder so they wouldn't have the energy to exert themselves when not under his direct supervision.

The pace was grueling. He had taught them a series of movements in both their human and dragon forms. Now, he forced them to go through them all, back to back, and switch between their two shapes relentlessly. It was exhausting and strangely disorienting to use one's human body to do sequences of punches, kicks, and flips, then be forced to perform maneuvers that required wings, tails, and dragon limbs that were more than twice the length of their human form.

Some of the other students had already collapsed from exhaustion. Not even threats of low grades could revive them, although their instructor still attempted this tactic. Kylara was already in good shape from the training sessions with her mom so she held up well enough, although her dragon healing ability had long since ceased to do anything about the stitch in her side.

Finally, when she felt she too might have to succumb to a

lower grade and a barrage of threats and insults from the Silver Bullet, he called for a water break.

Even these were odd at this school, however. Instead of a water fountain, they had a massive bag of water suspended on a wooden frame. Massive didn't accurately define the bag though. It was as big as a water tower and must have held thousands of gallons. Spouts protruded from the bottom that dragons could drink from or a human could shower under. She couldn't help but laugh when she saw these giant, fearsome, fire-breathing beasts sucking water from the bottom of the bag like calves nursing at a cow's teat.

Not all the dragons had stuck to that form, though. A few of them were in their human form so they could soak their sweaty bodies fully. Samuel was one of these, and she had to admit that he didn't look bad when he dripped with water, his golden hair slicked back.

She should have paid less attention to him, however, because when Kor called for them to line up for the dueling section of the class, she was watching the golden dragon instead of the person who sidled up beside her—Karl Midnight.

"All right, Tempest and Esme, God forbid you choose different partners but that's fine. Stoneflank and Saphire, that should be fun. Midnight and Diamantine." Kor continued to list other partners but her brain had stopped working when he'd put her with Karl.

"Go ask Kor to change our group," she whispered to him. She was not in the mood to duel with him, let alone stand next to him and critique the other battles as partners were expected to do.

"Why? Are you scared of facing me in a proper fight?" he demanded.

"Scared? I beat you one against three. Oh, my God—you stood next to me on purpose, didn't you?"

"You got lucky before using techniques I didn't know about. Mark my words. That won't happen again."

"You're a real creep, you know that, right?" Kylara knew that she shouldn't goad him but it was hard to resist. He was simply so slimy.

"And you're a nobody from a burned-out hole in the desert who has no right to be here. You know that, right?"

After that little tit for tat, they made no further attempts at conversation. She ground her teeth while he smoldered next to her. They watched Tempest defeat Esme. Her venomous claws were at quite a disadvantage with the distance between the pillars. Saphire made her opponent so cold he eventually collapsed off his pillar. This was met by sounds of concern from the students and cheers and whooping from Kor.

Finally, it was their turn.

"You're going down, Diamantine. If you agree to kiss my claws, I'll make it look like you had a chance."

"I guess after this, you'll be an official loser instead of an unofficial one," she snapped in response before she changed to her dragon form and took her place on the pedestal.

"All right, you lizards know the rules by now. Stay on your pedestal. The first one to leave their position for whatever reason loses. Now, let's see a proper fight!"

Midnight immediately launched into a series of shadow attacks. He sank his claws into the pedestal in front of him and more than twenty shadow cords whipped out from them and flailed to make their movements incredibly difficult to track.

Kylara had no choice but to go on the defensive as he lashed at her from all angles. Most of the tendrils lacked any real finesse and simply battered against her diamond scales, but it was impossible to tell which he intended to truly hurt her with from the distractions. Finally, she had to turtle up to protect the joints of her arms, legs, and wings as he split his tendrils into forty, then eighty, and he rained shadowy hell on her diamond scales.

It was like fighting a hundred snakes when she knew that only ten of them were venomous. She couldn't ignore any of the strikes, even though she knew that he mostly simply tried to keep her on the defensive. While she could think of no fighting technique that would help her in this situation, her mom's push to train her in aikido seemed especially useless right now.

Kylara drew into a tighter ball. She didn't know if Midnight could hurt her if she went fully defensive, but she also knew that he'd never stop crowing about it if she didn't go on the offensive and beat him.

The thought gave her the courage to unravel and attempt a blast of fire.

Karl saw her coming, however, and he pulled back half his whipping tendrils. Quickly, he spun them into a web that floated between them and very effectively robbed her attack of its momentum and heat. The dark webs vanished from the blow as well but that didn't matter to him.

He resumed his attack with a good thirty or forty tendrils, which he then split into double that with a grunt. Two them launched forward toward her neck, but a deft flick of her diamond claws severed them from their source and they vanished.

But even the attempted stranglehold was nothing but a feint.

Kylara realized this when her back leg was yanked out from under her. Her groin struck the pedestal painfully.

She dug in with her front claws and grasped the stacked marble pieces so she wouldn't be pulled off. While Karl had lashed and whipped at her face with his tendrils, he had sent another down his pillar to then wind up and around hers to catch her foot.

Infuriated, she tried to slash it with a claw and won herself a moment of temporary freedom, but because the tendril was coiled, it simply regrew from the closest loop and snatched her leg again.

"Call me master and I won't crack your face too badly when I pull you off of there," Karl taunted her.

That was the final straw.

With a roar, Kylara opened her mouth and light erupted from her throat to annihilate the tendril traveling from Karl's pedestal to hers.

His eyes widened at the assault. It seemed he had truly thought that Samuel had something to do with what he saw during their first fight. This despite her glowing fingers in the cafeteria. It was a mistake she was happy to remedy for him.

Now that she had called on her inner magic, it seemed to flow through her like a river. She called upon that power and used it to unleash a blast of light at Midnight.

He braced himself seconds before her attack hit. It took time to fill her lungs to release the energy, even though the blast itself was made of light and thus traveled at lightspeed. His tendrils all returned to him and spiraled out from his claws to wind around and crisscross the top of the pedestal.

His precautions were more than he needed. Her blast of light, as wide and broad as the beam of a lighthouse, lacked power and precision. It rocked Midnight but didn't knock him from his position.

"Try a tighter beam!" Samuel shouted from the ground. "And aim for his eyes!"

Unfortunately, Karl heard that too and immediately brought some of his tendrils of magic up his back and around his head. They gave him a mess of what looked like dreadlocks that he used to intercept her narrower beam of light.

He knew better than to let her try again and put him on the defensive, so he lashed out with tendrils as he had before. There were less of them now, however, as some of his efforts were spent maintaining the shadow dreadlocks he retained near his eyes.

But Kylara had begun to understand how his powers worked. He could only concentrate on a limited number of his tendrils at once, which meant that while he had to defend himself, she had an opportunity.

She focused on the magic coursing through her and channeled it into a ball of energy deep inside her chest. As weird as it was, she could almost feel it glowing.

Karl lashed at her face with his tendrils and she swiped them aside. She was pleased to see her diamond claws now glowed with light, which made short work of her opponent's shadow tentacles.

Before he could repeat his onslaught, she blasted him in the face with light. Samuel was right in that the narrower beam worked much better against her foe. Karl's shadow dreadlocks disintegrated and he reeled from the attack, but more strings of inky darkness emerged and tied his claws to the pedestal beneath him.

Kylara understood what to do now. One blast wouldn't do him in, but if she could catch him in the face, destroy the tendrils he used to hold onto his pedestal, and finally hit him a third time, that would probably do it.

She fended off more of his attacks. They had become wild and desperate, but that didn't mean they were less dangerous. If anything, it was the opposite. Karl used less of them now, but those he attacked with were much thicker and packed more of a punch.

But she now knew how to win. She took another deep breath and was ready to finish Midnight off, officially and in front of the entire class, when she saw, in the distance behind her opponent, a whirling mass of fire, smoke, and ash.

"Kor!" she shouted as Karl struck her across the face with one of his tendrils. It landed with such force that her neck cracked.

Their instructor turned and saw the fire moving toward them through the woods. It set trees on fire, threw ash in heated flurries, and generally burned the woods to the ground.

"All students back to their dorms! Now!" he yelled and

snatched a radio up. "We need backup in the fields. I repeat, we need backup."

"This fight's not over!" Karl raged and swiped at Kylara with another tendril of black magic.

She ignored him as she flapped her wings and took to the air. That monster was her worst nightmare. She had seen the swirling pillar of fire and ash before, as well as the face within. It was the creature of flame that took Hester Diamantine and Kylara wanted her mom back.

"She forfeits!" Karl screamed as she flew toward the fire. "Everyone saw that, right? Kylara forfeits that match, which means I win!"

"Damn it, Diamantine! Get back here!" Kor shouted at her. He knew as well as she did that it would take the other professors a while to get there. Their priority would be to get the students to safety but it only meant that while they were away, the fire monster had more time to destroy the campus.

Kylara didn't feel particularly generous toward it today. She would do what she could to hold it back.

But how?

She knew fire breath wouldn't do much against it. Her first thought was to try to burn a firebreak like her mom had, but they were in a canyon lined with pine trees. It would only need to get one ember past her to continue its incineration. Plus, she didn't want to escape it. She wanted to defeat it and force it to reveal where her mother was.

Finally, she decided she would try her newly discovered light powers and hope to hell that her diamond skin was as impervious to heat as Hester had always claimed.

The young dragon swooped toward the fire that raged relentlessly through the woods behind the training fields. She was still pumped from her duel with Midnight and as she flew, she focused on letting her inner magic surge. When she deemed herself close enough, she opened her mouth and focused a tight beam of light on the core of the fire.

The attack thrust it back, and the roar of the flames diminished for a moment—but only a moment. The being—seeing it again, she had no doubt that it was a being—rolled and pushed out two great limbs of flame that found nearby trunks. As the creature pulled itself up, the trees combusted into nothing and any damage that she had done to it was erased.

"Do not fear me, Kylara," the fire roared and she almost fell from the sky.

It stopped its race forward through the trees and toward the school as she spun in tight circles above it.

"What did you do with my mother?" she demanded.

"I am but a servant," the blaze roared rather than answering the damn question. It had formed a face again or a simulacrum of one anyway. It was essentially a great twisting mass of orange flame but at its center near the ground where most of the fuel was, a section of red fire looked like a gaping maw. Above that, two red points of flame danced like mischievous eyes. No other attempt was made by the being to appear as anything but fire, but that was more than enough to scare the living hell out of her. She had told the Steel Guard what she had seen but she had hoped she had been wrong. Now, she saw the beast of flame was real—and it could talk.

"Who is your master?" Kylara shouted at it.

"It is not my place to say. Know only that my master demands your presence and tires of your mother's insolence."

"Where is she?"

The creature didn't answer. Instead, it released a stream of flame that engulfed another tree to feed its power and make its flames burn brighter and the vortex at its core spin faster.

"Where is my mother?" Kylara shouted and blasted the monster's mouth—the base of the vortex—with another beam of light.

It toppled the beast, so instead of a vertical cyclone of flame, it collapsed and became a great wall of fire. This didn't seem to weaken it in any way, however. It merely gave it easier access to more fuel. It roared and the sound made her think of the same roar she had heard when her home burned on the other side of the mountain when she had fled. Then, it lunged toward her as a great pillar of fire.

Kylara was ready. She flapped her wings and ascended to evade the fire monster's strike. A plan began to form in her head. She knew she couldn't defeat it, not with her fire breath or her light powers, but if she could keep it slowed and focused on her, surely Kor would arrive with more help, right?

Before she could weigh the merits of her plan, a great blast of flame struck her in her wing, blistered it and shredded the membrane, and hurled her from the sky.

She landed hard with a thunk, righted herself, and vaulted skyward, but her wing screamed at her for her stupidity of trying to fly with a freshly burned wing.

Her gaze fell on the fire beast as it raced across the short section of the field between her and the trees that fueled it. It quickly became apparent that the distance between the trees wouldn't stop it. Like an eel keeping the tip of its tail in its cave, the fire monster stretched toward her and left a trail of flame to the forest, where it could continue to power itself with the abundance of resinous pine trees.

It moved too fast. Kylara wouldn't be able to escape. So, not liking it at all, she turtled up, wrapped her diamond-encrusted tail around her wounded wing, and tucked her head beneath her arms.

The fire monster fell on her like she was a pile of dried leaves.

Its flames crawled across her, looking for an ingress point between her scales. She knew it would not find one as she had practiced defending herself from blasts of flame since she was five years old. This was a more concentrated attack, but that didn't mean her ability to hold her scales tightly closed had changed. Try as it might, the fire monster simply couldn't reach her flesh.

In the next moment, she realized it didn't need to burn her flesh to kill her. Already, she could feel her diamond scales heating. Normally, they absorbed heat and dispelled it into the atmosphere between blasts of dragon fire, but there was no between with this monster. An inferno roared upon her as if to cook her inside her scales.

Worse, it became extremely hard to breathe. A dragon's blast of fire was fueled by the air in their lungs, but this monster took air from all around her. It might not burn her flesh but that didn't mean she wouldn't be cooked inside her scales after she asphyxiated.

Was this how she would die? Did the fire beast know how to do this because it had done the same thing to her mom? And what had it meant about Hester's insolence? Did it mean she was alive but being tortured? It became harder to think and breathe. Maybe it would be easier if she simply went to sleep. After all, it was warm—warmer than lying on the hottest rock on the hottest day of the summer. Maybe, if she simply slept, everything would get better.

A blast of cool air surged across her face and she shook herself from the stupor induced by lack of oxygen.

"Get behind me, Ky!" Samuel was in his dragon form and glowed like the sun itself. She scrambled to her feet and stumbled toward him. It was like walking into the sunrise. Light poured from him and silhouetted her as she moved.

The fire monster roared and sounded like a freight engine as it lurched through the light toward her.

"That won't hold it," she wheezed.

"I know that! Now get behind me!" Sam ordered and she stumbled to obey.

The fire beast—furious at this chain of events—reached

toward her with one of its fiery limbs. Samuel seared it with light and severed it from the main body of the beast, but the monster simply incinerated another tree and attacked again.

"Light won't work. We need to run," Kylara said.

"That's why Tanya's here with the water bag from Kor's class."

Kylara looked up as Tanya soared overhead, the massive, water-tower sized bag of water clutched in her claws. It was so heavy that she struggled to stay airborne under its weight.

She moved past the two young dragons and let the bag go. As it fell, Samuel blasted it with a tight beam of light that made the rubbery material rupture. A swimming pool's worth of water was unleashed on the fire spirit.

It hissed like the world's greatest bonfire being doused and retreated to the woods.

Kylara watched Tanya regain speed and height and realized that despite being best friends with her, she'd never taken a good look at her dragon form. She'd flown here and there across campus with her, of course, and rescued her from Karl Midnight's tendrils of magic. But now, with droplets of water in the air and the late afternoon sun shining, she truly saw her roommate.

She was a beautiful turquoise dragon, the color of a cold sea. Three ridges down her back were all webbed and her wings were so delicate that they looked like they were made of paper. Oddly, the wings and ridges reminded her of her friend's obsession with parasols. Truly, the dragon was as beautiful and delicate as one.

"Can you fly?" Samuel asked her and drew her from watching Tanya.

When she stretched her wings, they reminded her quite painfully that she couldn't. "I'm sorry, it burned my wings."

"It's no problem," he said and placed a claw gently on her wounded appendage. His claw glowed and a flood of energy enhanced her healing powers to mend the injury almost instantly.

"I don't mean to break up the snuggle session, but that monster's not dead!" Tanya shouted as she swooped overhead. Kylara's gaze lowered from her friend, beyond her delicate tail and the spiny fan at its end, and onto the forest.

It was burning in its entirety. The fire creature had been driven back but it had left a trail of flame to a place where it knew it could regroup and strengthen itself. It did so now and expanded into a vortex of flame that grew taller and wider as it swallowed more and more trees. A great pillar of smoke and ash erupted from its top and filled the sky with soot. Soon, there would be nothing left of the forest but ashes.

In the next moment, the fiery tornado toppled and closed the distance between itself and Kylara in a second.

Samuel blasted at it as it fell, but his light powers could only punch holes in the vortex, not cause it to split apart.

It landed decisively in a great shower of sparks that all swarmed together and into her eyes to blind her.

"Come for me, you overgrown candle!" he shouted.

She couldn't see but she heard the whoosh of one its fire limbs as it hurled the golden dragon away.

"Kylara, it wants you. Get out of there!" Tanya shouted overhead.

Seeing the truth of this, she tried to obey. She vaulted upward and pumped her wings to take flight, but the fire monster caught her tail to drag her down as if it were a cat toying with a rat. She pounded into the surprisingly hard earth and her attacker pulled her back. When she dug her claws into the soil, it accomplished little besides ripping burned grass from the ground.

Honestly, she had no idea how flames could pull a dragon—some type of vortex effect, perhaps? It didn't matter, of course. The monster's hold was as solid as any dragon's but far hotter. The scales of her tail heated as it engulfed more and more of her. She had been through enough training sessions with her mom to know she was in trouble.

But that didn't mean she would simply give up, not with Samuel and Tanya there and not when defeating this monster meant she might be able to find the location of her mother.

Kylara reached within to find her magic and used it to ignite her scales with glowing energy. The fire monster seemed undaunted and the glowing scales did nothing to slow its attack. The blasts did have some effect, but now that it was enveloping her, she didn't see how she could use light to thrust it away.

But what if that wasn't her only power?

What if she truly had made that bolt of lightning strike Tempest?

If she had, it meant she had storm powers.

And those, she told herself, meant she could make it rain.

She let the stream of magic flowing through her grow into a raging river. Her teeth gritted, she allowed every cell in her body to succumb to the magic to empower and strengthen her. Finally, she called on the sky itself for help.

Thunder rumbled in the distance as white clouds formed in the sky above her. Tiny, marshmallow-sized puffs swirled together to form a gray thunderhead. She sensed it stretch even higher than a normal cloud would.

Calmer now, she called on the wind and the moisture in the air itself—something she often wished for in the desert—and felt it respond. The thunderhead grew upward and outward and in moments, the entire area was darkened when the sun was blotted out.

Then, with a mighty roar, she made it rain.

The first few fat, tentative drops did nothing to the fire monster that tried to engulf her, but the storm soon began to rage in earnest.

Truly, it was no different from the desert storms she had grown up with. One moment, the sky was gray and the air thick with accumulated moisture and in the next, there didn't seem to be air anymore, only water everywhere.

The cloud, quickly formed, now went about its business of dumping all its water onto the earth below it.

Under this torrent, the fire beast had to retreat. The limb of pure flame wound around her tail was doused to nothing. The monster hissed in pain and tried to escape to the burned forest using the trail it had left while it still could.

Even though she could taste her freedom, she didn't let the river within her stop. She focused on the storm cloud above her, knowing that clouds like this in the desert could cease their downpours as quickly as they started. This one wouldn't, however. Not on her watch.

She refused to let the storm relent until Professor Sharra arrived and used her magic to force the bulk of the clouds to move over the forest, where the rain could extinguish any embers that lingered.

Kylara sagged, utterly spent, and rolled onto her back. The mud and the stream of water that now flowed around her felt utterly and unbelievably wonderful after battling the fire beast.

# CHAPTER TWENTY-FIVE

"What the hell were you idiots thinking?" Kor roared at Kylara.

She had only closed her eyes for a second. When had he come so close and become so angry? He was in his silver dragon form and each word boomed while he punctuated it with a flick of his tail that launched a silver spine across campus.

"That monster took my mom," she said.

"And your plan was to let it take you too?" he demanded.

"Sir, if Kylara hadn't acted as quickly as she had, it would have reached the U," Tanya protested.

"Where do you think the security team was digging in?"

The three young dragons shared a look. Their instructor took it as a confession of their idiocy.

"I guess I did wonder where the team was," the golden dragon admitted.

"We were doing what we have trained to do. Goddamn students. Every one of you has a god complex. Every damn one. It's a miracle we graduate any students at all, to be honest. I'm shocked that most of you don't simply crush yourselves with a goddamn mountain."

"I'm sorry. It's my fault," Kylara said.

"You're damn straight it's your fault," he grouched. "Which is why your defeat by Karl will stand on the books."

"What? Sir, please. I'll never hear the end of it from that asshole."

"Language, young lady. That asshole happens to be from a family that helps to keep this school afloat financially and that's why I'm giving him the match."

"Because he's well-connected?" she demanded indignantly.

"No. Because he'll continue to remind you how stupid you were for not going to the dorms with the rest of the students like I told you to do. Now, I'll take a look around with the other students. You three are to stay here on penalty of expulsion. Do I make myself clear? Or do I need to fetch Karl Midnight to make sure you listen?"

"That won't be necessary, sir." She sighed.

"We'll make sure of it," Tanya said, and Samuel nodded as well.

It seemed Kylara had burned up any good graces she had earned from the Silver Bullet as he left once only Tanya and Samuel had agreed to his orders.

"He's right, you know." The young golden dragon gestured at Kor. "That was a crazy thing to do, rushing in to face that fire monster, even if you did know it wasn't a regular fire and that light powers could work against it."

"Ky, you told me about your mother's run-in with it and you didn't mention anything about light powers. You didn't know they would work, did you?" Tanya asked.

She shook her head in shame. To her surprise, Samuel laughed.

"You truly are brave!" He smiled.

"You two came as well."

"Only because it was obvious that it wanted you and not us," her roommate said, but there was something in the way she smiled that made her think she was proud of her part in the fight as well.

"What was it, anyway?" he asked. "I thought it was a wildfire at first, but when I saw it attack, I assumed it was a mage. But it wasn't, was it?"

"I don't think so," Kylara said. "My mom always said fire magic was rare among mages and she never said anything about fire talking."

"It...talked?" Tanya asked.

She nodded. "It did. And I'm very sure it has my mom."

"What did it say?" Samuel asked, but before she could answer, Amythist circled above them and descended to land near the three young dragons. She took her human form and gestured for them to do the same.

To Kylara's shock, the headmaster was grinning. "All right, then. Does anyone have any boo-boos or did Samuel already take care of those with his light power?"

"I think I'm fine," she said, checked her body, and saw no burns or anything else.

"Kylara was the only one who got hurt," Tanya explained. "Samuel and I are fine."

"Very good, very good." The old dragon beamed. "I've already sent a message to the North American Dragon Council asking for backup, so help should be here soon. While we wait, tell me about that storm. Who summoned it? Tanya, have you finally gained a power?"

The girl hung her head. "No, Headmaster. I wish it was me, but it wasn't. I didn't even try to use any powers. I simply snatched the water bag."

Amythist nodded and rubbed her chin. "Using your brain is a power many dragons forget they have. But if it wasn't you, who was it? Somehow, I doubt that young Tempest came to your rescue so soon after you blinded him."

Kylara stepped forward. "I think it was me, Headmaster."

"Of course it was you!" Samuel snorted and sounded a little

jealous but mostly impressed.

"How sure are you that you summoned the storm, Kylara?" Amythist pressed.

"Very sure. Certain, to be honest. That monster had me by the tail and the light wasn't working, so I tried to use my magic to summon a storm like I did when I fought Tempest."

The headmaster's eyes twinkled at this revelation. "Ah…how wonderful! How truly astonishing! Three dragon powers in one dragon. Not even the Steel Dragon herself has mastered such a feat."

"Has anyone?" Samuel asked.

Amythist didn't answer but there was a twinkle in her eyes again. Kylara thought back to her time in the headmaster's office. How did she heat her tea? She had seen her make a spoon stir by itself. What powers did this ancient and venerable dragon possess?

"I would like to run a few tests on you, Kylara, simply to determine what's going on. You seem to have a much greater affinity for a wide variety of magic than most dragons. In fact…" The old dragon tapped her chin while she thought. "Would you be averse to me slotting you into some of the mage-specific classes? It might help you to learn more about what you can do since your powers are so diverse."

"If you think that would help," she said and recalled her three dullest classes. "Although I'd like to stay in Practical Dragon Powers and Magical Theory."

Amythist laughed. "Child, you drove back an efreet. I don't know what more you hope to get from the Silver Bullet's instruction, but if you wish to continue to suffer his verbal abuse, I won't stop you."

"What did you say it was?" she asked, but the old dragon was already pacing and ignored the question.

"Truly, your powers are more akin to how the mages use them

than most dragons do. I think those classes could serve you well. You already did wonders with the storm, but if you could master some of Professor Sharra's ability to move water, you would truly be a force to be reckoned with. Curious. Curious indeed..." She now mumbled quietly as if talking to herself. "The pixies said the first dragons were mages, but what if they were mistaken? They're the youngest of the magical races, after all. What if dragons and mages have a link or a dual history? How truly remarkable you are, Kylara."

*Great.* Just when she thought she was starting to fit in and understand how all this worked, she went and did something to make herself into a freak all over again. Instead of the weird girl from the desert with no money and no clothes, she was now the dragon with a weird link to mages.

"Is something wrong, dear?" Amythist asked. "Your aura is as impregnable as ever but your face does a poor job of concealing your disappointment."

"It's only...well, most dragons treat mages like they're not as powerful."

"Most dragons are imbecilic, my dear. Tell me, did you inherit this attitude from your mother?"

"What? No way! My mom always supported mage rights. She thought Kristen Hall was a real hero. She even named me after a mage she used to work with, a woman named Lara."

"Truly? How fortunate you are to grow up outside the umbrella of bigotry so many dragons are never able to escape." The headmaster patted her on the shoulder. "Truly, we couldn't be luckier in finding a dragon of your upbringing with abilities like you have. I hope you can enjoy yourself while you explore your potential. You are a special and unique young lady."

"Thank you, ma'am," she replied and hoped she sounded like she meant it.

Amythist looked as if she wanted to begin the questions then and there, but a disc of mist suddenly appeared, then opened into a window that overlooked a city from some other corner of the world.

Even though Amythist, Kor, and Professor Sharra were all nearby, she couldn't help but brace herself for another fight. In her experience, an unannounced arrival was never a good sign.

# CHAPTER TWENTY-SIX

Kylara's caution proved to be unfounded in this case. The robed individuals who stepped through the portal did not summon another...what was the word Amythist had used? Friti? But the thought vanished from her mind when she recognized who had come through the portal.

"Oh, my God. That-that's Amy Williams," she stammered.

Samuel and Tanya didn't seem to know who she was as they continued to look at all the mages as if there might be a dragon in their midst.

Amythist knew who the woman was, though. She wrapped her in a warm hug and immediately battered her with questions about the Steel Dragon.

"She's fine. As busy as hell with the Council, but fine," Amy Williams said.

"Who exactly is that?" Samuel asked.

"Amy Williams?" Kylara said again. She said the two names like they were only one—Ameewilleeums. "She's the most powerful mage in the world. Kristen Hall recruited her to join her team, and many analysts say she changed the entire trajectory of the technomages' secret war."

"Oh, right! She was there to help the Steel Dragon fight the Masked One, right? Didn't she bring a group of dwarves or something?"

She was appalled that her friends didn't seem to have as firm a grasp on the events that changed the entire world, even though it had been barely a year since they had taken place. "She brought dwarves to fight those the Masked One had recruited. She leveled the playing field."

"So you think it's fine that the Dragon Council didn't send an actual dragon?" he asked.

"Of course it's fine. Amy could probably defeat any dragon in one-on-one combat. She almost defeated the Masked One himself. For all we know, she could take on the Steel Dragon." She only realized belatedly that he was teasing her.

"Ky, don't look now but your hero is coming here." Tanya pointed and she followed the gesture to where Amy Williams approached her.

Kylara didn't know whether to kneel, bow, or curtsy, so she did a combination of all three.

"O...kay..." Amy said and bowed. "You're...uh, Kylara Diamantine, right? Do you mind if I ask you a few questions?"

"Not at all, Mage Williams. It's such an honor to meet you, ma'am." She bubbled with excitement, her fatigue from the fight gone, at least for the moment.

"Cool." The mage did not sound as if she thought it was that cool. "You can call me Amy, by the way. No one calls me Mage Williams. Like, no one."

"No problem, Amy Williams—Miss Williams...ugh, I mean Amy!" She reddened and had never been so thankful that her aura was hard for others to read. But she remembered that the mage couldn't read auras and was thus far more likely to understand the naked embarrassment on the teenager's face.

"Okay, so before we begin, can you take a deep breath and calm down?"

Kylara nodded, focused on her breathing, and tried to face another of her heroes. "If there's anything I can do to help, I'd be happy to."

"Sure. First thing, did you sense any dragon aura abilities?"

The question floored her as she was, of course, was not the best at detecting auras.

Samuel, fortunately, came to her rescue. "There weren't any, ma'am. I detected nothing. If it was a dragon, it was a master of its aura. I...thank you, by the way. I know you worked with my great-great-great-grandfather, Lumos. I should have recognized you sooner."

"You're one of Lumos's descendants?" Amy Williams smiled. "Those are big boots to fill, kid. You made a good start on that today. All right, so not a dragon, which makes sense. I didn't think this looked like a dragon attack anyway. Did you see a mage anywhere?"

"No, ma'am," Kylara said. She had decided that the more words she said, the more likely it was she would mess some of them up.

"What did you see? Anything unusual about this...being?"

"It had a face, ma'am—a face in the flames. It was like the fire had a mind of its own."

"Is that right?" Amy asked the other two.

"It had targeted Kylara," Tanya said. "And she said it spoke to her."

"What did it say?"

She took a deep breath. "It said it had a master and that it had my mom."

The mage nodded, although her face wore a stern frown. "That's not good. If it could speak and had intention as you say, it could only be a—"

"Enough of that," Amythist interjected and robbed the young dragon of information she desperately wanted, mainly because she'd already forgotten what the headmaster had called it.

"They're only students—students who should be getting back to their homework."

The mage nodded. "Thanks for your help," She turned away and extended a hand to the swathe of destruction left in the wake of the fire. Tendrils of mist drifted from her hands and spread gradually. Something moved through it that almost looked like Kylara. Another form flew overhead—Tanya, with her bag of water.

The three young dragons watched in amazement, their orders to return to their homework forgotten.

After a moment, Amy shook her head. "I can't detect any trace of it. Whoever summoned this was good at what they did. And clever too. It was a smart move to use one as an intermediary. The water dousing also did a perfect job of wiping away any trace."

"A win-win situation for them," Amythist said ponderously. "If the creature was successful, then of course a victory, but even in defeat, any traces of it would be erased."

"Are you saying it's my fault we can't use it to find my mom?" Kylara demanded.

"Child, what are you still doing here?" The headmaster looked at her with a warning expression.

"I can't simply go away, not when I finally know that the monster that took my mom is real."

"I'm sorry," Amy said placatingly. "I was too focused to realize you're the girl from the land that was burned near here. Look, we are working tirelessly to find out what happened there. The Dragon Council sent me because we suspect a mage is involved and quite frankly, I'm the best they have. We will find whoever did this. I promise you that."

It was a promise that Kylara had heard before, one the Steel Dragon had yet to keep.

"Thank you," she said, but the wheels were already spinning in her head. "We should go. Tanya, will you come with me to the library? There was something from Dragon Law class that I wanted to read up on."

"What? No! I don't want to read another word—"

"Tanya, come on," she insisted and her friend's face reflected her sudden understanding.

The two set off across the campus. With their backs to the burned forest and field, it was almost like nothing had happened. If it weren't for the mud and ash at their feet, she might have been able to believe that.

"This isn't about Dragon Law, right?" Tanya pleaded. "Because I don't care about my grade in that class. It's not helping my powers."

"Where are you two going?" Samuel asked when he caught up to them.

"Yeah, Kylara, where are we going?" her roommate asked and batted her eyelids mockingly because she knew full well they were going to the library.

"There's something they're not telling me," she replied, "and I want to know what it is. It has to be some kind of magic, which is why I thought Tanya could help since she's in so many mage classes. Sam, I wouldn't want to inconvenience you."

"It's no problem."

"Excellent!" Tanya agreed before she could say anything else. "The more the merrier, that's what I always say. Plus, the magic tomes can be tiresome. If you two work together, you'll probably cover far more ground."

"I don't know about that—"

"It sounds good to me." Samuel smiled broadly at Kylara, and she no longer had the heart to protest any further.

The library was located in the main building of the U and behind a door as nondescript as a janitor's closet. But once they entered, she gasped as she always did at the size and scope of it.

Enormous was what came to mind, and certainly larger than the building that housed it. The doorway they entered through led to a tiny landing. From their position, they could see down a flight of rickety stairs and out over dozens of high wooden shelves crammed with books bound in everything from leather, to tree bark, to dragon scales.

The walls, distant in the gloom, towered above them and were all lined from floor to ceiling with bookcases or maps that looked faded with age yet showed the earth in shocking geographic clarity. A perk of being a creature that could fly was that one could see the land beneath them, she decided. Near the far wall, an odd pocket-like space looked like it led into another basement. Tanya led them there without hesitation.

They moved through the stacks of books until they reached the alcove. Kylara's dragon vision could pierce the gloom but there were no chandeliers like those illuminating the main room. "Are you sure what we're looking for is back there somewhere?" she asked.

Her roommate shrugged. "No. Not at all. But the books out here are mostly dragon histories, stories of conquest, lists of estates and holdings, stuff like that. If we're looking for esoteric mage logic, it'll be down here somewhere."

Samuel made his hands glow enough to pierce the gloom, then looked through the dusty shelves. Tucked away there, instead of a vaulted ceiling high above them, any of the three could easily touch the mildewed surface above them. "There's another set of stairs there. How deep does this go?"

"If we have to find the answer to that question, I will be seriously pissed off," Tanya protested. "I've never been below the second basement level. Professor Sharra says it's not safe."

"Why not?"

"We're down here because you're looking for a living fire creature, right?"

"Or the spell that summons one, yeah," Kylara agreed.

"What if fire creatures aren't the only living spells?"

That gave the three of them pause.

Finally, it was Samuel who broke the silence. "Okay, but these are merely books, right? What could a book do?"

Tanya exhaled through her nose. "Just...don't read anything aloud, okay?"

The next few hours blurred together as they searched with total determination for information on fire magic. True to her word, Tanya proved herself to be much more adept at looking for information than her two companions. After an hour, they shifted their search to her finding interesting books, which she would then deliver to them to skim through those that were in English or Latin.

Kylara spoke a little Spanish as well as English, but it was Samuel's Latin that proved to be most helpful.

They searched with no success and had fallen into a routine after a while. They'd look through a book Tanya brought, prayed for pictures, settled for diagrams, and deciphered what they could of the old, stilted language. As much as she wanted to find her mom, she was exhausted from the day's work and without meaning to, leaned wearily against Sam.

Despite Tanya's warning, he was reading aloud in Latin and his words seemed to blend appealingly. He had a nice voice, she had to admit. It was deep and strong but had the slightest resonance of emotion when he read something he found particularly compelling. It made him seem strong but vulnerable, something she decided she liked.

He continued to read and she tried to not fall asleep. Finally, she heard it—Efreet. All the other words were a jumble, but that one struck a chord.

"Wait. Wait, what did you say?"

He rubbed his eyes and repeated the passage.

Kylara stopped him when he said it again. "Efreet. That's it! That's what the headmaster called it. What does it say it is?"

"It isn't much," he said. "It says it's a kind of...a spirit or something from Islamic mythology."

"You don't read Arabic, do you?" she asked.

He shook his head. "No, but I think I saw that word a few books earlier. There weren't any pictures, though, so I flipped past it."

"Which book was it?"

Tanya found them working much more energetically the next time she returned with a fresh stack of books. "Did you guys find something?"

"We're trying to," Kylara said as Sam flipped through more books. "Do you know what an Efreet is?"

"An Efreet?" The other girl frowned and reached for a book Samuel had already rifled through. She opened it to a passage on them. "Sure. Professor Sharra says they're a type of...demon, I guess? An elemental. Mages can summon them to do tasks, I think."

"What do they look like?" she asked.

"It says here that they come in many shapes, but that Efreeti are a form of fire elemental. They come from another dimension."

"What dimension is that?" Samuel asked.

"Whichever. There are all kinds of dimensions. Some people call them realms or worldly kingdoms, but the idea is the same. We live in a world of magic and matter, but some worlds are all air, or stone, or magic. In Advanced Magic, Professor Sharra told us about a group of mages who used water elementals to help them sail across an ocean. Although they were northern Europeans, so they didn't call them that. It seems elementals are fairly strong in this realm as long as they have matter from their realm nearby. So once the beings reached land, they couldn't help as much."

"What did they call them?" Kylara asked as her eagerness took hold.

"Water elementals, I guess," her friend said with a shrug that made her blond pigtails bounce.

"Tanya! Is it possible that the monster we fought could be an elemental from a fire dimension?"

"Yeah. It's possible," the girl said and her mouth fell open as she stared at the page. "But why?"

"Well, it worked well against dragons," Samuel pointed out.

"That's what it had to be," Kylara said. "A fire elemental. It makes sense. It took the form of its dimension and it said it had a master."

"But, if Tanya's right and it is an elemental, it's not from here at all."

Kylara nodded. "Which confirms that the fire beast isn't our true enemy. Whoever summoned it is."

# CHAPTER TWENTY-SEVEN

When Kylara next returned to Kor's class, she found that the headmaster, despite all her kind words and promises, had transferred her out of it and moved her to another.

"Check in with Professor Sharra." The instructor didn't spare her a glance. He was too busy making the dragons transform from their human shape to their dragon form and back again repeatedly.

"And don't come back!" Karl Midnight shouted at her back while she walked away. She didn't bother to turn and give him the satisfaction of knowing that he affected her, mostly because he did.

She understood that something more than simply unusual was happening to her—downright weird and possibly unique or at least of particular significance in dragon history. Yet she couldn't help but feel like she was being punished. She knew that Headmaster Amythist wanted what was best for her and the professor's schedules were what they were, but it was still frustrating to lose the one class she felt she was excelling in to be put in another where she felt like an outcast among outcasts.

Somewhat disgruntled, she trudged to the room where she

attended Magical Theory but it was deserted. A note on the door directed her to another room in another building of the U.

Kylara hurried to this new location, well aware at this point that she was late and that Professor Sharra would not care about her not knowing where she was supposed to report.

She opened the door to the class and immediately saw that it was the same kind of room as the library. It was much larger on the inside than the outside, maybe as large as the building itself. Like the library, it was also set below the level of the door, so she had to walk down another rickety metal staircase to take her seat in the class.

It did not much help that this staircase creaked. By the time she reached the bottom, every student stared at her either openly or clandestinely, including Tanya. She should have realized that her friend would be in this class as she was studying Advanced Magic instead of Dragon Powers, but it was still a pleasant surprise to see her. Too bad she was already seated at a table with someone else. The girl waved and smiled awkwardly before she shrugged and pointed to one of the two-person tables that were empty. Everyone else pretended to not see the two dragons communicating.

It wasn't like Kylara expected the other students to welcome and befriend her. The dragons and mages didn't mix yet. She knew a few faces from her morning classes but no names and not even any reputations.

By the time she had moved past the other students to sit at the table in the back, she knew many of the murmurs and whispers were about her but honestly, she didn't care. It was better than being reamed out by Professor Sharra, who had a tongue as barbed as the Silver Bullet's tail.

When she was finally settled and looked at the front of the room, she saw that her fears were unfounded. The professor wasn't there. The name of the class had been scrawled on a chalkboard so students would know they were in the right place.

Kylara relaxed. In the back of the room, no one could stare at her openly without turning in their seat. When anyone tried, she made eye contact with them—no glare needed—and they turned quickly to face the front.

While she played this little game with the mages—without realizing until much later that the most likely reason for them avoiding eye contact was because she was a dragon and for centuries, mages had been little more than servants to dragons—she studied the room. It wasn't nearly as crowded as the library was. About thirty two-person student tables stood near the front. A chalkboard and a teacher's desk with some bric-a-brac were placed facing the class, together with a tall wall along which the stairway led into the space.

Behind the student tables was a large open area with a tiled floor that was scuffed here or scorched there. It didn't take a mage to see that most of the class's practice took place in the back section.

Kylara had turned her attention to the walls of the room—mostly adorned with some kind of geometrical diagrams, it seemed—when the door opened again and she prepared to take her turn ogling the latecomer as they tried to find their seat.

It wasn't a student who hopped on a skateboard and ground down the ancient handrail to land next to the teacher's desk but Amy Williams.

"Morning, everyone. Sorry. I was running late. I decided that this school's been attended by only dragons for so long, it needed to be skated and broken in."

A good number of the mages laughed. It was common knowledge to anyone who had followed Amy and the Steel Dragon's exploits that the girl often traveled and even fought by manipulating her skateboard telekinetically.

"I'll be on duty here for a few days, so I offered to take over some classes while I'm here."

"Where's Professor Sharra?" a student in the front with tattoos on the back of his hand asked.

"Professor Sharra's skills are best used…elsewhere for the moment," Amy said.

A dozen more hands raised. Kylara noticed that more than half of the students already had a few simple tattoos of lines or intersecting circles or tessellations of shapes on their arms despite their youth.

"Look, before we start taking questions, I am well aware that everyone here knows about the freaky weird incident with the fire attack in the forest yesterday. I didn't attend this school, but that doesn't mean I don't know how the rumor mill works."

Everyone laughed at that, and Kylara smiled as well. Maybe she could fit in there. She and her mom had followed every step of Kristen Hall's rise to power and had both been fascinated by Amy's part of the story. The dragons didn't seem to know who this mage was, but all the students in there recognized her by sight.

Their unexpected instructor levitated her skateboard behind the desk and sat on top of it. "The first thing I want you to know is that you're safe here. Well…scratch that. The first thing I want you to know is that I won't call on any of you goobers before I even introduce myself, so put your hands down."

A few awkward chuckles ensued as the students who had still been keen to ask questions lowered their hands.

"All right. Now that no one's arms are in danger of falling off from fatigue, let me tell you about yesterday. Yes, the rumors are true. There was some type of attack."

"What do you mean by some type?" a student blurted.

"Exactly that. We're fairly sure, based on how the fire spread and on eyewitness reports"—her gaze flicked from Tanya to Kylara—"that the fire was magical in nature. We're still not sure if a mage or a dragon or something else was behind it, but we're working on it."

"But how can we be safe if you don't know what it is?" another student asked. Kylara thought they were taking advantage of Amy's relaxed nature. Professor Sharra never allowed outbursts like that.

"Because I have a team of combat mages here in case whoever tried to get into this academy returns. Although honestly, the staff here are more than competent enough to keep you all safe. Lumos told me—God rest his soul—that they defended this school and its grounds from many threats over the years. In fact..." She cleared her throat as her gaze darted at the two friends again. "There's no reason to think that any students would have been involved at all if everyone had simply listened to their professors."

Tanya's head lowered to her desk. Kylara wanted to do the same but resisted the urge.

"But while we continue to investigate, there will be extra security. Still, simply because we're safe doesn't mean we shouldn't practice defending ourselves, correct?"

The mages nodded at this, although not emphatically. The reminder of defending themselves seemed to make her assurances less than sterling.

Amy ignored the confused students and turned away from them with a flourish that spun her robe wide enough to reveal that she wore cargo shorts and a t-shirt with the image of a duck skateboarding under it. She went to stand behind the teacher's desk, noticed that the front of her robe had come open, and closed it with a flourish of telekinetic energy that Kylara thought looked simple enough. She could tell, however, from the student mages' reactions that tying the sash into a knot with her mind must have been one of those tricks that looked easy but had taken a ton of practice to master.

"Whatever that creature, it was undoubtedly fire-based magic," the mage instructor said and with a flick of her wrist, lit a candle on the table in front of her. "Fire is not an easy thing for mages to master. It's fairly rare to have a knack for it, in fact. Does anyone here have the ability?"

One hand rose a little shakily.

"That's what I expected." Amy made the candle flame split into two. One of them stayed on the candle but the other danced to a ball of cotton inside a brass lamp. She closed the door to the lamp with nothing more than a nod of her head. "Fire wishes to consume. That's its nature. Like far too many Americans, it simply can't help it."

Awkward laughter followed at the political joke.

"Which is why we won't focus on controlling fire today but extinguishing it." A blast of air puffed into the vents in the lamp and the light inside went dark. "If you face a fire mage, the chances are good that they will be significantly more advanced than you. That means you won't be able to take control of their fire." She made the candle flame dance up her arm, then hop to a twisted piece of driftwood on the desk. "Even this level of control took me months to master. I could never have controlled that fire in the forest."

"Then we're not safe at all," a student blurted.

"Not true," she said and a cup of tea on one of the desks in the front levitated into the air and emptied onto the fire. Instead of simply splashing over the driftwood, the water droplets swirled and stuck to the wood to completely extinguish the flame. "If you can gain even some level of water magic, you will be substantially better equipped to fight a fire mage—or, for that matter, defend yourself against a dragon."

Amy stretched toward the two side walls and swung her hands to the center. A dozen tubs of water scooted into the middle of the room. "I don't have a knack for water but with my telekinesis, I can control it easily enough. Your goal today is to extinguish a candle with water. Now, get into groups of four, come get a candle, and go to a tub. There's no one right way to do this. You can control the water itself, use wind to make it splash the candle, or use telekinesis to control the water and make it extinguish the candle. Your grade will be based on how much water you use. Whoever uses the least water to do the job gets the best grade."

Tanya and Kylara teamed up with two girl mages who both were quite good with telekinesis. Within a few minutes, both the mages had discovered how to make a rope of water and used it to splash the burning wick of the candle. As long as they kept the rope connected to the tub, they could do all kinds of things with it.

Kylara and Tanya fared much worse.

"Is it all right if I simply splash it?" Ky asked in an attempt at a joke.

Her friend laughed but one of the mages frowned. "If you want to try that, I want Miss Williams to see my attempt first. Otherwise, you'll get the floor all wet."

The other mage was more useful. She was at least willing to show the young dragons some of the physical gestures useful in telekinesis. No matter how zealously the two friends tried to repeat the gestures, their efforts had no effect on the water. At some point, Kylara thought she felt her inner magic start to flow as she made the action, but when Tanya nudged her in the ribs, she realized that she had simply made her hands glow.

She put them out as Amy approached the four of them. The two mages completed the task and she gave high marks to both, then asked the young dragons what they could do.

Tanya tried valiantly to reproduce the gestures the mage had shown her, but the surface of the tub didn't so much as ripple in response to her attempt.

"Good form." Amy praised her with a smile. "You simply need practice. What about you Kylara? I hoped that after summoning a storm, water magic might feel somewhat familiar to you. Any luck?"

"No, ma'am," she said, reluctant to repeat all the same actions

Tanya had done, simply to achieve the same result. "Jasmine and Latoya have been very helpful, but I can't get it to work."

"Did you try to use the moisture to make a raincloud?" their instructor asked.

"You can do that?" She was surprised.

"Sure you can. Clouds are merely water droplets. You created one from the moisture in the atmosphere, but there's no real reason you can't use a body of water. I've learned that much of being a successful mage is learning how to use what powers you do have. Jasmine and Latasha—"

"Latoya."

"Latoya, sorry." Amy nodded an apology. "If you two could keep practicing, I'd like Tanya to follow your gestures as you work. While you three do that, I want to show Kylara a few things."

"Yes, ma'am," Jasmine replied and took charge of the group.

Amy led Kylara to another tub of water. "The first thing you need to do is tap into your inner magic and reach out to make a storm. Do you think you can do that in your human form?"

"In here?"

"Yeah, sure. This room is big but it's not big enough for a dragon."

She tried and found that it was easier to find the magic stream inside her than it had been before. Thunder boomed outside the building. It was the nature of the magic room that it shook a fair amount.

"That's odd…" Amy said. "I can almost feel what you're doing."

"Is that bad?" she asked.

"No, not at all, merely unusual. Normally, I can't sense dragon powers at all, but this is good. Okay, reach for that energy. I don't want you to do anything with it, only to feel what I do, all right?"

She extended her hands like her instructor did and followed her movements as the mage cut her off from the stream of magic connecting her to the weather outside. She pruned it little by little until all Kylara's magic felt contained in only the room they were in.

"Okay, I feel that." She shuddered. "But I don't like it."

Amy chuckled. "Now that sounds more like a dragon. Using the greatest amount of power available to you is not always best. Often, it's better to cut yourself off from some of your magic or channel some of it elsewhere. We don't want it to rain on campus again, so I redirected your flow into this room. It's odd, though. I've never done this with a dragon before."

"Odd, yeah," she said and tried not to feel embarrassed.

If the mage noticed her discomfort, she didn't show it. Instead, she asked Ky to focus on her magic. "Before, you were able to make droplets of water appear out of thin air. I want you to try to do that but this time, focus on doing it right on the surface of the water. You got it?"

"Sure." She was glad to have something to focus on besides how odd she was. She reached out with her inner magic and tried to summon a cloud like she had before when she faced the fire. The attempt failed.

"You're still thinking about the sky," Amy explained. "Which makes sense since that's where weather usually is. But focus on the water."

Kylara tried again, although it was awkward at first. It felt more limited and much smaller but in a moment or two, whatever she was doing materialized on the surface of the water and a great plume of mist streaked upward like a pile of dry ice had been dumped into boiling water.

"Excellent!" The mage grinned and used her telekinetic powers to keep the mist contained while she tried to gain control of it. "Now, focus on making a thunder cloud exactly like you did last time. Don't feel bad if it doesn't feel as strong. It should be damn close to impossible to make a thundercloud in here, but if you go through the same motions, it should start to—"

"Rain!" Tanya shouted and opened her parasol as it began to sprinkle on the class.

"Very good!" her instructor said. "Now try to work with me so you don't completely soak all your new classmates."

Kylara reddened at her knowledge about the change in her schedule. That could only mean the headmaster and Amy had discussed her, but she focused on making the same sweeping movements with her arms that Amy did and found that the cloud obeyed. It grew denser until it was only a puff the size of a van above the teacher and student. Tiny crackles of electricity—somewhere between a static shock and a thunder crack—moved through the cloud.

"Awww..." Tanya smiled. "Those are, like, the cutest little thunder rolls ever!"

She beamed, encouraged by the fact that she'd used a power to do something instead of simply reacting.

"Excellent. Seriously excellent," Amy said, although she looked curiously at Kylara.

"Is there a problem, ma'am?" she asked.

"No... No, nothing like that. It's only that I've never worked with a dragon who could use magic like you do. I'll keep checking on the class and I want you to keep at it, all right?"

She nodded and continued to practice, but she couldn't stop thinking about her words. Amy had never worked with a dragon like her. Could that have something to do with why her mom had forbidden her to meet other dragons? Did that have something to do with her newfound abilities of light and storm magic?

Honestly, she didn't know the answer, and not knowing worried her. It made it difficult to get the tiny rain cloud to stop grumbling with thunder.

# CHAPTER TWENTY-EIGHT

Advanced Magic took up Kylara's entire afternoon, which wasn't a bad thing. It was exhilarating to learn how to use a dragon power in her human form. First light and now storm magic? She wished she could teach some of it to Tanya and vowed she would after dinner. Right now, she couldn't as Amy Williams—*the* Amy Williams—walked beside her toward the cafeteria.

"I wish we had an update on your mom," Amy said.

"You don't know anything, then?" She didn't mean to sound rude but it was hard to have a hero fail you and not come across as thankless.

"I'm very sure it's not a dragon. The way the fire moved and your description of it doesn't sound like any dragon power I've ever heard of. Honestly, this is beyond my expertise. One of the reasons I agreed to teach a few classes was because Professor Sharra is much better at tracking than I am. I'm more of a—"

"Kickass combat mage?" she finished for her.

Amy smiled. "Yeah. But I wish I could use my powers to help you find your mom."

They walked on for a minute in companionable silence. Kylara wanted to find Hester but she also knew people were working on it, and that provided some comfort. She merely hoped that this fire elemental—it could only be that—would be tracked to whoever had taken her mom.

"Do you think it could be a fire elemental?" she asked.

"It's possible," the mage admitted, although she raised an eyebrow at her. "How do you know about elementals? That's fairly esoteric stuff."

"Maybe you should tell professor Sharra to give Tanya extra credit for research skills," she replied.

Her companion smiled. "Maybe I will. Yeah, an elemental is a good guess, but they're hard to control and especially fire ones. Even fire mages don't usually mess with them."

"Why not?"

"They're damned hard to defeat. That's the real problem. If even a spark survives or a single smoldering coal, they can regenerate themselves once they come into contact with fuel."

Suddenly, she smelled smoke. "Wait, so if only one spark survives, they can come back."

"That's right..." Amy trailed off and turned to look past the dragons that flew toward the cafeteria after Kor's class. Smoke was visible behind them, coming from one of the sides of the canyon. "Get to the cafeteria, Kylara."

"Do you think it's the elemental? I can help."

"You can help by getting to the cafeteria and making sure the other students stay safe."

The Silver Bullet uttered a great roar and she understood that the fire elemental had returned.

"Kylara, promise me you will go to the cafeteria."

"But that monster took my mom," she protested as a mage rocketed overheard on a pillar of air, followed by another who sprinted as fast as any dragon could.

"Which is why you can't face it. That being wants you—that was what you said. We can't give it what it wants. Do you understand? If it catches you, we're toast. It's already proven that it's hard to track. If it can't find you, we might have the time we need. Part of using your powers is realizing when not to use all of them, right? This is one of those times."

"But I can summon a storm."

"So can I. Now, promise me you won't fight this."

"We promise!" It was Samuel. He swooped down in dragon form and transformed, his slicked-back hair wet with sweat, no doubt from training under Kor. "We'll get her to the cafeteria."

"That's right," Tanya added.

Amy took them at their word and hurtled into the sky atop her skateboard.

"Come on, Kylara." Her roommate took her hand. "We need to get inside."

By the time they entered the cafeteria, it was already crammed with students. There were empty seats here and there but not three of them together at any one table so they remained standing near one of the walls.

In all honesty, that suited Kylara fine because she had a good view of the battle outside through the window.

Storm clouds grew overhead as Amy shouted orders to her battle mages that couldn't be heard through the glass. Their strategy seemed to be containment, as any time the elemental approached any of the mages, they threw up a wall of wind or sheet of water to stop the fire in its tracks. Kor and some of the other dragon professors swooped in behind the invader and seared the ground behind it with fire to burn away its fuel and escape route to the trees on the side of the canyon.

She had to admit that the mages and dragons had the situation well in hand. They were all masters of their powers, working together in harmony to overcome a beast that was able to do less and less as they denied it fuel, its power source.

"Hey! These shoes cost more than you make a month, mage!" A splash was followed by the sound of plates being knocked to the floor.

Kylara yanked her attention away from watching the battle outside to see that Karl Midnight now yelled at the kitchen staff while water flooded around his shoes. They were soaked.

"I'm so sorry, sir," the mage said and attempted a gesture she had seen him use to pull water from dirty cloths or dishes.

Unfortunately, it didn't work.

"Is this a joke to you?" Karl shouted at him as one of the dragon professors came to assess the situation.

As soon as the dragon entered the growing puddle coming from the kitchen, he slipped and fell as if his feet had been pulled out from under him.

"Did you see that?" Kylara asked.

"That's not a spill," Samuel said and pointed to an overflowing sink. Oddly enough, the water didn't spread across the floor. It surged into the rough shape of a human, albeit a fifteen-foot-tall human made of water. "That's a water elemental!"

"What... What is the meaning of this?" Karl demanded before the water being drove into him and he sprawled across the cafeteria floor in a great wave of water.

"Mages!" Tanya shouted. "Send that water down the drain."

The mages from Advanced Magic hurried to obey, but their magic did little to the water besides send a few ripples across its surface.

The elemental, noticing this, swept their feet out from under them with sheets of water.

Some of the dragon students transformed into their dragon shape, which made the huge cafeteria suddenly cramped. They blasted the elemental with fire but it did little and less to its watery body.

Samuel, having already fought one elemental, took to his dragon body to sever limbs from the being with his light powers. But unlike the fire elemental, it didn't slow the water elemental. The water merely splashed on the floor, only to be immediately reabsorbed. The sinks in the kitchen were still running as well, which meant the being grew larger by the second.

Kylara, not knowing what else to do, tried her storm powers. She focused her magic on making a cloud and centered the source of the water on the elemental itself.

The creature turned its watery face to her, surged toward her, and transformed into a huge tidal wave as it did so. It swept into her, hurled her from her feet, and thrust the air from her lungs as she tumbled inside its body.

# CHAPTER TWENTY-NINE

Growing up in the desert and not being allowed to leave her home unsupervised meant that Kylara had spent very little time underwater. Her mom had taught her to swim and deemed it an essential skill, but once she had shown proficiency, they had moved on like they did from any competency. So when the wave swept over her and the sound of screaming students and bellowing dragons was replaced with the dull roar of water in her ears, it wasn't exactly a familiar sensation. She knew that she had to swim clear before she ran out of air but she didn't exactly know the best way to do that.

At first, she tried to pump her arms and kick her legs against the current, but she quickly realized that the water elemental surrounding her could direct the current inside its body whichever way it chose. There was little hope of overpowering the forces within it.

Her lungs burning, she reversed direction, hoping that if she went with the current, she could reach the outer edge of the elemental's body. Unfortunately, the being clearly understood its internal workings far better than she did and it simply reversed the flow of water to trap her in the center.

She resisted the desperate urge to draw breath, although her lungs now ached for air. Her sight—already distorted from being inside the beast and the flashes of light or possibly magic that caught its surface—closed in to cut off her peripheral vision.

Kylara needed air. Her body struggled to survive without it and already, her healing powers were shutting down. Dragons were powerful creatures but, like every other animal on the planet, they needed oxygen to function.

In the next moment, she had some. The water directly above her head turned into a piece of ice and sloughed away. She sucked the air in, willed her vision and healing powers to return, and almost cried with frustration when they didn't obey immediately.

"Good aim! I want another blast all around her this time. Ready, and, fire!" Tanya was still in her human form and used her parasol to direct some of the mages from the Advanced Magic class. They released blasts of energy from their fingertips that froze the water all around Kylara.

The angry sound of the surf pounding against a rocky shore followed when the elemental lost hold of the block of ice that now surrounded the young dragon.

She fell out of its body but her head caught the corner of a table and she lost consciousness for a moment. When she opened her eyes again, her roommate continued to coordinate an attack on the water elemental but they didn't seem to be able to destroy it. When any of its body froze, it simply struck it with its wave to shatter the great pieces of ice into something more like a slushy. These little pieces of ice—once again suspended in the water elemental—didn't seem to slow it at all.

"Ky!" Samuel flew over and knocked tables and chairs aside as he did so. He landed next to her in his dragon body, his claws already glowing. He touched her, his claws melted the ice around her, and she was free. "Are you all right?"

"I am now." She pushed herself to her feet, only to stumble and almost fall on her ass.

"No, you're not," he said, his dragon gaze locked on her head wounds. "Here, let me give you a dose of healing energy." He extended his hand to touch her head with the tip of a claw.

He never managed to make contact. The elemental surged into an attack and battered him with a tidal wave of water and chunks of ice, plus tables, chairs, tools from the kitchen, and even a goddamn refrigerator.

Despite being in his dragon form, Samuel was knocked from his feet and he twisted and twirled as the wave crashed over him.

Kylara knew she couldn't do anything with her head pounding and her body still gasping for extra oxygen, but could she use her newfound light powers to heal herself and get her powers back? She touched her head and tried to will her hands to ignite with glowing, healing energy like Sam had taught her.

In response, her head screamed at her that she would be better off sticking a dagger made of dragon claws through her temple than using a power she had only barely managed to use a few times. She'd never tried it when she had been injured, and it clearly wasn't a good idea.

Tanya and her mages proved to be far more effective.

"Freeze the water coming from the golden dragon and going back to the kitchen," the girl ordered.

Samuel was pushed up against a wall of the cafeteria, completely submerged in a huge bubble. It took almost all the water in the room to encompass his dragon form. But, as Tanya had pointed out to her mages, there was indeed a kind of umbilical cord of water connecting that which so obviously attempted to drown him to the faucets in the kitchen, where more continued to stream out to join the battle.

The mages directed their icy blasts to this umbilical cord and froze it instantly. The large bubble of water that had been wrapped around Samuel released him, splashed to the floor, and flowed over the shoes of everyone in the cafeteria.

For a moment, Kylara and everyone else in the room thought the water elemental was defeated. They looked at the water flowing over their shoes with expressions of mingled relief and distrust.

The distrust was the wiser emotion as the water elemental—reunited with the water that had been taken away from it by a bridge of ice—surged into a giant humanoid form in the middle of the room. In doing so, it knocked the feet out from under every human in the room, including the two roommates.

Kylara—whose head still pounded and healing power didn't work at full strength—found her feet in time to take a punch in her chest from the beast. She managed to remain standing this time and realized quickly that it wasn't trying to knock her over but rather to encapsulate her again.

"What do you want from me?" she screamed as she pushed out of the water and forced the elemental to let the limb collapse and flow into itself as it launched another water tentacle at her.

"My master wishes your presence," it said in a voice made of splashes and churning waves.

"Doesn't your master know it's proper to send an invitation to a dragon?" Samuel blasted the tentacle that surged toward her. He was able to channel his light to a razor-thin line that sliced through the water so the part was no longer connected to the elemental puddled on the floor.

"Mages, on your feet!" Tanya yelled but the mages—lacking healing powers like the dragons—were slow to right themselves.

The creature ignored both her friends and launched wave after wave toward Kylara.

Samuel and Kylara blocked each of them with a coordinated defence. They were both clever enough to notice that if they severed the water from the core of the creature, it splashed into pools and so they focused on this technique.

"Kylara, get out of here!" he shouted.

"I won't leave you guys!"

"It's after you, Kylara. You have to get out of here!" Tanya yelled.

"No way!"

"We can hold it off!" Samuel replied, then gestured at two students who had taken their dragon forms. "Hit it with fire!"

They complied without hesitation. It didn't drive the water elemental back at all, but any of its tendrils that it tried to send through the inferno simply evaporated. The beast roared in frustration and tried to attack her again.

Kylara, despite her injuries, took her dragon shape and prepared to fight, but she wasn't given the chance.

Samuel and Tanya did too good a job directing the other students. It was honestly amazing to watch her friends issue orders and the other students listen.

"I want alternating blasts of fire!" he instructed. He had returned to his human shape to make room for the dragons who had more potent fire breath. "Don't let that monster get through."

"Mages! Hit its back with ice. If it tries to retreat, freeze it in its tracks."

She rubbed her head, tried to shake off the concussion she'd no doubt suffered, and waited to engage.

But her assailant—and probable kidnapper—was contained. Between the alternating blasts of dragon fire and the wall of mages who froze the other side of it, the beast could neither approach nor retreat.

The water roared and whipped into a spinning waterspout. It grew steadily tighter and made the alternating attacks of fire and ice less effective. But that didn't matter. For now, it was contained. It took up less and less floor space in the cafeteria and Tanya had already cut off its retreat.

It still had a good supply of water at its command—easily enough to surround a dragon—but it had nowhere to go.

The defenders exchanged glances of both relief and victory, but these were short-lived.

Maybe there were some who didn't believe that water could break stone, but they hadn't grown up in the desert. There, it was obvious in every rock, every canyon, and every arroyo that water worked against stone. Normally, it took hundreds or thousands of years, but not always. A strong storm in the desert would easily move enormous boulders.

The water elemental more than qualified as a strong storm. It spun itself even tighter until it became a kind of spinning drill bit that created a hole in the roof.

Once that was accomplished, the water spout it had formed collapsed.

"Don't let it go to the kitchen!" Kylara shouted, not wanting it to escape.

But the creature hadn't tried to escape through the roof. It had made an entrance for an ally.

A high-pitched shrieking began to keen from the aperture. Dust and sand blew in with more force than she had ever seen, and she sensed another presence in the room.

"Tanya, watch out for the air—"

Before she could finish her warning, her friend was swept off her feet and tossed into the air. With her elaborate dress and parasol, it looked like the wind elemental didn't even have to struggle to lift her off the ground.

"Mages!" she shouted, although the wind stole the rest of her words.

The water elemental used that opportunity to surge past the distracted mages.

Kylara tried to work out why it was retreating instead of targeting her when the air elemental swung and hurled Tanya into Samuel. In a tangle of limbs, the two were scooped off the ground and thrown through a window.

"No!" She screamed, bounded out the door after them, and

took to the air on her wings. Even that caused a searing spike of pain in her head and she realized she had hurt herself badly. Her healing powers were returning, but it wouldn't be enough. Her friends were being whisked away far faster than she could follow.

"Help!" she shouted at the scene below her. The team of mages and some of the professors had contained the fire elemental. They had it surrounded, but when Amy saw Kylara and followed her gesticulating talon to her friends, she let her guard drop.

In an instant, the fire spirit swirled around itself. It extinguished in a puff of smoke and sent a lone ember into the sky that was whisked away inside the currents of the air elemental.

"I'm on it!" the mage shouted and hopped on her board to give chase, but from her vantage point, Kylara could see there was no way the mage would catch the elementals.

They had taken her friends and they were gone.

# CHAPTER THIRTY

Kylara followed Amy as the mage pursued the air elemental. They raced over the burned forest that clung to the canyon walls, but by the time they burst over the top of the canyon, Tanya, Samuel, and their captor were gone.

"Which way did they go?" she roared. There was fury in her veins. The elementals had taken her friends because of her. She was certain of this, which meant that—once again—people she cared about were in danger and yet again it was her fault.

Amy—levitating on her skateboard hundreds of feet in the air —extended her hands to the vast landscape below them. Motes of light streaked out in a dozen different directions. They zig-zagged like well-made fireworks, but after a moment of search-ing, they returned to her hands. Kylara could tell from her grimace that she had been unsuccessful.

"Goddammit." At least the mage didn't apologize. Strangely, she liked that about her.

"Is there nothing you can do?" she asked and already tasted the bitter answer as she flapped her wings to fly around her companion.

Amy shook her head, "I have no experience tracking these.

Mages have a kind of signature to their magic. It's not as pronounced as a dragon aura, but it can be tracked. But these are not mages. They're something else. Their signature—if they have one at all—is much more difficult to sense."

"They're Efreet or elementals, which means they were summoned from another dimension to do a mage's bidding."

Amy gave her an appraising glance. "How much did Amythist tell you about them?"

"Nothing. I found a little information in the library," she replied.

Her companion nodded and looked impressed. "Did you see how the air elemental snagged them?"

As they flew back, she related how the water elemental had come through the water pipes and how it had broken a hole in the ceiling for its ally to enter and snatch her friends. Before the girl had finished, Amy had begun to curse. She continued to do so now and punctuated everything the young dragon said with colorful little invectives that did not seem at all becoming of her station.

"They wanted me," Kylara finished. "I'm sure of it. The water kept coming for me and only stopped when the two people doing their best to defend me were snatched."

Her companion didn't stop swearing at this, nor did she attempt to disagree or tell her she was overreacting. Instead, she took her cell phone out and made a call.

"Yeah…hey, Kristen. It's me," Amy said into the device and gestured for Kylara to follow her to the ground. With the wind, it was hard for her to hear anything on the other end of the line, although Amy made some kind of air bubble around herself so her words could be heard more easily.

"I'm telling you there were three of these fuckers. Yes! Fire, water, and wind. Yes, it was a distraction. No, we didn't catch them. Yeah, I'll keep her safe." The mage hung up.

"Will the Steel Dragon come?" Kylara asked.

"She's tied up with the damn Council. I swear, if I knew how much her position there would cut into her free time, I would never have arrived with those dwarves to help her."

"You don't mean that."

Amy shook her head. "No, I don't. It's merely gallows humor. I learned it from Kristen's cop friends but it doesn't matter. It was a tasteless joke. What does matter is that she is sending more support as soon as possible. This school is important to her. It's important to all of us, so we'll make sure this doesn't happen again, all right?"

"It'll keep happening as long as I'm here," she said as they landed.

"What will?" Amythist asked as she approached in her dragon form. In this body, it was obvious why she was called Amythist Skyjewel. Her scales were a glorious crystalline purple color, and in the light of the setting sun, they seemed to sparkle with an internal light.

"Kylara is convinced that these attacks are focused on her." Amy explained what had happened in the cafeteria while the staff had battled the sentient fire.

"So it was only a distraction." The headmaster rubbed her chin, a strange gesture to see a dragon do. "I cannot say I refute your logic, Kylara."

"I think they took Sam and Tanya because they want me."

"But why?" the old dragon asked.

She shrugged. "I don't know! The fire elemental told me that its master had my mom. The water one also said it wanted me to come with it."

"Maybe it wasn't trying to drown you, only capture you," Amy said.

"That would make sense," Amythist agreed. "If it got water in your lungs, you would have fallen unconscious, at which point it could have simply extracted the water, put you in a bubble of air inside it, and waited for the air elemental to come and fetch you."

"But why does it want me?" she pleaded. She wanted to understand so badly. Not knowing what was going on had become extremely frustrating.

"I wish I knew, child," the headmaster said. "My first instinct is that your mother must possess some knowledge she is unwilling to part with, and that if they can capture you, they hope to use her relationship with you against her."

"Did your mom ever tell you why she wanted to live a life of isolation out in the desert?" Amy asked.

"Not really, no." Kylara sighed. "I wish she had told me something. Her most important rule was for me to never speak to other dragons."

"Why?"

"I don't know. In fact, we were arguing about that the night before all this happened," she admitted.

"Diamantine isn't exactly unknown," Amythist said. "She served on the Boston SWAT team for years. One can't have that job and not earn a few enemies."

"Do you think she was hiding from one of them?" Amy asked.

"I cannot say. All we know is that she was hiding from someone. But I also cannot fail to see that Kylara is a part of this as well. Your new powers are remarkable, child. Unique, in fact. If it were not for you and your mother's history with these things, I would be inclined to think that it was your...unprecedented nature that attracted the attention of this hidden master. As it is, I cannot be certain that is the case." Amythist exhaled a deep breath and craned her long dragon neck to watch the sun sink behind one of the mountains that surrounded the school.

"So we have no idea what to do next?" Kylara asked.

"Ah. Spoken with the impatience of youth. I know precisely what we will do next."

"Excellent." She was ready for this. Transforming into her dragon form had helped speed up her healing powers. Her headache was gone and she was ready to join Amy and her combat mages and track these monsters. "What's the plan?"

"The plan," the old dragon said and turned from Kylara to address the professors and security team, "is to lock this campus down and ensure the safety of all our students, including yourself. I want mage and dragon guards placed on every building until whoever is behind this is caught. Twenty-four-seven shifts and no one works alone, since our foe is obviously skilled at infiltration and deception."

"Do you want me to help guard, or should I go with the search team?" Kylara asked.

"You are likely the target of these attacks," Amythist said. "You said so yourself. You'll return to your dorm where you will be kept safe."

"What? That's ridiculous!" she protested.

"Sorry," Amy said with her arms folded firmly. "But she's right. It's the most logical thing to do."

"But I can help. I have three dragon powers."

"None of which saved your friends." The words were like a knife delivered to Kylara's chest.

The strength she had felt, the courage building in her chest at the prospect of going after her friends and finally finding out who had taken her mom, seeped away and left her feeling empty and vulnerable.

"Come now, child. Let's return to your room, all right?" Amythist said, took her human form, and gestured for her to do the same.

She knew she wouldn't be able to change either of these powerful women's minds. They were people who often went toe-to-toe with the Steel Dragon in arguments. She didn't stand a chance against them. The next best thing was to simply go and do it herself, but she didn't see how she would evade the teachers, let alone the combat mages.

Kylara thought of all this while Amythist led her to her dorm and chatted amicably to her.

"Ruby, be a dear and show Kylara to her room, all right?" the headmaster said and dismissed her deftly but also made sure she would be escorted in the process.

"You got it," Ruby said and walked with her down the hallway to her room.

"With dinner being...uh, interrupted would be a euphemism, I guess, we're ordering pizza."

"There's delivery out here?" she asked. The question sounded so empty compared to what was happening on the other side of these walls.

"We're sending another dorm monitor to pick it up. We ordered every pizza they had—over a hundred. It will be the biggest pizza party this school has ever seen. Everyone will have to remain in their rooms but it still should be fun."

Kylara gave her a withering look.

Ruby's ever-present smile faded like a flower left in the desert heat. "Right. They told me about Tanya. I'm sorry about that, Kylara, I truly am, but they'll get her back."

"How can you know that?" she asked as they entered her room.

"This school has a long history. Many things that should have been impossible happened on these grounds." The girl smiled kindly.

She knew that the other dragon was older than her and more experienced. More than that, she'd surely seen things that Kylara —growing up in the middle of nowhere—had never seen. But right now, she couldn't help but feel pissed at how stupid and naïve Ruby seemed.

"What about a dragon who keeps getting new powers?" she demanded, snatched a bottle of water, and gestured at her companion with it. She knew she shouldn't take out her frustration on her. She was simply doing her job, but Kylara was also confronted with the reality that if she wanted to escape, it would be Ruby who would either stop her or raise the alarm. She was confronting her jailor, in a sense. At least that was how it felt after losing her friends, her mom, and being locked up in the dorms.

"But Kylara, getting new powers is great. That's why we brought a dragon like you in, after all."

"That's not true," she said, pissed at Ruby for pigeonholing her. "I'm merely a dragon refugee. I'm only here because my mom was too embarrassed about me to let me meet any dragons and now, she's gone." She went to sip from the water bottle in her hand but stopped when she realized it was scalding hot. Surprised, she grimaced and shook the bottle, soaking her companion.

"Ruby! I—"

"You've made your point, Kylara," the girl said, both dripping wet and steaming from the inexplicably hot water. She was a Firedrake so the heat didn't bother her, but she looked hurt in other ways. "Don't leave your dorm tonight at all. Understood?"

"Ruby, I'm so sorry!"

The older girl gave her the world's tightest smile and left, shutting the door behind her.

Confused, alone, and feeling both betrayed and like she'd hurt one of the only nice people she knew, she collapsed onto her bed in a flood of tears.

She felt weak, naïve, powerless, and plain worthless. Her mom and her friends were gone because of her. Ruby was pissed because of her. Amy and Amythist had ordered her locked up. That was her fault too. Kylara had no idea what was going on. She didn't know why the water she'd held had become scalding hot or why she could make light or summon storms. In all honesty, she didn't understand what or who she was anymore.

All she knew was that she had caused harm to the people she loved and there was nothing she could do about it.

With these thoughts weighing on her like chains, she cried herself to sleep to the sounds of the other rooms all having private pizza parties.

# CHAPTER THIRTY-ONE

Kylara woke to the buzzing sound of insects. She rubbed her head and wondered where the hell the sound had come from and where the hell it had gone.

It started again, then stopped almost immediately.

Stopped.

She realized that the buzzing was not insects but her phone. They had purchased a charger during their shopping spree, so at least she could still use the device. She fumbled for it in the darkness of her room and glowered at the unlisted number on the screen. Her scowl deepened when she realized it was barely past midnight.

Her first thought was that this must be the master behind the elementals, and she steeled herself to answer. Amy and Amythist had been right. She was the target of these attacks, although she had thought the hidden master's next attempt would have been more subtle and clandestine than a phone call.

The phone rang once more before she forced herself to complete the connection. "What do you want?"

"Oh, I'm glad you're awake. Time zones never cease to confuse me."

"Kristen...Hall?" she asked hesitantly.

"In the flesh. Or, well, on the phone. I wanted to check how you're doing."

Kylara's mind vacillated between honor that the Steel Dragon was checking on her and complete confusion as to why that would be the case. She finally said, "We were attacked again today."

"I heard and that's why I'm calling. It was my idea for you to attend the Lumos School. I told myself it would be safe for you there, but...well, I had ulterior motives. I wanted an outsider at the school and you fit the part."

"That's okay..." she said hesitantly, not sure what her role was in this conversation.

"It's truly not," Kristen replied and thus eliminated "comfort the most powerful being on the planet" from the possible purpose of this call. "I risked your life by sending you there. It was foolish to think that whatever took your mother wouldn't come for you. And it was even more foolish to put you somewhere that was only a few hundred miles away from where she was taken. I endangered your life and the lives of your classmates because I tried to win the culture war."

"Well...the culture here does suck," Kylara said. "The dragons treat my roommate like crap simply because she doesn't have any special powers."

"I heard about that too," Kristen said. "About how you developed light powers?"

"Yes, ma'am."

"You should be very proud of yourself, Kylara. You've already gone well beyond my expectations and it hasn't even been a whole semester yet."

"Thank you, ma'am."

"Kylara, are you all right? You know we will rescue the two students who were taken. It's our top priority."

"Maybe it would make more sense to simply offer to trade me for them and my mom," she suggested despondently.

"What? Kylara, no way! Negotiating with monsters like these is never an option."

"But this is all my fault." She began to cry again. "My mom kept me hidden for my entire life because I'm some kind of freak. I couldn't even respect her rules, and when I broke them, she paid the price, not me. If I had only listened to her, I would never have put everyone in danger."

"Hey, now, I understand how you feel but you must let go of the guilt. Believe me when I say that."

"How can I let go of it when it's all my fault?" Kylara raged into the receiver.

"It's not your fault. You're a victim in this. The fault lies with the asshole who took your mom and your friends."

"But they took them because of me."

"I know, and now, my team will rescue them for you. One of the things I struggled with the most was accepting help, Kylara. You have to let us help you."

"But *I* can help."

"You can't do anything while you're wracked with guilt about what happened. If whoever took your friends is really after you—"

"Of course they are," she interjected.

"If they have targeted you—and I admit it seems very likely—then you rushing off is exactly what they want. They want you, for some reason, and the more eaten up by guilt and doubt you are when they find you, the better for them. Guilt is a poison, Kylara. You have to let it go."

"I can't simply pretend nothing happened. I can't go to class tomorrow while my friends are out there in danger."

"I agree," the Steel Dragon said and surprised her completely.

"You do?"

"Yes. I do. You being at that school right now is not safe—not for you and not for the other students or the professors. I don't want you there, blaming yourself for this mess."

"But I thought you said I couldn't help."

"I want you to come to my base in Detroit. It's not perfectly defended, of course—nothing can be—but I assure you we have tighter security here than at the school. It appears that it would ruin the architecture of the building to mount any more anti-aircraft weapons on the roofs." The young dragon could almost hear Kristen shrug. "Amy will have a portal to transport you in the morning, all right?"

"No way! I won't abandon my friends." She couldn't believe that this was what she wanted to do. The woman had practically made a name for herself by rushing into situations and now, she told her to retreat?

"It's not abandoning them. Think about it, Kylara. It's making a smart choice. If you are the target, you being in Detroit makes you harder to capture. That will give my team the breathing space they need to catch whoever is behind this."

"I already started going to this school while my mom was out there," she fumed. "You can't expect me to run away again while my friends are missing too."

"I don't expect anything of you, Kylara. Consider this an order. You are to stay in your room until Amy comes for you. Is that clear?"

"As clear as diamonds," she snapped and hung up on the Steel Dragon.

She regretted doing so almost immediately. It was never particularly prudent to hang up on someone more powerful than oneself, especially when that person was in charge of dragons and mages and could turn themselves to steel.

Kylara tried to call the number back but it didn't go through. She rubbed her face, uncomfortable with what she had done. Maybe Kristen was right and the guilt was getting to her. She shouldn't have reacted the way she did and should have talked to

Amy instead. After all, the mage could create portals that let her travel anywhere in the world. Being in another city wasn't hours away but only moments, she reminded herself.

Her phone—still in her hand—buzzed and she pressed the answer button before she checked who was calling. She knew it was probably Kristen, ready to give her the earful she deserved.

"Hello, Kylara Diamantine." The voice belonged to a woman who sounded older than the Steel Dragon and more controlled in the way she spoke.

Kylara yanked the phone away from her face. She hadn't so much as looked at the number but she did so now and realized with sinking dread that this was one her phone could identify. Whoever was speaking, they used Tanya's phone.

"Who is this and what do you want?"

"I'm the person holding your little dragon friends prisoner," the woman said. "And if you ever want to see them alive again, you will do exactly as I say."

# CHAPTER THIRTY-TWO

"You're crazy if you think I'll listen to you," Kylara said into the phone. "How can you expect me to believe my friends are even alive?" She hated saying it aloud but there it was. There was zero evidence to support the idea that her mom was alive. The only clue she had was the word of some type of demon monster from another dimension. There was little reason to think her friends had fared any better, especially not with Kristen's warning going through her head.

"But of course. Dearie!" the woman yelled to someone who must be in the same room as her. "How do I set the speaker-phone? Oh, there it is." The quality of sound coming through the device changed. "Say something for your friend."

"Ky, hang up and go get help! This lady is crazy, Ky. She's crazy."

The sound changed again and she assumed the caller had turned speakerphone off.

"So? I'll admit that she sounded a little deranged but that was the voice of your friend, was it not?"

"Let them go and I'll do what you say," she said.

"No, no, no, Kylara, you misunderstand. This is not a negotiation and it's not a conversation. This is me talking to you only long enough for you to accept that you will do exactly as I say if you want the people you love to live."

Kylara took a deep breath and tried to ignore the fact that what she planned to say next might hurt her friends. Still, she had to try. "They're not my friends. To be frank, they're merely dragons I've found useful. Do whatever you want to them. It doesn't matter to me."

The woman laughed so loudly it came out distorted on the phone. "Oh, Kylara, you just told me you'd do whatever I say if I let them go. You are as dense as the scales of that dragon bitch who snatched you away from your family and slaughtered your parents."

She was speechless, stunned by these words. Snatched away from her family? Hester Diamantine was her family. "Are you talking about my mom, Diamantine? She's alive, then?" She couldn't keep the concern out of her voice. For as long as she could recall, her mom had been her life. It hadn't always been stress-free, but she had always cared for her, always made her stronger, and always been there for her. And now, this woman voiced the unthinkable.

"Do you honestly believe that dragon is your mother?" The caller laughed. "How can you think that? You two look nothing alike. She has her blonde hair and yours is dark like your mother's. I wonder if Hester even noticed when she killed your mother and father how much you look like them. I guess it must have been easy to keep you in the dark out there in the desert."

"You're lying," she said. "You're merely a crazy mage who got on the wrong side of Dragon SWAT. My mom told me she made mistakes. She told me about people like you too. I was a fool to not believe her."

"She told you about me? Did she truly? And what did she say about your mother? Did she say how she caught up to her in a fishing shack? Did she explain how hard your father fought and how he gave her that scar on her hand?"

Kylara didn't know what to say. Her mom had never explained where the burned hand had come from.

"Did she tell you how your real mother either drowned or froze to death? I was too late to know which one. By the time I found her and your father, they were both frozen solid. I had hoped to find you but you were gone. I feared you were dead for so many years. I had nothing to hope for, so I set my mind on revenge. What a surprise it was to discover that my niece was still alive. You give me meaning again, Kylara, now that vengeance is so close to being served."

"You...you're lying. You're not my aunt."

"I am your aunt. I even have a matching pendant. I still remember when your mother and I got them. We were still so young then, sisters without care—except a longing for freedom. How long ago that was. I thought everything was lost but now, I have you."

"You're making this up. I'm a...a dragon like my mom. I even have her diamond scales."

"I'm not making any of this up, Kylara and you know I'm not. Think about it. I've seen what you can do through my elementals. Summon a storm? Make light? Are those things your classmates are learning in school?"

"You can't prove any of this."

"Oh, but I can. I truly can. Come to me and I'll prove it to you. I'll show you my pendant, I'll show you the fishing shack—or what's left of it, anyway—and I'll show you who you truly are."

"I...I can't."

"Yes, you can, and if you want to see the bitch who stole you from your family alive, you'll do exactly as I say. You will leave and fly north. Once you're a few hundred miles away, you will enter a gas station and find a map, then come to these exact coordinates." She gave Kylara some numbers which she scrambled to write down.

"You will not look up the location on any device. You will tell no one or the dragon bitch who stole you will die and her blood will be on your hands. I have an air elemental there, watching the academy even now. One misstep and the news will reach me far sooner than any dragon ever could. You will come to these coordinates alone and immediately, and then everything will be clear."

# CHAPTER THIRTY-THREE

The woman hung up.

Kylara knew she had to go. She had been left with no choice in the matter but would have done so anyway to save her friends and her mother. Besides, she would have gone simply to find out who she was. The woman had struck a nerve and stirred up so many questions.

She almost wished it felt like a choice, but it didn't. It was her only option. She had to save the woman who raised her—her mom, she told herself firmly. The woman on the phone had to be lying, right? She also had to save her only friends so she would go and she would go alone. If the woman said she had an air elemental watching the academy, she saw no reason to doubt her. She had already proven her ability to infiltrate the campus with powerful magic elementals. It wasn't a stretch at all to think one still remained.

After a deep breath, she looked at the coordinates she'd written down. She didn't know longitude and latitude coordinates offhand, but these looked like they were extremely far to the north. In Canada, most likely, but that would come later. The beginning of this mission would be the most difficult part.

Somehow, she had to get off campus and past a team of combat mages and a group of extremely powerful dragons without being seen.

It didn't seem possible, but it also felt impossible to simply ignore what this woman had told her. The problem was that her mom had never been particularly forthcoming with details of her past. She had never talked about her father and had never explained why she wasn't supposed to leave their land. Ky knew that Hester was her mother. She had raised her, cared for her, and taught her to survive. They even had the same scales in their dragon form.

And yet, she couldn't dismiss everything the woman had said. Why bring up the pendant? Why mention a fishing shack in the north? If she wanted to do something to Kylara besides tell her about her past, she'd had all the opportunity she needed. The wind elemental could have taken her and the water elemental could have drowned her. That didn't mean she trusted the stranger, but it was relevant.

It meant enough to the young dragon that she wanted to know more. And that meant sneaking off campus.

Kylara turned her light off and let her eyes adjust to the dark before she eased her window open and peeked outside. A dragon flew overhead and scanned the green spaces between the buildings. Another perched atop a neighboring building. She knew that others would be perched on every roof. And there were Amy's mages to consider. They would have powers and methods she could only guess at, and every one of them would be out and actively looking for anyone moving across the grounds when they shouldn't be.

While she considered what to do, another dragon flew overhead and confirmed that her escape would not be easy.

With a grimace, she withdrew her head and this time, stood to open her door quietly and look down the hallway. It was empty so she braced herself, wrote a note explaining that she was going to go make things right, and left her room.

She hurried down the corridor and moved as quickly as she could while she kept as quiet as possible. Most of the rooms were silent—it was after midnight, after all—although she did hear a few voices of girls still up, gossiping, complaining about how bad the pizza was, asking for more pizza, and any number of other conversations.

When she reached a side door, she tucked herself into the alcove leading to it barely in time as a door opened in the hallway. Three agonizing minutes and a toilet flush later, the sound of a door clicking shut told her it was her time to move. She stepped outside and hurried out of the light illuminating the door.

Kylara slid against a wall of the building that was out of the light without any dragon sounding the alarm. For all she knew, the mages might be secretly conversing about her pathetic escape attempt right now, but she had no reason to think that if someone had seen her, she wouldn't immediately be intercepted and returned to her room.

Cautiously, she crept along the side of the building toward the corner closest to the burned remains of the forest the fire monster had laid waste to. It would require a long run to reach cover, but it seemed like her best option.

Before she could come anywhere close to the corner, however, a dragon swooped into the airspace above her. It circled slowly and its flight path would soon take it directly over her. She flattened herself against the wall and leaned against a pipe that shunted rainwater away from the building, knowing perfectly well that she was as good as caught.

Dragons could see in almost perfect darkness. There was no way the one Amythist had selected for guard duty in the middle of the night didn't have keen night vision. She was done. It was only a matter of how many seconds were left before she was caught.

Kylara had no idea what to do. Running was not an option. She was too far from cover and dragon eyes were too sharp. If she ran and somehow managed to avoid the dragon flying toward her—which was impossible, she decided—one of the others would surely see her.

A little desperately, she tried to sink into the tiny shadow the drainage pipe provided. She knew it wouldn't work. It couldn't work, but maybe, just maybe, if she stood perfectly still, the dragon wouldn't notice.

The young student willed it to be so with every fiber of her being. Her inner magic churned within her, tried to help, and failed.

A moment later, however, the shadow from the pipes seemed to expand. Like the first drops of water that clung together in the sand at the start of a desert storm, rivulets of shadow crept out from the darkness behind the pipe and enveloped her.

For the briefest of moments, she began to panic, but she fought the urge as the tendrils of darkness eclipsed her completely. This didn't feel like an attack. When Karl Midnight struck with his tendrils of darkness, she could feel his malice. This felt like...well, it felt like magic.

The dragon flew overhead. If it noticed that a section of shadow was a little darker and more enveloping than it was elsewhere, it didn't react.

But hugging the wall wouldn't get her out of there. She needed to move.

Kylara stepped away from the wall and willed herself to stay hidden, and the shadow remained with her. She could see out of it fine but as she moved, it expanded before her as the spot on the wall where she had been hiding was reabsorbed into the glob of dark that now kept pace with her.

It was dark powers, she was sure of it because it looked and behaved exactly like Karl Midnight's powers did. Tendrils of dark energy—like liquid shadow or solid ink—seeped from her fingernails and surrounded her to blend her into the night.

She honestly had no idea how this was possible as she had never had dark powers. In fact, she hadn't even known that powers like those existed until recently. She knew the Masked One had shadow powers, but there were no descriptions of him making ropes of shadow or darkness, a power that—if he had possessed it—he would have undoubtedly used against the Steel Dragon in their infamous final battle.

But the time to find answers was later. She had to fly a hundred miles before she could even confirm where she was going.

In the meantime, she would use these powers, exactly like she had the others that had come to her. For now, she would use them to escape.

Slowly and quietly, she adjusted her course toward the burned forest. She no longer hugged the wall of the building—an obvious place for someone to be in mid-escape—but meandered through the middle of the field.

The tendrils of dark energy instinctively searched out the darkest patches of the field, so she let them guide her on a random course as she proceeded to her target location. She didn't know enough about the powers to know what it would look like if she stepped into a pool of light, but she did know that she had seen Karl Midnight's darkness under a tree. That had been during the day but still, caution now might cost her a few moments, while getting caught might cost her the lives of the only people she cared about.

Kylara finally reached the woods. It was easier to move there. The blackened trunks of trees provided easy cover for her to sneak between them. The dark magic seemed to work even better out there and expanded to encompass more of the area around her.

She thought she was in the clear when she reached the part of the forest that grew up the side of the mountain, but a glowing orb of light appeared in the hands of a mage she hadn't seen.

"Who goes there?" The man had swirls tattooed on his forehead that looked rather frightening in the harsh glare of his ball of light. "I heard you break a branch and I've already alerted the others. So come out now and the consequences won't be as dire."

The young dragon hesitated, uncertain as to what to do. The forest floor hadn't been burned there, which meant it was littered with branches, dried oak leaves, and pinecones. If she moved, she'd be heard. She briefly considered trying to knock the mage out but decided against it. For one thing, she didn't know enough about their powers to be sure she'd be successful. And besides, she didn't want to start hurting people simply because a mysterious mage had told her to come when she called.

In the next moment, her decision about what to do was made for her.

A great gust of wind toppled a nearby tree and almost crushed the mage. He managed to stop it with a burst of magic that let him kick through the trunk.

"Air elemental!" he yelled, his voice unnaturally loud and augmented by magic.

"Go," the wind whispered in Kylara's ear as it kicked up leaves, branches, and pine needles and threw them at the guardian, who knocked them away with a blast of his wind.

She wasted no time. The noise from the being masked the sound of her footsteps as she raced up the mountainside and she didn't slow until she reached the top.

When she looked back, three mages were engaged in a battle with a creature that even in the moonlight, was practically invisible. At night, it looked like they simply hurled spells at branches and leaves.

Her instinct was to help, but there was nothing she could do if she wanted to escape. She could see more mages coming. They would either overpower the elemental and capture it—she didn't know if they even could be captured—or it would retreat.

Either way, this was her only chance to save her friends.

Kylara transformed into her dragon form, built a web of darkness around her, and leapt into the night before she swooped down the other side of the mountain and veered north.

After a hundred miles or so, she stopped and checked a road atlas in a gas station. The attendant seemed more concerned that she was walking over his freshly mopped floor than the fact that she was a young woman alone in the middle of the night. She took that to mean that if her disappearance had been discovered, the dragons were not using human networks to find her. If they had, this guy would surely have received some type of alert on his phone.

Hoping she was in the clear and that she hadn't wasted too much time, she continued north toward what appeared to be a lake nestled between the mountains in the far north of Canada.

It would be a long and lonely trip.

# CHAPTER THIRTY-FOUR

Kylara flew all through the night and into the morning. She stopped and slept when she neared a city. It wasn't big but she still didn't want to risk being seen. She slept through the day, tracked a herd of deer at dusk in her human form, then transformed and killed and ate in her dragon body. After her time at the school, the dragon-fire-roasted meat didn't taste as good as it once had but at the same time, there was something almost nostalgic about hunting and killing her food. She and her mom had done it hundreds of times.

As dusk fell, she took to the sky again. She flew over Nebraska, South Dakota, the northwest corner of Minnesota, and into Canada. Fortunately, the location she had been given hadn't been beyond the Rocky Mountains. Given the late fall weather, she didn't know if she would have been able to make it over those.

As she traveled, she thought about the task ahead of her and the abilities she now had to face it with. It was bizarre that she had multiple powers. She knew Amythist had learned new powers, as had the Steel Dragon, but no one else had. No one but

Kylara. And while they had learned their powers through instruction by the pixies, she had developed hers at random.

Except it wasn't haphazard, was it? It didn't feel random but rather like some kind of natural progression, which made no sense when she thought about it.

She had diamond scales like her mom. Was Hester her mother? Even thinking the word sent her mind into a spiral of confusion if she let it. Now, she also had light powers, storm powers, and most recently, dark powers. Plus, there was the night with Ruby when the bottle of water in her hand had somehow heated to near scalding.

All the powers belonged to dragons she had recently met. But there was an even more clear link than that. Kylara had met many new dragons. She had met some with poison claws, others that could launch ice crystals, dragons who could turn parts of themselves to stone or shoot metal barbs from their tails and she didn't have any of those powers. No, all her new powers came from dragons who had used them on her.

Samuel had used his light powers to heal her. Tempest had battled her in class and struck her with lightning. Midnight had used his tendrils of darkness against her when she'd saved Tanya and in class. Even the bottle of water getting hot could be explained in the same way. When she had first met Ruby, the dragon's hands had been hot from using her powers to dry her nails.

It seemed logical that she could somehow absorb powers that were used against her. One or two might have been a coincidence, but four? There was no way any of them could be a random occurrence. She must have somehow reacted to these powers being used on her.

But what did that mean? Her mom had told her many stories about apprehending dragons with odd powers. She had never said anything about a dragon whose powers could change, much less evolve like this. No one in the school had ever mentioned anything like that either. Tanya attended the school to learn new abilities. Surely, if other dragons knew that some of their kind could absorb different powers, the professors would have sought them out if their goal was to teach dragons how to gain such powers.

Kristen and Amythist had learned new abilities, she reminded herself, but her situation seemed very different than theirs.

As she flew farther north, she turned these questions about what she could do over in her head repeatedly.

Still, that wasn't the only line of thought she pursued as she continued toward a rendezvous with the woman who claimed to be her family.

Her aunt, she had said. A mage claimed to be her aunt.

Not only that, she insisted that Hester Diamantine wasn't her mother at all but the murderer of her parents. A murderer who had then adopted her and raised her as her own and...somehow turned her into a dragon?

It made no sense. In fact, none of it made sense.

Kylara was a dragon. She had wings and scales and a tail and she could breathe fire. She had her mother's dragon speed and strength and now had other powers from other dragons. This was all proven fact and rooted in a non-negotiable reality.

But then why did this woman claim to be her aunt? If she had an ulterior motive to hurt her or her mom, why invent such a glaringly impossible story? Why not tell her something more plausible?

Because there certainly were gaps in her past. Her mom never talked about her father and had no photographs of him. No stories had slipped out when Hester was tired or allowed herself to get a little drunk with a bottle of wine. From a young age, she had told herself that the reason her mom clammed up anytime she asked about her dad was because the topic made her sad.

But was there any evidence of that?

Hester Diamantine never became emotional when she had

asked about her father. She simply changed the subject without elaboration or quietly refused to answer any of the questions. Could it be because she simply didn't know her dad? As the young dragon grew older, she came up with the theory that maybe her dad had gotten her mom pregnant and either run off or been killed. She had told her that her dad was dead. That was the only thing she ever said about him.

Would this woman have answers for her? Would she be able to explain not only her past but what was going on with her body? Was it possible for a mage to know how a dragon was able to absorb the powers of other dragons? After all, mages learned new magic abilities. Did her so-called aunt know what she was capable of? Was it those very capabilities that had made her mother keep her hidden for so long?

Kylara's biggest fear was that the woman would have answers that made sense and she wouldn't like them.

It was enough to make her want to turn back and forget about the whole thing.

But she couldn't do that, of course. Not with Tanya in the woman's clutches. Her roommate was the first friend she had ever had. She had taken her under her wing despite the obvious risk—for a dragon whose reputation was already in question—of befriending an orphan from the desert. The smart thing for her would have been to ignore her or better yet, treat her like a pariah and make friends with the rest of the student body. The girl had never given any indication that she ever even considered that, though. Instead, she saw a person in need and offered to help. For the sake of their genuine friendship, she couldn't let her come to any harm.

And there was Samuel Lumos to think about. While her loyalty to Tanya was simple and unquestionable, her relationship with Sam was more complicated. When she had first seen him, she had been desperately curious, but when he'd pursued her, those feelings had evaporated into storm clouds of distrust.

When she discovered who he was at school, she had thought him arrogant and aloof, but she no longer felt that way.

The golden dragon had consistently come to her aid. He had stepped in to help her any time she'd needed it and seemed like he would have done the same for Tanya if Kylara hadn't been there, not because he liked her but because he was simply a decent man. Dragon. And it didn't hurt that his golden hair was perfect and that it was hard to tell what was more attractive, his human or his dragon form.

Now, both were in trouble simply because they had fought against the water elemental that had tried to take Kylara. She had to save them and her mom.

And find out if there was any truth to the mage's version of her past.

She scowled when she considered the implications. If she messed up, she would likely have to battle at least three elementals in a frigid northern wasteland where no one would be able to hear her screams.

No matter which train of thought she pursued, one thing was clear. This trip would be trouble.

# CHAPTER THIRTY-FIVE

On the dawn of the third day, Kylara finally reached the coordinates she had been given. Despite the long journey, she felt fine and even well-rested. She had hunted along the way to stay fed. That, plus sleeping during the day and doing little else besides flying and mulling over her situation meant she felt ready for anything.

It wasn't much of a comfort that anything could be waiting for her and she had no insight to enable her to prepare.

Still, she was glad to be there—or proud, at least. She would save her friends and her mom and would confront this woman who claimed to know something of her past. Her mind was made up. She would do these things or die trying. That was the kind of person Hester had raised her to be.

Her only regret was the chaos that no doubt consumed the school in her absence. She hoped the air elemental had ceased its attack once she left, but she couldn't know for sure. In an effort to reassure herself, she focused on what seemed probable—that by leaving she was keeping the school safe. With her gone, the mage's elementals would leave too. Of course, that might simply be wishful thinking.

She didn't think it was because she knew she was central to all this and that leaving had been the right decision. That aside, she hoped Ruby had found her note and shared it with Amythist and Amy so at least no one would think she was kidnapped.

All these thoughts battled for dominance when what she needed to do was clear her mind.

The coordinates seemed to be centered on a lake surrounded by mountains and she looked at the snow-blanketed landscape below her. She circled the shore in search of a house, a shack, a message in the snow, or anything to provide a clue. There wasn't much to see, though.

Kylara was about to widen her search to the mountainsides when something in the center of the lake caught her eye. At first, she thought the dark-blue spot in the center of the frozen lake was simply a small area devoid of ice or that it had yet to freeze. But as she flew toward it, she realized it was a hole in the lake itself.

Tense and wary, she flew in tight circles above it, transformed into her human form, and landed as gently as she could on the ice next to this impossibility.

She approached the hole and stepped carefully on the ice at first, not being familiar with it and quite concerned about falling through. But when she reached the edge, she saw that her concern was unwarranted.

It existed because the sides of it were solid ice. Her first thought was that it was like a great frozen tornado had drilled into the depths to clear the water away and freeze it out of the cavity it created. It was a bizarre and impossible sight, made stranger still by the stairs that seemed to be carved into the icy wall. It was hard to see into the gloom at the bottom of the frozen pit, but she thought she could make something out down there. A structure, she decided after she'd peered at it long and hard. A house had been built at the bottom of a lake.

Kylara swallowed, steeled herself, and proceeded down the

frozen steps. As she descended, the light changed from the harsh white of sunlight reflecting off the snow to the softer blue of the sun shining through the water.

The ice was thick and lined with cracks that looked like they had been broken and refrozen many times. She had the sense that this pit of ice had been there for some time—years, most likely. Powerful magic had no doubt been used in its creation.

She wondered if the entire lake was frozen solid. It would make the most sense in that if there was a crack in the walls that framed this inverted spiral ice staircase, no frigid water would flow in, but she saw that this was not the case.

Something on the other side of the ice watched as her she descended the frozen steps. It was large. She could tell that much from the way it displaced the water it moved through, but she could see little else. Through the less than transparent ice, she saw snatches of movement and flurries of bubbles, but no fins, no flippers, no spines or shells, and nothing else to give the impression that it was an animal or a dragon.

No, it was most likely an elemental, Kylara realized. It was also probably responsible for the frozen lake, she thought at first, although she also toyed with the idea that it might be waiting there for some poor hapless soul to explore this obvious death trap so it could consume them or drown them or whatever elementals wished to do.

The being didn't attack, though. It merely followed her as she proceeded down the steps. Finally, she reached the bottom of the lake. The ground was covered in a light dusting of snow that was thicker near the walls.

At the center of the frozen circle of the vertical tube was a house. Well, house might be a generous term. It had a roof and walls but it was little more than a shack. Worse, the wood was blackened by fire.

To think that it had been burned like her home in New Mexico filled her with a flood of pain and discomfort.

Still, Kylara approached it and stepped inside. It seemed logical that it hadn't always been at the bottom of a pit in a frozen lake. From the look of it, she decided, it had once been a type of glorified fishing shack that had been erected on either the surface of the frozen lake or the shore. It appeared to have been destroyed in a fire and somehow reassembled down there. Pieces of wood were held together not with nails or notches in places but a clay-like substance. Compared to the burned wood, the gunk that held it together looked relatively fresh.

It was hard to tell much about the structure. The fire had almost burned the wood to nothing, so any things inside were long gone, consumed by the blaze or eaten by rot.

Kylara pushed around a corner and found one thing of interest.

It was a type of canoe that looked like it could double as a sled, but in its center was a bassinet carved of wood and lined with blankets and what she assumed were seal pelts.

She had never seen anything like it before and had never even heard of such a thing. Even thinking about a canoe bassinet sled was frankly ridiculous, yet she couldn't help but feel an overwhelming sense of familiarity with it.

For a long time, she stared at it, although she made no attempt to approach or look away. She wondered again why she was there. Why had the mage brought her to this museum to lives lost at the bottom of a frozen lake? And why did she sense that—even from across the room—she could feel the seal fur and sense the gentle rock of the bassinet as it was dragged across the snow?

"It was yours, of course."

Startled, she whirled to see...herself. Her eyes narrowed and searched out the differences. The woman was much older than her but she had the same dark eyes, dark hair, and coppery skin. She had the same strong nose and big eyes. It was like looking into her future, or—if the mage could be believed—her dead mother's past.

# CHAPTER THIRTY-SIX

"That's where you once slept. In fact…" The woman who looked like Kylara chuckled softly. "It was the only place you would sleep. Your mother used to chide your father for doing too good a job in making it. You would never sleep anywhere else."

She wore layers and layers of furs. The young dragon thought her pants might be made of deer or elk leather. Her boots were handmade and appeared to be dense, shining seal fur. Over it all, she wore a white fur coat that might have been a polar bear once or a dozen foxes. She got the sense that this woman had learned to make all this herself. There was a refinement to some of the less worn garments, but it all spoke of someone who had survived on the land for a long time.

"You're lying," she said. The words were weak on her tongue and lacked force and substance. They still robbed her of the strength she had felt when she first saw this frozen lake.

"I'm not, Kylara. In fact, I'm the first person who will tell you the truth."

"I don't even know your name."

"I had always hoped to be your Aunt Cassandra. Now that you're here, it would honor me if you called me that." The mage held her arms out and beckoned her in for a hug. It felt bizarre for this woman who kidnapped her friends and mom to expect one while inside a burnt fishing shack at the bottom of a frozen lake haunted by a water elemental.

It was hard to form words, but she tried as she shook her head firmly. "You can't simply claim all this. You have nothing to prove what you're saying—nothing."

Cassandra lowered her arms slowly and brought a hand to her chest. Instinctively, the young dragon readied herself to defend against an attack—she was good enough at aikido that she had little doubt she could break her arm—but instead, the woman took something out of her shirt.

"Our father—that's your grandfather—made these for me, your mother, and our sisters." She held a perfect replica of the silver and turquoise pendant the girl always wore around her neck. Even the stone looked like it had been cut from the same piece of rock.

"That doesn't prove anything. There could be a hundred of those. You could have bought them or seen them in a photo or...or..."

"Of course, it proves nothing, not by itself," Cassandra agreed and took a slow step forward with the pendant outstretched. "But my father did make these. Tell me, at that school, how were your dragon aura abilities? Did they develop as much as your other skills?"

"That's none of your business." Kylara took a step back.

"They didn't develop because the pendant is enchanted to interfere with dragon aura abilities. He gave them to us once he realized we had the gift and made sure the enchantment was strong before we all fled the United States to get to the relative safety of Canada.

"We were all mages, you see, the whole family. And back then, before the Steel Dragon came along and tried to stand up for us and defeat that pointless group of terrorist mages, being a mage meant servitude to a dragon or an existence on the run.

"Or death, I suppose." Cassandra sighed and gestured at the burnt wood of the shack.

"Is that why you brought me here? Because you wanted to take revenge and kill me at the bottom of this lake?"

"No! Kylara, I would never hurt you. Not more than I have for being too weak. When you were a baby, they came for your parents. The dragons did. I was out hunting," The woman clenched her teeth and shook her head. "I didn't need to be out hunting. We had food but your mom wanted something fresh and…" She shook her head again. "I returned too late. By the time I got here, our home for the winter had become their final resting place. I searched for any signs of survivors and found the bodies of our family, all burned or frozen in the ice, but I never found my niece. It took everything I had to reconstruct the shack. I wouldn't have been able to do it without the help of the water elemental you saw during your descent."

"The dragons who hurt these mages…was my mom with them?"

"Your mother was a mage, Kylara. But to answer your question, yes, the woman who raised you—Hester Diamantine—was there."

"But why?"

"For no reason other than the fact that we were mages and did not wish to serve dragons. We tried to build a life on our own here. Nothing more and nothing less. We weren't fomenting rebellion. Lord knows your father wanted to join the techno-mages, but your mother and I were strongly opposed to that and he respected our opinion. Simply existing outside of dragon control made us a threat, so a team was sent to eliminate us. Diamantine is the last dragon still alive from that team."

Kylara's heart jumped into her throat at the admission that

her mother was still alive. "What happened to the others? My... that is, Diamantine said they were all killed."

"That is because I killed them. Vengeance for the loss of my sister and my niece was all that fueled me. Tracking and slitting Diamantine's diamond-encrusted throat is all I've dreamt about for years. I'm not proud of this, Kylara. I was a bitter, hate-filled woman but I won't lie to you. Not like she did and not like those dragons who tried to keep you locked in their precious academy. It wasn't until I finally found her that I learned you were alive. Your existence gives me a reason to live for something besides vengeance, Kylara."

"You burned my home to the ground."

"I know." Cassandra hung her head in shame. "And if I'd known then that it was the home of my niece and not only hers, I never would have sent that fire spirit there."

"But...none of this can be true."

"Kylara, you need only look at our faces to see it's true. You look exactly like your mother, who looked exactly like me."

"But I'm not a mage, I'm a dragon. I flew here on wings. I have dragon strength and speed. In my dragon body, I have diamond scales identical to my mother's."

The woman nodded. "All of this is true, of course, and it is exceptionally curious. I don't doubt that you are gifted. I have seen you through the eyes of the spirits I sent to bring you to me. Not only do you have diamond scales, but you have light and storm powers as well. That's truly exceptional. For a dragon, anyway."

"They're dragon powers. No mage had diamond scales."

Cassandra shook her head slowly as if she didn't want to correct her misconceptions but knew she must. "I will not lie to you and say that I understand exactly what is happening inside you. I only know that you are the person who grew up from the baby I loved like my own. That baby was the daughter of a powerful mage who had many different kinds of power. It's an acknowledged fact that all mages can learn more powers as they go along."

"But dragons can too," she protested.

"Sure they can. There are what? Two famous examples? The Steel Dragon and the headmaster of your school. Compare those two with the vast majority of mages who can usually learn at least a few kinds of magic if not some level of control for almost all of them."

"No... No, this can't be," Kylara muttered and shook her head vehemently in an attempt to push out the narrative that her aunt —not her aunt!—tried to put into her head.

The problem was that she could no longer deny that it had begun to make sense. Despite the persistent voice within that insisted it didn't, she had also begun to believe it.

## CHAPTER THIRTY-SEVEN

"Come with me, Kylara. There's so much more I need to show you and tell you. I want to teach you everything there is to know about your family—our family."

"Even if you are my...my aunt, I want nothing to do with you. You took my friends and my...that is...the woman who raised me...and used them as hostages." She scowled when she heard her lack of force and conviction. It was all too much to understand but was it so outlandish? Looking at Cassandra was like looking into a mirror that showed her the future. But even if they were related, the woman had kidnapped her friends.

The mage sighed. "Your friends are nearby. Would you like to see them?"

"They're not hurt?"

"They had a few bruises and scrapes but nothing that their dragon powers couldn't make short work of," the woman explained. "Follow me and I'll take you to them."

Kylara merely nodded as she didn't trust her voice to not crack. She was surprised when rather than exiting the shack, her guide led her deeper into it. In a corner at the back, she muttered something above the floor and revealed a hidden passage that led even deeper beneath the lake bed.

"Your mom designed this passage," Cassandra said gently. "She even had it enchanted so it went to the house when it was still on the top of the frozen lake. No one could make magic quite as beautiful as she could. When the dragons came, they attacked too quickly and she didn't have time to flee here and escape."

"You can't keep making these claims and expect me to accept them!" She allowed a brittle edge into her voice.

"What more evidence do you need, Kylara?" Cassandra snapped. "We have the same face. The same pendant. Take yours off and use your dragon aura to sense if I'm telling the truth."

"I won't let you trick me," she said, her tone sharp and heated. "Many dragons don't have perfect control of their aura. I won't give you all I have left of the woman who raised me. You still haven't explained how I'm a dragon. You still haven't explained how any of this can be true."

"And Diamantine explained all that?" The mage's words were laced with venom. "Did that dragon bitch say anything about your father, or that pendant, or why she kept you hidden for your entire life? Did she tell you anything at all?"

"She told me how to fight," Kylara retorted and her hands began to glow with light energy. It had not escaped her notice that Cassandra had not mentioned her having dark powers earlier. Was it possible the air elemental hadn't seen them? "She told me to respect mages and that justice was a difficult dish to serve. She told me she loved me every damn day."

The woman took a long, slow, deep breath, held it in, then released it slowly. "It sounds as if...as if Diamantine saw her errors, even if was far too late for your mother."

"Let me talk to her. Let me see her so we can all talk about this together," she pleaded.

Cassandra shook her head. "It would be my word against hers. And besides, there is a better way." The mage exited the shack and left the tunnel wide open as she went outside to sit cross-legged at the bottom of the icy shaft. "I know of only one way to give you the proof you desire, but it will take a minute or so. Please, give me a little more time to make things clear to you."

"What are you talking about now?" she asked as she followed her outside. She didn't want to believe her, not at all, but she couldn't help but want to know the answers to questions she'd had for her entire life—questions her mom had always refused to answer.

"Emotionally driven events leave an impact on a place," the mage explained. "Remnants of their energy lingers long after the event. A talented mage can draw on that energy and bring it to life. The more powerful the event, the longer the traces will linger."

The ground beneath her rumbled and shook and suddenly, they rocketed upward through the icy shaft and past the water elemental that swam in the lake beyond the wall. Kylara slipped and landed on her ass when they settled on a piece of ice that levitated above the lake.

A pillar of mist billowed directly above where the house now stood. It stretched higher and expanded over the lake in tendrils. Mostly, it clung to the surface but here and there, it looked as if there was something within it, an area it couldn't fill even though there was nothing there.

The vapor slowed and what might have been described as an absence of mist in the shape of a house took its place. It was the silhouette of the fishing shack, Kylara realized, when it had still been on the surface.

She narrowed her eyes and looked closely. The outlines of three adults moved through the tiny home and a baby tried very hard to crawl with very little success. A fourth appeared and seemed to say something to the others. He gestured wildly.

In the next moment, they all went still as the silhouette of a dragon flew overhead, transformed, and landed as a human jumped off her back.

What followed was hard to understand. There was some kind of conversation during which the dragon yelled at the people inside, who huddled and whispered amongst themselves.

Finally, someone stepped out of the house and began to hurl energy at Diamantine.

Kylara knew it was her mom's silhouette now because she had sparred with her thousands of times. She recognized the way she picked apart the man's technique and the way she moved closer and closer. When he threw a blast of energy that injured her hand, that was all the confirmation she needed.

So that was how her hand had been burned, she thought ruefully.

Cassandra grunted from her cross-legged position atop her floating island of ice as the battle became harder to follow. The woman with Diamantine had to be the mage Lara that Kylara had been named after. She battled with a woman until she vanished into what appeared to be the ground.

"She drowned," the young girl said.

"I always thought so." Cassandra grunted. "It's a pity. Your mother was truly gifted with her control of water."

Her stomach dropped unpleasantly. She had been talking about Lara, the woman she'd been named after, who had been drowned by—if the mage could be believed—her real mother.

The battle grew more complex as dragons rained fire and the surface of the lake melted. The mages were all either incinerated or slipped into the frigid water. It was hard to be sure with the mist and the tears now streaming unbidden down her face.

It ended with the mages dead and the dragons retreating—all but one. Hester Diamantine remained. The misty images seemed to fast forward through what must have been a long and arduous search in her human form. The dragon, she realized, must have tried to find Lara, although also seemed to verify the deaths of the mages along the way.

When she transformed into her dragon body, the images slowed. Hester flew around the lake, swooped low, and picked up something that might have been a log but the girl knew was not.

Cassandra sent her disc of ice into the woods to follow the silhouette of the dragon and her parcel.

They landed and Kylara stepped off the piece of ice and stumbled closer to the figures in the mist. She watched as Diamantine peered inside the canoe she had picked up and found a baby swaddled in blankets next to the corpse of one of the people who had given his life to save hers.

Hester reached out and touched the baby.

When she did, it changed. Its legs extended and grew claws. Tiny, stumpy wings appeared on its back. It grew a tail and a tiny frill around its head. And even in the mist, she could recognize the shape of diamond scales.

It was her, she realized. She was the baby the mages had died to protect. It was the only possibility. She was the reason why her mom had fled and isolated herself.

Somehow, she still couldn't fully accept that she was a mage rather than a dragon.

"Of course," Cassandra murmured as the misty form of Diamantine bundled the baby in a carrier she found in the canoe. "You must have taken the magic to change into dragon form and the diamond scales from that touch. I haven't heard of such a thing happening in millennia."

Kylara could hardly process the woman's last words. She thought about her new powers. The light power she got when Samuel touched her. The storm powers when Tempest blasted her with lightning. Dark powers from Midnight and heat powers from Ruby. It was both horrible and wonderful to finally have a way to explain where she was from, who she was, and what she was all at once. It meant her entire life was a lie but that was balanced by the relief that she might finally have the truth.

She watched as Diamantine transformed into a dragon again, scooped up the carrier with the infant, and headed south in a slightly different direction than the other dragons had chosen.

Was she watching an echo of the moment when her mother had decided to reject her place in dragon society to save a lost little girl? Had she thought about building them a home together in New Mexico even then? Did she grieve for Lara, the mage she had lost and think about the tiny mage she now carried?

Suddenly, the mists dissipated and Cassandra stood and wiped the blood from her nose. It stained the white fur on the cuff of her coat a bright scarlet.

"I know that does not answer everything, Kylara, but I hope we can find the answers to the rest of your questions together. But first, shall we go see your friends?"

She nodded shakily and followed the mage without argument.

# CHAPTER THIRTY-EIGHT

The walk below the lake was a long one. First, they had to descend the spiral stairs cut into the walls of ice all around them. Once again, they entered the home itself. Kylara could no longer think of it as a shack. People had lived there—her people. She could no longer deny the truth of that either. But that didn't mean she would simply give up on the woman who raised her or her friends. While she could no longer deny that Cassandra was being honest, she had still taken innocent people prisoner simply to prove a point and had killed those she deemed guilty.

Although she trusted her more than she had before—how could she not?—she didn't want to hear anything else she had to say until her friends and her mom were free.

The slope of the tunnel changed and now moved upward rather than downward. After a while, the walls became solid rock instead of rock lined with ice. They reached a set of stairs that took them up a series of switchbacks. The route was dark, lit only by Cassandra at first. After a while, the girl couldn't help but ignite her fingertips with light magic so she could also illuminate the way ahead.

It made sense to her to have her magic primed in case her

guide didn't let her friends go. Plus, it wasn't like her aunt didn't know what she was capable of. The only power her elementals hadn't seen yet was the dark magic she'd drawn from Midnight. There was no point in trying to play coy.

"It's truly remarkable," the woman said with a look of something like rapture on her face.

"You're making more light than I am," she replied. "Plus, yours is a ball that you can send where you want it to go."

"This is true, but only because I have studied this form of magic for decades. You use similar magical pathways to make light but you do it instinctively the way dragons do."

"Do mages use magic in a different way?" she asked. It was a question her instructor had never tried to explain. Professor Sharra said dragons used magic one way and mages used it another, end of story. She threw a wrench in that little theory, though.

"I don't believe so, no, or not at first anyway. The ability to harness magic energy is a gift. It comes partly from the blood— your mother was a gifted mage—and partly from study and determination. We have an instinct to harness power, exactly like the dragons do, but we must study far more than they do."

Kylara didn't know if that was true. She knew that she only defeated other dragons in duels because she had practiced so many times with Diamantine. Although she had used some powers instinctively, it was with little success. Practice was the key to her dragon body. Even her diamond scales weren't particularly useful if their limits were not understood.

Cassandra took her silence as a request to continue. "You, of course, might prove able to pursue both paths of study. Kylara, with your skills as a dragon and my help to become a mage, you could rival the Steel Dragon herself in sheer power."

"Rival her? Why would I want to do that?" she asked. "She made the world a more just place for all races but mages especially."

"That's what she says, yes." The mage's voice was bitter. "But the world has not changed so much since she assumed power."

She intended to point out that the world had changed considerably and continued to do so, and that maybe it was Cassandra and her vendetta of vengeance that needed to be updated. Before she could speak, however, they reached a cave.

At first, the girl thought she had let her dark magic leak out somehow because the light coming from her and her aunt—still a weird thought for her, even if it was true—seemed to be swallowed. Then she realized that it was merely that the size of the room was massive compared to the narrow tunnel they'd walked through.

Her guide sent her ball of light ahead of her. It traveled close to a hundred feet before it elevated and came to rest perhaps another fifty feet above their heads. The room was very clearly a lived-in space with a big fire pit in its center with a large kettle above it.

The mage spoke quietly and the fire crackled to life under the kettle and spread more illumination around the room.

Now, Kylara could see a bedroll against a wall and a few storage containers—some made of terra cotta and others of plastic—stacked against a rocky wall. Another passage led from the cavern, presumably to an exit somewhere in the mountains that surrounded the lake where the house had been.

All of this was an afterthought, though, as what caught and held her attention now that the light was bright enough for her to see was her two friends. Tanya and Samuel were secured against a wall in their human forms.

It wasn't only physical chains that bound these humans who could change to dragons whenever they desired. A mass of water covered every inch of their bodies except their faces. That it was a water elemental was obvious now that she understood what they were and had faced them a few times.

She recoiled instinctively, appalled that a wall of water pushed against her friends or held them frozen there. Worse, the water seemed to undulate, ripple, and move as if invisible fish swam through it to nibble her friends' bodies and make sure they didn't move too much or try to struggle.

"Run!" Tanya yelled, and the creature promptly slid a mass of water over both her and Sam's mouths.

"Let them go," Kylara said forcefully.

"You know I can't do that," Cassandra said, crouched on her haunches, and warmed her hands by the fire.

"Isn't that why you brought me here?" she demanded. "To let my friends go?"

"I didn't bring you here, Kylara. I invited you. You came of your own free will."

"I came because you kidnapped my friends."

"You don't have to be friends with these creatures anymore. Now that we have each other, we can build a new family and make new friends together. I know I'm not your mom, Kylara, but I also used to tease her about how badly I wanted to raise you like my own."

"You're not my mother."

"I understand that this will take time, but I won't betray you or lie to you, not ever. Do you think these two will talk to you now that they know what you are?"

"They know?"

"Not everyone was as hard to convince as you were." Cassandra gestured to the elemental and the water that trapped her friends moved and flowed away from their mouths.

"Get out of here, Ky!" Sam shouted.

"I won't leave you," she said.

"See? It is as I said," Cassandra said to Samuel. "Now that she knows who she is, you will not be able to leave. It's simply too big a risk. I am sorry."

"That's not what she meant," he shouted and water splashed

into his face. He struggled against it as waves seemed to assault his face.

"Stop it. You're drowning him!" Tanya screamed. Her voice sounded hoarse like she'd screamed continually.

"He cannot be drowned if the spirit binding him can simply suck the water from his lungs before he dies," Cassandra said and gestured at the elemental to do exactly that. Samuel stopped thrashing but now, his face was entirely covered except his nose.

"Tell Kylara what you told me," the mage said to Tanya.

"Kylara, you have to get out of here and get to safety!" her friend yelled as the water elemental surged around her. She couldn't be sure, but she got the sense that it was crushing her.

"You have to stop this." She growled at Cassandra.

"Of course. There's no honor in drawing this out," the woman said. She gestured again and the water elemental stopped doing whatever it was doing.

"Tell her," the mage said as if this was all part of the threat.

"I told her that you would never lie to me," Tanya said. "I told her that I've seen you use dragon powers to defend people who needed help. I told her that you're not a mage!"

"It's okay that you lied to her," Cassandra said and the water splashed over the young dragon's mouth and ears again. "I have lied many times in the pursuit of lore capable of killing even the mightiest dragons. We must not lie to each other because we are family, but we will build a wall around ourselves to protect us from the world."

"Sure, Aunt Cassandra, whatever you say," she said. "Those dragons murdered your family. They need to be punished. But Tanya and Samuel have nothing to do with that. You need to let them go."

"They know your secret, Kylara. They know what you are and are a threat to our security."

"Are you saying you want to kill them?" she demanded.

"I do not think it will come to that," the mage said. "There are spells I have uncovered. Methods, one could say. It will not be simple and the results are not guaranteed, but we may be able to destroy their memories of you."

"No! Cassandra—Aunt Cassandra, we can't do that," She hoped the familial title would help to talk the woman down from literal brainwashing. "They had nothing to do with what happened to your—to our family. We can let them go. We'll all go to the authorities together. The Steel Dragon won't tolerate this. Those dragons—Diamantine included—murdered those mages. Justice can be served."

Kylara didn't ask where her mother was, not yet. If Cassandra wanted to destroy the minds of two innocent students, what did she want to do to her mother, the woman she held directly responsible for these crimes? She had to keep her talking and get her to release Samuel and Tanya so she could find out where Hester was.

"I've tried that, Kylara, I truly have. But the Steel Dragon herself is against justice. Part of her new world order was to create amnesty for actions in the past. She will not punish dragons for past crimes, no matter how painful those were."

"But that's good," she told her. "Back then, it was a war between mages and dragons. Diamantine told me all kinds of horrible stories."

"She told you nothing," Cassandra retorted.

"You're right. I'm sure you're right," she said, held her hands up in a neutral gesture, and took a step toward her friends. "But things have changed. There are mages at the Lumos school, not only dragons. They might not...not banish me or whatever if we simply tell them the truth."

"They will hang me for the crimes I committed," the mage said. "All the Steel Dragon's treaty did was give amnesty for the horrors the dragons perpetrated for centuries. We have no protection—we never did and we never will."

"No, mages are respected now! I've met Amy Williams—*the* Amy Williams. She's the Steel Dragon's right hand."

"Is that what you think she calls the messenger she sends to tasks less important than her precious Council meetings?" Cassandra pushed out of her crouch to stand with her hands raised, one toward the fire and at the water on the wall.

"Please, we don't have to wipe their minds and you don't have to kill Diamantine." Kylara had tried but she couldn't wait any longer. She had to know where her mom was.

"My intention is no longer to kill," the woman said. "Diamantine has...confided things to me, things I had not anticipated a dragon guilty of her crimes was capable of feeling. That is largely why she is still alive. Together, you and I can decide her punishment."

"That sounds...fine." She tried not to lie because she didn't think her aunt was. If anything, the woman was being frighteningly frank. It wasn't technically a lie, anyway, as she wanted to help decide what happened to Hester. That seemed far wiser than leaving it up to her captor. "Where is she?"

"Not here," the mage snapped and the question caused a flash of rage to cross her face. "She is a strong beast. I knew she would be and she has proven her reputation sound. I wouldn't hold her somewhere like this."

Kylara desperately wanted more but she couldn't simply go off to see her mom—her adopted mom?—with her friends imprisoned like this.

"Okay, Aunt Cassandra. We can see her another day. Right now, let my friends go. We don't need to wipe their minds or hurt them. They're my friends. They want to help me."

"That was before they knew what you are. Now that they know, they won't be your friends any longer."

"They will, Aunt Cassandra. I'm telling you, they will. They don't feel like the old generation of dragons do. Let them go and I'll prove it to you." She tried to smile and to somehow make all of this okay. The truth was that she wasn't angry with the woman for telling her who she truly was. She was thankful. Kidnapping her friends was not acceptable, but her aunt had been desperate. She had acted without thinking. If she would only let them go, everything would be fine.

"I'm sorry, Kylara, but we can't let them go. They'll hunt me for my past crimes. No amnesty will be given to a bitter old mage like me."

This wouldn't work, that much was obvious. Cassandra was too entrenched in her beliefs and too paranoid. She wouldn't release the dragons.

"Let them go, Auntie, please. Do it for me."

The mage shook her head.

"I can't do that."

"I'm no longer asking." Kylara clenched her jaw as her resolve firmed. "Let them go or I will free them myself."

Cassandra smiled. "You're so much like your mother and I were at your age. The fighting spirit is strong in you."

She had heard enough. Her expression grim, she moved toward the water, made her hands glow, and readied a slice of light energy like Samuel had used to sever part of the water elemental. She didn't know if she could use her hands to do this instead of her dragon form, but she assumed that if she was a mage and he could do it, she probably could as well.

Her hands began to glow and the light narrowed to only her fingertips, then only her nails. Seconds before a blast of light could launch from her fingers, a great gale of wind swept into her. She sprawled heavily and her ray of light energy careened into the roof of the cave.

"I won't lie to you, Kylara, but that does not mean you get to do whatever you wish," Cassandra said. "You must respect your elders. It is your safety that we value above all else."

"Let them go, now!" She moved back toward her friends and transformed into a diamond-encrusted dragon. The air elemental drove into her again, but it wasn't ready for the gust of wind she brought down from the tunnel leading to the outside.

Thankfully, she hadn't spent the conversation with her aunt doing nothing but trying to sway the woman's mind. She had also worked to build a storm cloud outside. Now, it rushed into the cave and brought moisture, wind, clouds, and cracks of lightning that all hurled themselves at the shimmering air that buffeted her.

# CHAPTER THIRTY-NINE

Kylara roared as the air elemental tore at her scales and tried to rip them loose, to knock her over, or to dislodge her footing.

None of its efforts were successful. She launched the fury of a thunderstorm at the beast, thrust it back, and scattered its energy throughout the room.

"I won't let you disobey me, Kylara. I will stop you for your own good." Cassandra gestured to the fire she had been standing near and the small, crackling flames expanded and rose out of the fire pit to take the form the girl knew so well. Limbs of flame lunged toward her as the fire elemental used a nearby stack of firewood to power itself.

She knew her diamond scales would protect her from the heat for a moment, but she also knew she couldn't directly hurt it. The storm building inside the cave could, however.

Clouds condensed above her as she let the beast's flames surge into her. The clouds swirled with ever-increasing speed. The winds grew and thrust the wind elemental aside. When rain began to fall, the fire monster shrieked with steam and smoke as it tried to advance but found the path forward too wet and devoid of fuel.

Kylara turned to her friends. She filled herself with light energy, opened her mouth, and released a beam of blinding energy. The light rocketed forward, but as she had begun to learn, it was more than light. It was some kind of glowing coherent energy—light converted into a force via some translation of power that human physicists would no doubt call impossible. The beam seared into the water elemental that bound her two friends and sliced off a chunk of it that sloshed across the floor.

The beast reached a limb of water out to catch the liquid this glowing dragon had denied it and in doing so, freed the two young dragon's heads.

"Behind you!" Tanya yelled.

She barely had time to turn her head and raise a wing to block before a bolt of freezing energy blasted into her from Cassandra's hands. Well, that answered the question of whether the woman could use the more traditional mage powers. Clearly, she could.

"I don't want to fight you, Kylara. We're family!"

"Then let my friends go," she roared.

"I can't let that happen. They won't keep our secrets."

"We don't need to keep secrets."

"Oh, to be young again." The mage made a gesture and the air elemental gusted all around Kylara and pulled at her wings with such force that it threw her across the room. She impacted with the wall of the cave with such force that rocks and ice fell from the ceiling. The water creature crashed into her legs, and with another blast of freezing energy, her arms and legs were frozen to the wall.

She struggled against the bindings as Cassandra moved toward her friends. "I'll take them from here and attempt to wipe their memories. If it works, I'll release them. Then I'll find you again, do you understand, Kylara? It's what we have to do to survive. I know it might seem wrong now, but in time, you will see the light."

"Let her do it," Samuel shouted and made her heart ache for this sweet, stupid boy.

For a moment, she considered lashing out with her dark powers. She knew she could use them when bound. Midnight never had to move to make the tendrils extend, but something told her not to. Not yet and especially not when she had the perfect power at her disposal.

Kylara diverted the magical river flowing through her to her hands and feet. She thought about Ruby Firedrake, about how she heated her hands to dry her nail polish, and how she had done the same thing to a bottle of water without meaning to. The river of magic flowed easily into this new channel of energy. One moment, all four of her claws were frozen in ice and in the next, nothing held her in place except warm puddles of water.

Cassandra had thought she had captured the dragon form of her niece and now ordered the wind elemental to swirl around her friends. She wasn't paying attention and the girl had only one chance to surprise her.

Tanya was looking at her, quite aware of what she was doing and of how important this moment would be in the fight.

"Hey, Cassandra!" Kylara yelled.

"No!" her friend shouted as the mage turned to look at her.

But her attention was exactly what she wanted. As soon as Cassandra's gaze found hers, she opened her mouth and a blinding blast of light escaped her throat to fill the room with white light.

"Close your eyes!" Samuel shouted but it was too bright to see if Tanya had been able to obey.

It didn't matter that much, not yet anyway. Her friends were still bound by chains and Cassandra was blinded.

Kylara knew what to do. She summoned whips of dark energy, lashed out with them, and wound multiple tendrils into two cords that were strong enough to slice through the chains connecting the two young dragons' wrists and ankles to the wall.

They fell forward, off the wall, and onto their knees.

"Tanya, dragon form! Samuel, hit the water elemental with light!"

The other girl nodded and he pushed to his feet and held his hands out toward the approaching tidal wave of water.

Surprisingly, nothing happened.

His fingers didn't glow and his palms remained dark. All that happened as the water beast raced forward in a cresting wave was that his look of triumph changed to one of horror.

Tanya fared no better. She extended her arms, ready for them to change into claws, but they didn't.

The creature surged into them and swallowed them with water.

"You didn't think I would be able to bind two dragons with nothing but iron?" Cassandra said. She motioned at the water elemental to swirl in circles so her friends, no matter how hard they tried to swim, couldn't escape it.

"Stop this!" Kylara said and seared the mage with a streak of light energy that the woman deflected with an ice shield she pulled from thin air.

"The cuffs on their wrists hold the same spells that the dragons used on our people for centuries. While wearing them, they cannot use their powers nor take their dragon forms."

"But then they can't heal," she blurted and the full revelation of this pounded into her like an avalanche in the chest.

"Which is why you need to stop this pointless tantrum," Cassandra said patiently.

Kylara knew she had to act fast. She had to save her friends or they would drown. While she could try to slough pieces of the water elemental off with light magic, she knew from prior experience that if the creature touched any of the water, it would reabsorb it. It wasn't a great strategy in an enclosed place like this cave. She could channel the energy from the clouds she had brought in there to blast the water elemental with electricity, but that might very well kill her friends.

Instead, she defaulted to what she knew best.

She raced forward with a burst of dragon speed. Cassandra's eyes widened as her niece raced toward her but she didn't flinch. Calmly, she lined her forearms and shins with ice and defended herself from the flurry of blows.

It was immediately obvious how the woman had managed to kill multiple dragons. She fought with magic-augmented skills. Every time Kylara tried to grasp a limb and pull her off balance as she'd learned during her years of aikido, her adversary blocked her with a slab of ice or a used wind to prevent her fingers from closing around her clothes.

Frustrated, she put everything she had into trying to overcome the woman's defenses and get her in a hold. It was damn difficult. Aikido had always worked against Diamantine because she had possessed such ungodly strength and been more than willing to inflict all kinds of damage with it during the training sessions. Hester had fought like a great white shark and delivered massive blows to her daughter. But blows like that could be redirected and used against their creator. Not so with Cassandra. If Diamantine fought like a shark, Cassandra was an eel.

No matter how hard she pressed, the mage evaded easily and slipped through her hold with boosts of water, air, or magics Kylara couldn't even name.

As she pressed her attack, she realized that Cassandra hadn't so much as let her touch her. She was a skilled fighter and must know that letting her land a weak blow could give the older woman the opening she needed to defeat her, so why didn't she?

Was it because she knew she could absorb powers?

Could it be that she could absorb the woman's powers?

She decided she had to try and she knew exactly what to do.

Again, she struck at Cassandra but this time, when the mage moved back, a rope of dark energy had grasped her ankle. Her eyes widened as Kylara caught her by the neck and lifted her off the floor with her dragon strength. She could feel her opponent's pulse and her very life in her hands. It would take nothing to kill her. All she had to do was squeeze. The mage's life and her quest for vengeance would be snuffed out to nothing. The location of Diamantine would die with her, but surely her mom would be able to escape any prison. It made sense. All Kylara had to do was squeeze and she gritted her teeth to settle her resolve.

With a deep inward sigh, she accepted that she couldn't do it. She wouldn't kill.

Instead, she hurled Cassandra across the room and into a wall of the cave, and the woman sagged.

Kylara spun toward the water elemental. Her friends were still inside and continued their attempts to swim out of the whirlpool inside the creature's body. Samuel looked like he was doing better than Tanya, whose strokes seemed weak and uncoordinated like she was almost out of air.

"Release them!" she screamed at the beast, held her hands out the way she had seen Cassandra do, and focused on the form inside the water that moved through it and left waves in its wake.

"You...are...not...my master," the beast protested in the voice of a raging river, but its whirlpool body seemed to slow.

The girl stepped forward and forced all her magic and will into her hands and her voice as she ordered the water elemental to obey her, release her friends, and return to whatever dimension it had come from.

She said this not with words but with a deep guttural roar. It was the language of willpower, the language of demand translated across dimensions from her eyes and posture to the intelligence that was able to move water like she could use her body.

The water slowed and the whirlpool stopped. Sam and Tanya somehow reached the surface and sucked in desperate breaths of air.

In the next moment, a fire tornado pounded into her and threw her into a wall.

Kylara—awash in flames and wind—watched in horror as the water elemental swallowed her friends again and then saw nothing else as she was swung into a wall with enough force to knock her unconscious.

She wasn't out long. It couldn't be more than a few seconds at most, but it was long enough for Cassandra to regain control of her elementals. The girl opened her eyes to see that a wall of flame and a literal tornado were now between her and her friends, who were once more swallowed by the body of the water beast.

The mage stood behind the tornado and the fire but in front of the wall of water that seemed determined to drown the two young dragons. "It was clever of you to keep the shadow powers in reserve but naïve to think you could overpower my control of these spirits."

The fire and wind elementals battered the young dragon. Her diamond scales prevented her immediate death but it quickly became clear that even now, Cassandra wasn't trying to kill her. The wind elemental sucked the air away from her as the fire elemental surrounded her to deprive her of oxygen.

But she had expected such an attack and had a lungful of air. If she were simply a dragon, she might have used that single huge breath to blast her foe with fire, but she now understood that she was no simple dragon. She was a mage but she was also more than that. As impossible as it seemed, she was unique, a mage with abilities like no other.

Kylara reached out to the storm that still filled the ceiling of the cave. Wind ripped at the surface of the water elemental, sucked water from it, and evaporated it so it could condense into the cloud. This poured sheets of water on the fire elemental. The wind tore at the air elemental as well, and she could breathe.

"You are so stubborn!" Cassandra shouted. "But no matter.

Your mother was the same and she eventually listened to reason." Blasts of force, ice, lightning, and wind that cut like blades issued from the mage's fingertips, .

The girl fought back with everything she had. While her storm powers struggled to keep the elementals at bay, she launched streaks of solidified light at her opponent and tried to bind her with tendrils of dark energy.

The woman deflected the light with shields of ice. She fired rivulets of flame at the tendrils of shadow that crept across the floor and snatched constantly at her ankles.

She missed one, and Kylara bound one of her legs in a criss-crossing black web. Now that the mage was restrained, she had a clear shot at her face and she delivered a beam of light with such force that it hurled the woman to the ground.

"I'll say it again. It was clever of you to hold some of your power in reserve," Cassandra said, her eyes squeezed shut. "We are so alike."

In the next moment, the ground beneath Kylara gave way. What was once rock was now liquid. Her claws sank into the stone before it solidified again and locked her four dragon legs within.

Her aunt—still rubbing her eyes and still blinded—pushed to her feet. "You fight very well, Kylara. I will tell Diamantine that she trained the child she stole very well."

"You will not go anywhere!" the girl screamed and released a great ball of dragon fire at her captor.

Before it could strike the mage, a wall of stone erupted from the ground. The fiery projectile struck the barrier and puffed away to nothing.

"I will give you time to accept your new reality. I know it must be a shock that you are a mage, not a dragon. You will come to see that your allegiance should be to your family—the family that was taken from you by dragons—but I can see today is not that day. I will leave you to consider what you have learned as I have no desire to continue this battle. I love you Kylara. I always will. Sooner or later, you will see that I am right."

A bubble of stone rose from the floor and surrounded the mage. Kylara blasted fire and light, lashed out with tendrils of dark energy, and willed lightning to strike the ground itself, but none of it slowed the escape of the earth elemental and the mage who was its master.

# CHAPTER FORTY

As soon as the bubble of stone vanished beneath the surface of the cave, the other elementals ceased their fight. The tornado of wind spun itself out. The fire let itself be fully extinguished by the flame. The water elemental that had tried to drown her friends collapsed and became nothing more than a couple of inches of water that ran slowly down the tunnel Kylara had entered the room though.

Her feet were still bound in stone but that was a simple fix. She changed into her human form, freed herself from the rock, and rushed to her friends.

Both lay on the ground, soaking wet, their lips blue and chests disquietingly motionless.

She yanked the cuffs off their wrists and ankles with surprising ease. Iron cuffs hadn't been used to bind the dragons but surprisingly dainty ones made of something like silver. Still, their chests didn't begin to rise and fall.

A little desperate, she tried not to panic. Her friends weren't breathing. They weren't breathing because of her. She couldn't let them die and had to save them. But how?

Her mind sifted through what her mother had taught her of

first aid and all she had been through. Finally, it settled on Samuel's light powers. He had used them to heal her. Could she do the same?

Quickly, she knelt beside her two lifeless friends and put a hand on each of their chests. She tried to breathe evenly and stay calm as she willed the river of magic inside her to flow into her hands and illuminate her fingertips. Her hands began to glow and she maintained her steady breathing. She could do this—she had to do this.

A little calmer now, she willed the light into their bodies. At first, it did nothing but glow as if the magic didn't understand what it was supposed to do, but then it began to flow. Slowly at first, a thin sheen of light crept out from her fingertips and across her friends' bodies.

It spread and wrapped them in a cocoon of shining brightness but it didn't seem to be enough. It was protecting but not healing them. She needed it to soak in so she could share her energy with her friends.

"Please," she begged, not knowing if she was talking to herself, her magic, or a higher power from another dimension. "Please let this work."

Suddenly, Tanya sat, clutched her stomach, and coughed to expel the water in her lungs. She rolled on her side, gagging and sputtering as it sprayed on the floor. "That sucked..." she wheezed.

She would be okay, so Kylara turned her attention to Sam.

"Come on, Samuel. Come on!" she whispered to him. "Please don't be dead...not now that I...that I feel..."

"Yes?" he said, opened one eye, and smiled.

"You jerk!" she said and slapped him in the chest, which dragged a groan of pain from him that made her only slightly regret hitting him.

"What were you saying?" he said as he managed to sit.

"I was merely hoping you didn't suffer any brain damage, but I can see I was too late."

He made no response and simply smiled with a somewhat smug expression.

Kylara forced herself to not roll her eyes at him and helped Tanya to her feet.

"Oh no," the other girl said as soon as she stood. "Oh no, Kylara. She's coming back."

A circle of blue light swirled in the middle of the room. It increased speed and the middle of the circle began to resolve. Before Kylara could see what was on the other side of the portal, robed figures streamed into the cave.

They moved quickly to surround the wounded dragons and the exhausted mage who had unwittingly masqueraded as one.

She clenched her teeth, ready to fight, but Amy busted a double kickflip as she emerged from the portal and splashed into the water still pooled on the floor.

"What? Seriously? I just got this board!" The mage levitated the board into her hands, which then caused her skater shoes—normally hidden beneath her robes—to get soaked. She grumbled at this and made herself levitate up and out of the water by a few inches.

"Amy Williams!" Kylara blurted.

"Kylara Diamantine," she replied with a smile. "Seriously, though, Amy is fine."

"How did you find us?" Tanya asked.

"Honestly, it was your phone," the mage explained. "Kylara received a call from a cellphone that used a cell tower way up in northern Canada. It took us a while to pinpoint the exact location." She winked at the young dragon-mage. "Although the raw magic pouring out of this cave made that a little easier."

"You tracked my call?" she asked, a little shocked, a little offended, but mostly thankful that such pedestrian technology had saved her from a magical foe.

"Kristen's brother is like a god with tech." Amy shrugged. "It wasn't that hard for him. We would have come sooner but like I said, we only had a tower to work with. When we sensed the magic, we feared the worst, but from the looks of things, you had it covered."

She nodded and suddenly, in a flood of words, she revealed everything about the call, flying there, finding the house at the bottom of the lake, and the vision in the mist.

"And you believe her?" the mage asked when she finally stopped talking long enough to take a breath.

"I do," she admitted. "A part of me doesn't want to. Seriously, she kidnapped my mom, but...so much of it rings true," Her hands had found the pendant around her neck. "I don't think I'm a dragon. I'm merely a mage who can mimic them. I'm a fraud and I don't belong at the Lumos School. I don't belong with any of you."

"Oh, my God. Teenagers!" Amy laughed. "You guys can be so dramatic! So you're a mage, not a dragon. That's great. You do realize that this very ability has been lost to mages for over a thousand years. This is so much more awesome than you being a dragon. Of course, I'm biased but, like, team mage for life!"

"You...you think I can still go to the Lumos School then?"

The mage laughed heartily. "Are you kidding? You're kidding, right? My best friend is a dragon raised to think she was a human who developed special powers and became a bridge between the worlds. You being a mage who can change into a dragon...it's perfect! The only thing better would be if you didn't understand dragon society."

"She doesn't," Tanya pointed out.

"She truly doesn't." Sam grinned.

"You're talking about the Steel Dragon, aren't you?" Kylara asked.

Amy nodded. "Her powers are formidable but they're not what made her change the world. Kristen was only able to do that because she had a unique viewpoint. Being able to see things from different angles than everyone else is an asset, not a problem."

"But my entire existence is a lie. How could anyone still want to talk to me?"

"Could you seriously do us a favor and stop making our decision to be your friend for us?" Tanya glared at her. "I already knew you were a social outcast when I saw you try to put a dress on. If I could be friends with someone like that, you'd better believe I'm still your friend after you saved my life."

"We don't care how you were born," Sam said and slung an arm around her shoulders. "Only what you do. And that means you now officially have two friends for life."

Her roommate nodded enthusiastically before she wrapped her in a hug.

"Oh, teenagers," Amy said again and smiled. "Hugs and tears until someone doesn't want to see the same movie as you on a Friday night, then it's all backstabbing."

"Ma'am, do you want us to close this portal?" one of the mages asked.

"Absolutely not." She gestured to the swirling magic and the school campus on the other side. "We need to get back before these kids start fighting again."

"I can't leave," Kylara said, and Amy frowned at her. "Cassandra still has my mother—the woman who raised me, I guess. Now that my friends have been rescued, I have to try to find her."

As the others lined up to move to through the portal, the mage fixed her with a firm look. "And nothing will happen to her, not yet. Diamantine is her trump card, the one thing she still has that will ensure that you won't simply turn your back."

She grimaced and had to acknowledge the truth of the words. "Okay...she did say she had decided not to kill her, and although she was angry, I think she meant it. Besides, she could easily have trapped me and taken me with her, but she didn't."

Amy nodded. "And you need time to heal and to adjust to what happened and what you have learned. It makes no sense to begin a hunt when you are at a disadvantage. We now have a location from which to begin our search, and I'll have teams on it as soon as we return. I know you're frustrated, Kylara, and you feel like you're abandoning your mother but you aren't. The worst thing you can do is track Cassandra when you're weak after the battle. You want to face her from a position of strength, or she will have both you and your mother, which is the worst thing that could happen. I also have the feeling that she will come looking for you again. It serves her purposes to keep Hester alive as a weapon to compel you if she has to."

For a long moment, she thought about all she had learned. It was painfully hard to accept that she wasn't who she thought she was, but it was also less of a shock than she had thought it would be. The fact was, there were so many gaps in her identity. Hester Diamantine had never told her everything about herself. Aunt Cassandra—she found she now thought about her as family, even after the attack—had filled in the gaps.

She wouldn't forgive the woman for taking her friends and she wouldn't stop trying to rescue her mom, but she also had a feeling that if she spent a little time bolstering her new-found abilities, it might give her the edge when Cassandra came looking for her. She was quite certain she hadn't seen the last of her. Amy was right. The mage had her mom and was keeping her alive instead of killing her.

It was unclear if that was because her mom—as cantankerous as they came—was simply too strong, or if her recounting how she had raised Cassandra's niece had softened the mage's disposition. It was frustrating to still have so many questions, but she finally felt like she had the tools to begin to answer them.

That, plus her friends, was more than enough for now.

The story continues with Dead Dragons New tricks, coming soon to Amazon and Kindle Unlimited.

And we're of on another adventure! First off, if you've read this far you've probably already finished the first book in Michael and my new series, *Dragon's Daughter*. Thanks so much for reading! I hope you loved the tale. With so many fans of the *Steel Dragon* series dying for more stories set in that world, we pushed pretty hard to get something new, different — and yet familiar as well — out to you all.

If you haven't read the *Steel Dragon* series yet, that's OK! You don't really need to read those in order to understand and enjoy the *Dragon's Daughter*. But if you want to go back and see how Kristen Hall got *her* start, it's a fast-paced, fun adventure.

This year has been a weird one, huh? I don't know anyone who isn't facing more stress in 2020 than they usually do. It's just been a messy, difficult, complicated, and emotional year, for a lot of different reasons. But stories provide an escape from all that.

When we sit down to enjoy a story we get to be transported away from whatever we're facing in our day to day lives. Human beings use stories for a bunch of different reasons, mind you. We use them to teach, to pass on knowledge, and more. But we use them for relief a lot, too.

Thing is, there's nothing wrong with that. It's a human thing to do, turning toward stories in times of stress. I for one am so glad for all of the artists whose work helped make this year brighter for me. I'm also glad to be a part of doing that for others as well.

With luck, this story gave you that relief from whatever worries weighed down your day. I hope so.

I'm not sure what Michael and I are going to work on together after this series (it'll be six books, we think), but we'll probably come up with something! I'll be busy as heck with my own books next year as well. I'm wrapping up two series and starting two new ones! *Valhalla Online* and the *Starship Satori* series will both conclude. But the new storylines are hot! One's science fiction, the other urban fantasy, and we'll see at least a couple of each come out next year.

Just something to look forward toward!

As always, thanks so much for reading!

Kevin McLaughlin

# MICHAEL'S AUTHOR NOTES
## NOVEMBER 11, 2020

First, THANK YOU for not only reading this story, but to the author notes in the back.

I now live in Henderson Nevada. I'm about 25 minutes from my garage door to walking into the Aria Hotel on the strip where I used to live.

So, I'm close.

What that doesn't explain is that I'm higher in elevation, and can see the strip from the area I live now. Well, I can if a tree or a building isn't in the way.

I'm typing this from a restaurant that has a view of the valley floor and the strip. Often, the view has been pretty if we don't have smoke, or dust in the air. Today is dusty so the view isn't so fantastic, but yesterday it was super clear.

And it was beautiful.

It was also *uplifting*.

I don't normally feel the difference in my attitude or general mental well-being while looking around me. However, there is now snow on Mt. Charleston (west side of the valley – I'm more on the east side) and seeing that beautiful peak with white capping it for the first time since early this year really helped.

When I was writing from The Cave in the Sky™ on the Strip (Veer condos), I would often wonder if my VR headset (Oculus 1) would allow me to feel like I was somewhere else and not (to me) a tiny room 25 stories up in a concrete jungle.

I don't care how pretty the concrete jungle is, it isn't a spacious construct.

So here is the picture. I'm in a 12x10 room somewhat cramped with a glass desk and black executive chair I can swivel in. It's pretty messy with clothes and stuff crammed everywhere. I put the Oculus Virtual Reality headset on and suddenly, I'm in another 'world' inside a cabin on a mountaintop.

There's a fire crackling in a fireplace about 15 feet from me with a couch between us. I turn and the outdoors is beckoning me about 30 feet away where I will be able to look down the slope to the sea of trees.

I turn myself to the left and *CRACK!*

Pain blazes through my kneecap, my hands reach down to my knee that just stabbed itself against the glass desk. I try not to move too much because I've lost spacial awareness with the AR headset on.

Slowly, I get the pain under control and take off the headset. Here is my messy desk, the jumbled office. I shed a tear and wonder.

Am I sad because of the pain, or the loss from my sudden reality check? I'm not on a mountain, there is no view down the slope.

Am I saddened because I realize that no matter what we do as a society, there is only so much time before those of us who are anxiously hoping for new benefits from VR realize we have a way to go before reality will make you take notice?

Usually painfully.

*I'm not sure.*

I write science fiction in part because it allows me to play with societal norms that I hate dealing with and feel insufficiently capable of changing in my reality.

Then, like a user who needs another hit I reach for the VR helmet one more time. I check my surroundings a bit better, perhaps move my chair as appropriate. No matter what the chance is that I'll hurt myself I slide that helmet back on.

I need a hit.

I want that hope that the future CAN be better. I'll seek it one more time and perhaps by seeing the difference between where I am in reality, and the reality inside the VR headset I will find the path to *make my virtual my reality.*

Then, I just need to figure it how to move it at scale.

Ad Aeternitatem,

Michael Anderle

Book 11 - Brave New Worlds (2019)

Book 12 - Warrior's Marque (2020)

## The Ragnarok Saga (Military SF)

Accord of Fire - Free prequel short story, available only to email list fans!

Book 1 - Accord of Honor

Book 2 - Accord of Mars

Book 3 - Accord of Valor

Book 4 - Ghost Wing

Book 5 - Ghost Squadron

Book 6 - Ghost Fleet (2019)

## Valhalla Online Series (A Ragnarok Saga Story)

Book 1 - Valhalla Online

Book 2 - Raiding Jotunheim

Book 3 - Vengeance Over Vanaheim

Book 4 - Hel Hath No Fury

## Blackwell Magic Series (Urban Fantasy)

Book 1 - By Darkness Revealed

Book 2 - Ashes Ascendant

Book 3 - Dead In Winter

Book 4 - Claws That Catch

Book 5 - Darkness Awakes

Book 6 - Spellbinding Entanglements

By A Whisker (short story)

The Raven and the Rose - Free novelette for email list fans!

## Dead Brittania Series:

Dead Brittania (short prequel story)

Book 1 - King of the Dead

Book 2 - Queen of Demons

Raven's Heart Series (Urban Fantasy)

Book 1 - Stolen Light

Book 2 - Webs in the Dark

Book 3 - Shades of Moonlight

## Other Titles:

Over the Moon (SF romance)

Midnight Visitors (Steampunk Cat short story)

Demon Ex Machina (Steampunk Cat short story)

The Coffee Break Novelist (help for writers!)

You Must Write (Heinlein's rules for writers)

# CONNECT WITH THE AUTHORS

**Connect with Kevin McLaughlin**

Website: http://kevinomclaughlin.com/

Facebook: https://www.facebook.com/kevins.studio

Twitter: https://twitter.com/KOMcLaughlin

Instagram: https://www.instagram.com/kevins.studio/

**Connect with Michael Anderle**

Website: http://lmbpn.com

Email List: http://lmbpn.com/email/

https://www.facebook.com/LMBPNPublishing

https://twitter.com/MichaelAnderle

https://www.instagram.com/lmbpn_publishing/

https://www.bookbub.com/authors/michael-anderle

Made in the USA
Middletown, DE
14 December 2020